PRAIS

HOU
PARTY

'A slow burn romance with multi-layered characters and sizzling chemistry, *House Party* left me absolutely breathless. Clear your schedule to read this in a single sitting'

Annabel Monaghan

'Such a fun, sparkling, swoonworthy romance full of memorable moments'

Cressida McLaughlin

'*House Party* is dazzlingly electric! Chloe is a master of the romcom and this is an exquisite slow burn full of heart, friendship, and a brilliantly steamy romance that will keep you hooked at every page!'

Beth Reekles

'Funny and charming, with plenty of steam to warm you up on those cold winter nights... the perfect winter escape!'

Catherine Walsh

'*House Party* is everything I want in a romance — emotional, gorgeously written, and utterly addictive'

Carrie Elks

HOUSE PARTY

ALSO BY CHLOE FORD

Work Trip

HOUSE PARTY

CHLOE FORD

HEAD
of
ZEUS

An Aria Book

First published in the UK in 2025 by Head of Zeus,
part of Bloomsbury Publishing Plc

9 7 5 3 1 2 4 6 8

A catalogue record for this book is available from the British Library.

ISBN (PB): 9781035913244
ISBN (E): 9781035913251

Cover design: Gemma Gorton
Typeset by Siliconchips Services Ltd UK

Printed and bound in Great Britain by
Clays Ltd, Popson Street, Bungay NR35 1ED

MIX
Paper | Supporting
responsible forestry
FSC® C018072

Bloomsbury Publishing Plc
50 Bedford Square, London, WC1B 3DP, UK
Bloomsbury Publishing Ireland Limited,
29 Earlsfort Terrace, Dublin 2, D02 AY28, Ireland

HEAD OF ZEUS LTD
5–8 Hardwick Street
London, EC1R 4RG

To find out more about our authors and books
visit www.headofzeus.com

For product safety related questions contact productsafety@bloomsbury.com

To the New Year's Day babies who ring each birthday
in with fireworks.

ONE

In hindsight, spending Christmas Day alone in my flat might've been the smarter choice.

Instead, I'm sat on an uneven, wooden footstool that Mum foraged out of the garage this morning. She changed her mind at the last minute and decided to invite Granny after all, and Granny *cannot* sit on the uneven, wooden footstool. And of course, nobody ever has enough dining chairs for Christmas lunch. I mean, unless you're rich, which the Tycers are not. It's especially unfair since I'm one of the tallest people in this room and my knees are almost up to my chest. But according to Mum, I don't count as a guest in this house, even though I don't live here anymore.

Worse still: I've been bullied into wearing a ridiculous sweaterdress Mum bought with a giant Rudolf on it (adorned with a red bobble for the nose), along with a fragile paper hat from one of those corny Christmas crackers. I'm sweating my tits off, due to the combined heat of the oven in the open-plan kitchen and the radiators cranked right up. And now I'm having to watch my eccentric cousin, Dylan, stuff his face with another Yorkshire pudding, while his mother and my auntie, Maeve, harass me *yet again* regarding the whereabouts of my ex-boyfriend.

"I liked Adam," she says. The brass on this woman is astonishing. I've long thought it should be studied.

"That's nice," I retort, forking another carrot into my mouth.

"And he couldn't make it this year... Why was that again?"

Dylan gives me a pitying glance from under his light, curly fringe. His family always comes to ours for Christmas, but Mum can only stomach her sister's company for so long. Why must we suffer this meal every year? None of us enjoy it. And yet we do it anyway. I take my rage out on the turkey, cutting it with force.

"Mum, leave it," Dylan warns, giving her an imploring glance.

I catch his eye across the table and offer him an appreciative smile. He's well versed in my aunt's linguistic assaults. He's only a year younger than me, but, aside from our ages, we don't have much in common. He's never been in a relationship that's lasted more than a few weeks, he bounces around from job to job, and he makes wild, unpredictable decisions. During his mid-twenties, he was in crippling credit card debt, so what did he do? Got *another* credit card and took off to work in the Bahamas for a year.

But Auntie Maeve isn't done yet.

"Well, we just want to know what went so wrong, don't we, Martin?"

Uncle Martin is far too many sherries down to care

about Adam, but he nods anyway. He subscribes resolutely to a 'happy wife, happy life' mantra. "Yes, dear," he quips.

"I did warn her that you wouldn't want to talk about it," Mum finally chirps. And yet the expression on her face is one I recognise right away. She has never gotten to the bottom of it all either, and she too would like to know the whole story. As *if* I'm suddenly going to give them the entire rundown over Christmas dinner about how my shitty ex broke my stupid heart.

How fucking festive.

I sigh, dropping my fork. "And that's because it's incredibly difficult to talk about it. Honestly, I..." I pretend to choke up. Anything to get them off my back. I fiddle with a section of my curly hair, which has fallen over my shoulder, for extra effect.

Aunt Maeve reaches across the table and places her hand over mine. "Go on," she says softly.

"Well, you see... We were on this boat, travelling to the US for a long holiday and..."

Dylan looks confused.

"The boat hit an iceberg and, Adam... Well... He drowned." I finish in my usual dry style, dipping a roastie into the gravy and stuffing my face so I literally can't talk for at least two minutes.

Dylan hangs his head. I can see he's highly amused. Maybe we've finally found something to bond over. Maybe this is the year Dylan and I become friends.

Nah, I think.

I just haven't been single at Christmas in a very long time.

"Did Adam really drown?" Aunt Maeve asks, using the

same hand she touched mine with to cover her heart. She's aghast, the colour drained from her cheeks.

Mum scoffs. "Don't be daft, Maeve. That's the plot of *Titanic*."

"Oh, that's *very* bad taste, Hattie, very bad," she tuts. For absolutely no reason whatsoever, she looks like she's about to burst into tears. She loves to play the victim, especially after one of her notorious interrogations. Basically, she's a more vicious version of Mum.

I shrug, my mouth still full of potato.

"It's no laughing matter really, your being single," she says. "There's a reason there aren't many children in this house. Your mum and I left it too late."

"Good God, Mum!" Dylan retorts. "You can't say those things these days."

"Why not? She should know. I'm doing her a favour!"

It's official. All Christmas joy has been lynched from my body. I could've been watching *Elf* or *Love, Actually* in peace, tucking into a fruit-bowl-sized serving of those pigs-in-blanket-flavoured crisps.

I sigh. The baby chat isn't new to me. We've all heard Mum bleat on about how she wished she'd had more than just one child, how time really gets away from you. Sometimes, I feel bad for her, but it isn't something I want to worry about at Christmas. Especially the first Christmas at which I've been single for over *nine* years.

"Excuse me," I say, rising from my arse-chewing stool. "Think I'm going to grab some fresh air."

"Oh, don't make a scene, Hattie," Mum berates.

Me? I'm the one making the scene?

I give her a look and she relents, shrugging glumly as if

this wasn't her plan for the day and we're all ruining it for her.

I lock myself in the loo to discourage anyone from following me. I stare at my reflection and pull the paper crown from my head, balling it into my fist. The worst part about all of this is that while I'd love for everyone, myself included, to forget about Adam, that won't happen. Adam was a part of my life whether I like it or not. I run my fingers through my hair, careful not to frizz it up. It plonks back exactly the way it was: frothy. Mum used to say if I had dyed my hair black when I was a kid, I'd have been the spit of Tracy Beaker. Not exactly the vibe I was going for. Although I'd love to tell a few people to bog off right now.

I take a few deep breaths then stride out towards the back garden, grabbing my coat in the hall on my way.

Once I'm outside, sitting on the frozen garden furniture, I breathe in that fresh, winter air for all of two minutes before I hear the door open and close.

"Brr, it's sharp out here," Dylan says, rubbing his hands together. He draws a long puff from his vape. It's a festive one – apple and cinnamon spiced, or something similar. I don't mind second-hand steam so much when it smells divine.

"Thanks for sticking up for me in there," I say.

He shrugs. "Mum's a right nosy bitch. She's been wondering about your break-up for weeks." He shakes his head. "I'm glad you didn't give it to her." He turns and gives me a conspiratorial grin. "Welcome to the Black Sheep Parade. We march at dawn."

I snort. The thing about connecting with other *tragic* people when you feel particularly lost yourself is that you find yourself oversharing. It's like I want him to know I qualify to be in his tragic club. So, I tell him, "He thought he could do better."

Dylan makes a face. "Adam said that? What a prick."

"He didn't say that *exactly*. He said something along the lines of, 'You don't fit in with my new friends.' His new finance-bro crowd."

"Well, what a relief."

I laugh. "*Right?* Anyway, how's your recent venture going?"

"Which one? The dog-walking business or the clothes brand?"

"Both of those are new to me. You started a clothes brand?"

"Well, technically, it was just briefs."

I nod to show him I'm listening.

He shakes his head. "That's all there is to it really. I got bored and am now thinking of becoming a travel blogger."

I can't help the teasing smile that works its way onto my lips. "Thanks, Dylan."

He frowns. "For what?"

For helping me realise I have at least a little bit of my life together, even if it isn't quite all of it. "Just for cheering me up," I say.

We sit in silence for a bit, and I work over all the stuff I need to do before the gallery opens again after the Christmas break. Truthfully, it isn't all that much. It's part of the reason I love the job: the simplicity of it. Right on the sea front, it's owned by a lovely local couple who pay me to manage it. Adam always thought it was too 'provincial', and I could do more with my art degree.

I mean, he hated that I did an art degree full stop. What sort of business was I going to get into with that?

Hopefully, none, was always my first thought. Business always sounded boring to me.

But I've found myself in the art business and so far, I'm enjoying it. He belittled me for it, as if having wealth, or aspiring to wealth, was the only route to happiness. He didn't like that I wanted to "rot away in that little shop", as he so eloquently put it.

But I love art, and I especially love art that's associated with the sea or the seaside. Ever since we moved down to the south coast from the city, when I was fourteen, I've always loved the freedom of the beach: the seagulls, the sound of the waves crashing against the pebbles at high tide, the way you can taste it, hear it, breathe it. And anyone who can capture that beauty is my kind of artist.

But now I do occasionally wonder if there was some truth in what he was saying because, for example, he isn't at his parents' place for Christmas, moping outside and wishing the time away.

Well, at least I don't think he is… *Pfft.* Who am I kidding? I checked his Instagram this morning like an idiot. He's skiing in the French Alps. It's as if I'm chasing that gutless feeling it gives me whenever I go looking for updates.

He doesn't want me anymore. He doesn't love me anymore. And I have moved on.

Sort of.

"What's on your mind?" Dylan asks. "You're grinding your teeth and it's giving me shivers."

"I keep panicking that I've wasted my twenties," I burst out. *Maybe I really do belong in this tragic club, eh? See, look how pathetic I am.* "But so what if Adam doesn't want to be with me anymore? It's been a few months now and it's less sore. I'm ok. I'm enjoying having my own flat near the beach and being able to watch the TV I like without having to worry it will be too girly for him. I like cooking Thai and seafood in my own kitchen without having to think about all his undiagnosed allergies. And you know what? I like sleeping alone. He used to take up too much of the bed. You know?"

Dylan scrunches his face up. "Not really... but go on."

"What if he *stole* my twenties?" I say, my voice raising a pitch. "What if he never actually intended for us to be long term and I was just convenient? Hmm? And now I've gone and given him my entire youth? I'm going to be old soon, Dylan."

"You're twenty-eight."

"Yeah. *Right now.* But what about in two years? Next week will be the last birthday in my twenties."

My pulse is raising. Am I sweating? I can feel a lump forming in my throat.

Dylan looks restless, like he's regretting his decision to join me outside.

"I can't get those years back. And now all of the good men are gone!"

Dylan watches me, wide-eyed. "You do know I'm probably the worst person to be giving advice, right? I haven't got my shit together either. Hell, I don't even know where my shit is. How am I supposed to get it together? You've always been the golden child round here and now you're coming to *me* for advice?"

"I didn't ask for advice..."

"Maybe you need to let your hair down. Stop being perfect for ten minutes. Go and do something, or *someone*, recklessly. Screw rules. Screw that lot," he says, tilting his head towards the house. "Screw giving this final year in your twenties to someone else. Make it your own!"

I nod quickly. "Yes! This sounds right."

Dylan shakes his head. "Meh, it's most likely terrible advice."

"No! It's good. You're right. I need to take this year. I need to *own* it."

"What've you always wanted to do?"

"I want to see the seaside."

Dylan purses his lips. "Babe, you *live* in Seaford."

"I know, I mean *better* sea sides! Croatia, the Greek Islands, California and…" My eyes widen. "Shit! There are so many places I should go. Why haven't I been?"

"Didn't Adam hate travelling?"

"Yes! He only ever wanted to go skiing, and I wasn't invited."

I feel feral. He only ever wanted to go away with his mates, and his excuse was that I wasn't very good at learning new things (which I'm now convinced isn't true) and he didn't have time to train me while also getting out on the best slopes.

Dylan cups his hands around his mouth and blows to warm his fingers. "Are you coming to the family New Year's Eve party then?"

"Oh hell. I forgot they'd roped me into that too…" Panic sets in. But then I remember what I just said. "No! I'm taking back the final year of my twenties. New Year's Day is my birthday! I'm making plans for New Year's Eve,"

I proclaim, a little over-excited. "And you know what? I want to have another house party. I was meeting up with my friends after anyway at the pub. Might as well make a bigger deal of it."

"Isn't your flat more of a studio?"

I clap my hands at him. "You're becoming less helpful now, Dyl."

"I'm just saying. You being irrational is making me squirmish."

"*Squirmish?*"

"I don't know what it means, I just know that's how I feel."

"Ugh, maybe you're right." I lean back in the garden chair, the icy armrests sticking to my coat sleeves. "I should ask someone sensible first. I'll call Fliss; she'll know what to do."

"Good idea. Check in with someone sensible. Would you be open to signing a waiver that resolves me of all liability from giving advice?" he asks. He's being funny, but there's a nervous glint in his eye.

"No, sorry. You should've thought about that before you gave it to me."

"Crap. I better lawyer up."

I snort as I take my phone out to message my sensible person.

Fliss used to work for a high-end marketing firm in the city. Her mum is friends with mine, so we've always known each other by proxy. She's two years older than me so we didn't really cross paths as children, except for at family barbeques, and she was always too cool to hang out with me back then anyway. But recently, she's moved back to

Seaford and has been doing freelance work for the gallery's events. We've bonded over our shared love of fish 'n' chips and lunchtime cocktails on a Friday while staring out at the grey abyss that is Seaford seafront during winter.

Dylan blows out a long stream of apple-scented steam. "Come on," he says. "Let's get wasted before they ask us any more questions about our life plans."

TWO

The one where I first saw him

Three days before my fourteenth birthday, just after Christmas, we moved into a detached three-bed in Seaford near to my dad's new job. I never did know what he did back then. Something to do with analysis and computers. Although Dad didn't like to talk about it much, Mum had muttered a few times about me not making it harder for either of them, since it was bad enough he'd lost his job in the first place. The last thing he needed, according to her, was for me to be 'difficult' about us picking up and moving our entire lives.

No thoughts were given to how an awkward fourteen-year-old girl who wore glasses, had garish braces and hair cruelly akin to Sideshow Bob, would fare at a new school with no friends.

And to make matters worse, we had to attend a New Year's Eve party at Dad's new boss's place, a stoic, red-brick house with bay windows on a much leafier street than ours.

"Now, remember to be polite and try to smile, Hattie. Nobody likes it when you mope," Mum said as she ran her fingers over her dark bob. Dad was fiddling with his shirt sleeves, nervous energy practically oozing off him. He knocked on the front door as I hugged myself against the freezing night air.

Mum had made me wear the pink top and denim skirt she'd bought me for Christmas. It wasn't my style at all. I'd been pushing aside all the girly pinks and frilly shoulders she wanted me to wear more recently for darker colours and thick, wonky eyeliner. I'd also attempted to straighten my reddish-blonde hair, sick of it being so noticeable all the time, but I'd ended up singeing the ends and it had begun frizzing up again on the short, misty-aired walk from the car.

We were ushered into the house in a blur of introductions and offers of food and drink. Mum and Dad were told to make themselves at home while the boss's wife, who'd introduced herself as Mandy, tucked her arm in mine and showed me to where the 'other children' were.

Which – *rude* – I was practically fourteen.

"Sam, sweetie," she called, cracking the door open to a small bedroom covered in rock-band posters. "Lovely Hattie is here. The girl I told you about."

"Oh," was the less-than-excited response.

Mandy pushed the door open wider, and there sat a scrawny boy who I thought was younger than me, but then I noticed the birthday badge pinned to his t-shirt; he was fourteen today. A whole day older. To my surprise, the "other children" turned out to be just one and he scowled at his mum as if he'd made it abundantly clear he wasn't interested

13

in hanging out with some girl at a party he didn't want to be at. Which I guess is tricky when it's in your own home.

"Right then," Mandy said, ignoring her son's expression. "You two have fun." Then she turned and fled back to the adults.

"Nice badge," I said.

Sam looked down and frowned some more. "I forgot that was there."

"Is it your birthday?"

He blinked. "No. I just like wearing birthday badges."

I laughed. He was funny. "Same," I quipped. "It's my birthday tomorrow, actually."

"Really?" he asked, perking up slightly. "How old are you?"

"I'll be fourteen too."

"Weird."

"Why's that weird?" I asked, tilting my head.

"Just weird that we met today and have similar birthdays."

"Not that weird."

"It's a coincidence."

"A boring one."

Sam finally snorted, then shook his head. "Why are you called Hat?"

"It's not Hat. It's Hattie."

Sam continued to stare. He had bright-blue eyes that looked a little bloodshot – like he'd been staring at a screen for too long. He wore a white t-shirt with the AC/DC branding on the front and blue jeans that were scuffed in a way that looked more like they were hand-me-downs than in the fashionable sense.

14

"Hattie…" he said again, but slower, as if he was testing it out on his tongue. "I prefer Hat."

"Ok," I said. "That doesn't seem fair though as I can't shorten your name."

"You could just call me S."

"But that takes the same time as just saying Sam."

He raised his eyebrows as if he was considering this too. Then he shrugged. "So your dad is going to work for mine now, right?" he asked. I hoped it wasn't some weird power trip. I nodded anyway. "And you're going to the same school as me? Down the road?"

I shrugged. "I don't know what school you go to. But the one I'm going to is down the road, so maybe."

"Do you like rock music?"

"I like My Chemical Romance and Fall Out Boy."

He narrowed his eyes slightly. "You don't look like you like rock music."

I peered down at my pink top and sparkly shoes. "Yeah, well, my mum bought this for Christmas, and I didn't want to upset her by refusing to wear it. My parents have been a bit sad lately."

Sam turned back to the computer screen and hit save on his game before logging out. "Right. Want to steal a bowl of popcorn and a bottle of pop from downstairs?" he asked.

So, I guess he was done with conversation.

It was like I'd passed a test I didn't know I was taking. He bounced around a bit. I liked that about him. It felt like he had enough energy for both of us and I could take a back seat.

He strode out the door and I followed, pausing at each

corner as if there were people he didn't want to bump into. We were in cahoots. If he started to tiptoe, I copied. If he squatted down below a window, I did too. We were strangers but already so in sync. It occurred to me, as he was passing me bottles of Coca-Cola and Fanta through the hatch in the wall, that being forced to attend a party with my parents might actually have been a good thing.

Had I just found my new best friend?

We spent the next few hours on *The Sims*, creating houses for our characters and making up random back stories for them. But as the sugar took hold and our friendship settled in, we decided to make it funnier, putting them in pools and snatching the ladders away so we could watch the grim reaper show up as they drowned helplessly. We set fire to things and giggled as the worlds we created burnt to ashes.

I never did understand why that game let you do that. *Disturbing.*

"You're cool," he announced without looking at me.

"Thanks?"

"You want to walk to school together first day back?"

My eyes went round. He had to know he was offering me a power card of some sort, surely. "You want to walk to school with me?"

"I asked, didn't I?"

"Like we're *friends*?"

"Yeah. We're friends."

"Wow, that was easy."

Sam shrugged. "No point making it difficult."

I guess my experience with girls had thwarted my opinion

on friends in my old school. I'd found the social hierarchy difficult to navigate. But this felt genuine, so I agreed and decided that, even if his offer did turn out to be too good to be true, at least it was more than I'd had a few hours ago. I'd been having nightmares about walking into school that first day all alone.

Around quarter to midnight, Sam's mum showed up again, smiling at the sight of us, crumb-lipped and wide eyed. She encouraged us to come out to the garden and watch the fireworks.

We bundled on our coats, hats and gloves and made our way out to the Harrisons' long, townhouse garden that was sloped so you could stand at the top and watch everything going on further down on the lawn.

I followed Sam to some chairs, and we sat side by side.

My dad appeared, rosy-cheeked and smiling for the first time in forever. He handed us sparklers and we put our embarrassment aside to mess around with them.

When the first fireworks lit up the sky in reds, blues and golds, I caught a glimpse of someone else. A tall, slightly older boy with tawny hair blowing in the breeze and, although I couldn't make out the colour in the dark, I could tell he had bright eyes and a wide smile. He was in a blue shirt, with smart, black jeans and Converse, surrounded by friends who were all laughing at something he'd said.

There was something about him that made me not want to look away. Maybe it was the lines in his cheeks as he smiled. Or the way he dipped his chin when someone else was talking to show he was listening. Either way,

I noticed him like I'd notice a rocket exploding against a dark sky.

"Who is *that?*" I asked Sam.

He stumped out his sparkler in the sand bucket placed by our feet. "*Him?* That's my idiot brother. We don't like him."

My gaze flicked back to Sam, his long hair covering part of his eyes. I pulled my beanie lower in a hope of disguising the heat in my face. "He *does* look like an idiot," I agreed. Although he really didn't, of course. A warm, exhilarating sensation was brewing inside of me every time I looked his way.

Not that he'd noticed me noticing him. But I was *definitely* noticing him.

"How old is he?" I asked, working hard to keep my voice somewhat disinterested.

"Seventeen."

"Cool."

"He's not *cool*. He's an idiot."

"Why? What does he do?"

Sam scrunched his face up, glaring in his brother's direction. "What doesn't he do? He's Mum and Dad's favourite, to start with. He's on all the sports teams. I have to wear all his shitty clothes when he's done with them and worst of all, he messes up my room and then tells Mum I did it."

"That's rude."

"Like I said. He's an idiot."

"Right," I nodded. "What's his name?"

Sam paused to test my expression. "Why?" he asked with narrowed eyes.

I bit my lip guilty.

"I don't know. If we're going to be friends, I feel like I should know your brother's name. That's all."

Sam took another look at his brother before sighing. "Freddie. But just pretend he doesn't exist."

THREE

The day after Boxing Day, Fliss agrees to meet up at our local pub for brunch. I'm early and there's a steady flow of people milling about. It's that weird time between Christmas and New Year where nobody knows what day of the week it is and we're all still drinking eggnog before two in the afternoon. Luckily, we close the gallery for the whole Christmas period, so I get a good festive break.

Fliss has been a rock during my break-up with Adam, always making herself available to talk it over. She walks in through the main doors and pauses to look around. I smile at the sight of her. I find Fliss's dress sense to be a bit out there, and today is no different. Her dark hair has been pushed back by a bright-fuchsia headband which matches her long teddy coat. She's always the sparkiest person in any room. She exists in stark contrast to me, who likes to dress in dull colours so as not to draw attention to myself. I prefer to be unseen as much as I can help it. Unfortunately, my hair never got the memo.

It's also no surprise when I see she is being flanked by her unfairly handsome boyfriend.

I mean, really, she could work harder not to rub it in.

He's all dark features and long lines, with dazzling, blue eyes. He places a hand on Fliss's lower back and nods in my direction, having spotted me first. She lights up, flouncing over and sliding into the booth on the bench opposite.

"Hello," she says, smiling.

"Good morning, I see you brought James along to rub salt in my wounds," I say, but she knows I don't mean it. James has introduced a calmness to Fliss that has helped her really come out of herself. Going freelance was the best idea she's ever had, after her previous high-stress, corporate role all but burnt her out, but I'm not sure she'd have believed in herself enough to take the leap without his undying support.

"I'm more pepper than salt," James adds, standing beside us. "What can I get you ladies to drink?"

"Espresso Martinis?" Fliss asks me.

I nod. "Well, it's still morning, so if we're drinking alcohol, we really ought to make it caffeinated."

"Right you are," James says, turning and stepping up to the bar with a slight lean, hands in pockets. He's so smooth.

I eye Fliss. "So, that's going well then?"

She nods. "It's our first Christmas together. His sisters have been nice… I think. They're very protective of him. The younger one asked me what my intentions were with her brother yesterday evening."

I snort. "I'm sorry? Your intentions?"

"Like I said, they're a protective bunch. But his mum is

lovely, and his nephew is adorable. And so far, my parents are treating James like he's been in the family for years."

"In the family?! That's *very* serious."

Fliss's face colours. "I know but it just feels right. I hated him before I loved him…" She stops talking, twisting her gaze to James's back, who probably didn't hear her. I decide to torture her over it anyway.

"Love?!"

"SSHH!" she bats her hands at me as if to blow away the word.

"You said love!"

"SSSHH!"

"Oh, Fliss, that's wonderful. I'm sure he feels the same about you. I've seen the way he looks…"

"Oh my God!" she whisper-hisses. "If you don't stop talking right now, I'm going to throw my cocktail over you."

"But then you'd have to explain to James why you wasted a £12 drink on me."

"Worth it."

"To be honest, this is mostly payback for being so cute and loved up…"

"Don't say that word!"

"…when I'm so lonely and broken."

Fliss sighs and tilts her head. "That's not really what you think, is it? I thought you liked living alone?"

"It's true. It's nice. The novelty hasn't worn off just yet. But you know, my feet were really cold last night. The sort of cold where not even fluffy socks can help you and I couldn't be bothered to get up and find a hot water bottle, so I cried a little bit because I didn't have a man's hairy legs to warm them on."

"Fuck, that's sad."

"I know…"

"No, like you need to a get grip."

I laugh. "Well, ok. But I have a plan. Dylan made some great points at Christmas lunch."

"Dylan? Your perennially in-debt cousin whose been bailed out by his parents five times? The same Dylan who leant his car to a guy he met on Grindr and never saw it again? *That* Dylan gave you advice?"

"Well, when you say it like that…" I grimace. "In fairness, he let me join the Black Sheep Parade. It sounded right up my street."

"No, Hattie, we don't take advice from the resident black sheep. I'm *so* glad you called me because this could've been a disaster."

She pauses as James returns with our drinks. He squeezes in beside her, stretching his long arm over the back of their bench. Fliss leans into him instinctively. A hideous thing to behold when you're *this* single over Christmas.

"But humour me anyway. What was his advice?" she asks.

"I'm not sure what his exact advice was but I did conclude that I need to take back the final year of my twenties. You know, since Adam stole my youth from me."

Fliss and James blink at me for a moment before she says, "As someone in her thirties who still feels youthful, I find that statement offensive. But if we dodge past that for a second, I think you're onto something."

"Really?"

"Yeah, I do. I think you deserve to go a little wild. Why the hell not?"

James gives her a sideways glance. "Excuse me, have we met?"

Fliss ignores him. "So, what is your plan?"

"Ah there it is," James laughs. "Go wild, but have a plan."

Again, Fliss ignores him. "Make a list."

"Oh yes. A super-wild *list*," he adds, before he grunts from what I can only imagine is irritated-girlfriend elbow pressure.

"I have actually thought about this in detail," I begin. "First, I need to throw a party for my birthday. I was planning on a pub thing with Sam and the girls anyway after schmoozing with the family, but screw them, I think it needs to be bigger. It needs to be a whole trip. An adventure. Something Adam would've never approved of for all the many stupid reasons he always had. And then I need take a whole year and just make it mine. I want to travel, and I want to live on my own to prove to myself that I can."

Fliss leans forward, resting her hands on the table, while I take a sip of my cocktail. I swear you can never not look elegant whilst drinking an espresso martini. My pinkie finger is liberated.

"You've been living with Adam since you were twenty-one, yeah? If you feel like you need to prove your independence to yourself then do it. But own it. Don't let yourself be forced off-track."

"What do you mean by that?" I ask.

"Well... Ok, and don't take this the wrong way..."

"I love sentences that start like that," I quip.

"You definitely have relationship-girl vibes. I mean you're a very sweet, kind and attractive girl. Any guy would be lucky to have you, and I think they'd give it a good go."

"Adam didn't seem too bothered anymore," I point out.

"Screw Adam!"

"Yeah, screw Adam," James imitates but with a glint in his eye that says he's here and he's supportive even if he doesn't really understand why. In fact, he looks whiplashed by our whole conversation.

I hold my hands up in surrender. "Ok, well, I personally don't think it's going to be so difficult to avoid a relationship. I created a Tinder profile two weeks ago and within fifteen minutes, a man was requesting photos of my feet, so I deleted it."

"I think I'm going to get another drink." James shakes his head good-humouredly and gets up before I say anything else.

"Ew. Did he even flirt or was it just straight in there with the foot fetish?"

"In fairness, he did ask me what my favourite Disney character was."

"Which is?"

"Bambi."

"Oof. So, you basically insinuated you were an innocent little baby deer?"

"So, a fawn," I correct. "He didn't ask which character I *related* to most."

"Which would be?"

"Ok, also Bambi… I'm curious and occasionally naïve. And hey, that would make you Thumper."

"We're getting off topic," she says, before pausing and trying to remember what we were talking about. "We need to set some rules. Have you got any paper?"

"I have a napkin," I offer. Fliss, being Fliss, tucks her hand into her bag and produces three different colours of pen. "Always so organised."

"Thank you." She smiles.

"I don't know if it was a compliment, actually."

"I'm taking it as one anyway."

I swipe the black pen because I'm going wild, not psychotic – I can't use red or blue pen on pub napkin; that would be crazy. I write RULES at the top and underline it, only to rip some of it in the process. Never mind…

"First rule?" I ask.

"No serious relationships for the whole of next year."

"Right. No issue. Easy." I write it down, the ink blurring slightly on the dots. "Rule two?"

"Travel to at least four or five other countries?" she asks as if it's up to me how many it should be. I write minimum of four.

"I love it. Any more?"

"The living-by-yourself rule," she adds. "One whole year."

I jot this down too then sit back and proudly stare at my napkin of rules.

"Oh! And the party thing. You should do that. I obviously can't do anything for New Years, *sorry*, but you know Sam will and I'm sure your other uni friends will leap at it."

I frown. "I don't know… Priya has a nine-month-old baby and Sara has been really distant recently. Besides, she probably wants to hang out with her fiancé." I shrug. "I'm sure Sam would be well up for a trip away. Even if it was just the two of us, we couldn't do it at my studio anyway. It's too small."

"Great! Make it happen, Hattie," Fliss says. "Oh, and invite his hot older brother while you're at it," she adds with a mischievous grin.

26

I start. "I have no idea who you're talking about. But also no, he's *very* off limits."

She takes a large sip of her drink. "Even better."

That evening, while I'm watching the show *I* want to watch (*Modern Family*) and I'm eating the meal *I* want to eat (prawn Thai curry), I take out my phone and multitask like a bloody pro. I'm sat in my short pyjamas with the heating on because I can, and nobody can stop me. Ok, my bill at the end of the month will have things to say about it but for now, I'm happy. I open my uni group chat and think about how to start this conversation.

Butt Chat was devised in our second year of university when we all moved in together in Brighton. Priya, Sara and I lived together in halls during the first year and, because Sam sort of came as part of my furniture, they befriended him too and then we had enough people for a student house in the city during our second year. We moved into a three-bed terrace, the front room becoming our fourth bedroom, on the graffitied, ridiculously steep Butt Lane.

Hence, Butt Chat.

I fork a mouthful of noodles, enjoying the tanginess of the sauce as I type with my other hand. Like I said, professional-level multitasking.

Hattie
Anyone up for going away for NY to celebrate Sam and my birthday? I know it's last minute so you might not be able to, but I really want to celebrate properly.

Sam
Count me in.

Sam
No pubbing then? What you thinking Hatter?

Sara
Ooo. Where?

Hattie
I'm sure we could find a house to rent?
My flat is too small.

Priya
I'm in. I need to get away. This is perfect.

Sam
I'll look at places. Any requirements?

Priya
Hot tub

Sara
Own room.

Hattie
Fairly private

Sam
You planning on murdering us?

Priya
I need a fridge for BM

Sam
BM? Bondage…

Priya
Breast milk, Sam. Get a grip

Hattie
We should go tomorrow and make a real thing of it!
Sam, you book something, yeah? We can sort money
later. Plus ones welcome! The more, the merrier

Sara
Wow, ok. Cool of you to assume we're free at such short notice

Priya
I am

Sara
You're ruining my point Pri

Priya
Sorry was I meant to pretend I'm really busy and sociable
over New Year? Cause I think Hattie would see through that

Sara
Never mind. Mike had a thing but I didn't want to go anyway.
Perfect excuse to get out of it

Sam

So are we doing this? Are we actually doing a Butt Lane get together?

                                                                    Hattie

                                                            I think we are

Priya

WOOWOO

Sara

You guys are weird. No plus one for me

                                                                    Hattie

                            Mike won't want to change his plans to join us?

Sara

Nah, he's got a family thing.

Priya

But he's your fiancé…

                                                                    Hattie

                                        And he's no bother. We love Mike!

Sara

Thanks, but just me

Priya

And just me too. Issy will stay with her mum and baby Ollie

Hattie

I'll sort food

Sara

I'll get drink

Priya

I'll barely have time to get myself showered before I step out the door so count me out from organising. Hattie I'll send you a list of ingredients we need. I'll do a buffet. Can someone pick me up?

Sam

I'll borrow Freddie's car and drive us. Sara, you want to get the train into Seaford?

Hattie

We can't book a house in walking distance?

Sam

Not with a hot tub in our budget

The chat goes quiet for a bit as I clean the kitchen before more messages light up my phone. Sam has sent through pictures of a seafront apartment in Brighton. It's nice but I just know we'll end up going out into the city which isn't the vibe I was going for. I message back that, crucially, there's no hot tub.

Priya

Agree. Have my heart set on overheating in a fancy outdoors bubble bath now.

Sara

Tell me you don't actually put bubble bath in your hot tubs

Priya

Is that not a thing?

Sam

What about this one?

A link comes through of a modernised cottage in Surrey. It's expensive for what it is. Pretty. Very *The Holiday*. To be honest, I'm surprised it's even available at such short notice around the festive period.

Sara

Ceilings too low. I'll bang my head.

Sam

Good shout. I'm taller than you. Wouldn't need booze though. We could just get high off multiple concussions.

The links to potential house party locations don't stop, and we continue to critique Sam's choices. The worst being a rundown townhouse that is being advertised with literal mould on the walls. Sam swears it's just decoration. It is not. The best option is a London penthouse which Sam thought was priced per the whole stay instead of just one afternoon. Three grand gets you a fabulous three hours. I actually don't want to know why there's an option to rent a penthouse in the city for just an afternoon.

Sara

Well obviously it's an expensive shag pad.

Priya

They don't even stay the night?

Sara

No, they have to go home to their spouses, silly

Priya

Gross

Sam

What about this one then? I'm getting tired and you lot are the fussiest fuckers I know!

This time, he doesn't send a link, and I wonder if this to prevent further detailed critiques. Instead, he sends screenshots of the website. It's a lodge in a forest, all timber framed and like something out of a modern-day fairytale. And there's a hot tub.

To be honest, my eyes are feeling heavy and it's a miracle all of Butt Chat want to even come with us. So, in the spirit of jumping at opportunities for a whole year...

Hattie

Perfect. Book it

Sara

Why no link?

Priya

Yes to hot tub and friendly forest squirrels

Sara

Where does it say there are friendly forest squirrels? I don't want that. Don't sign me up for friendly forest creatures.

Sam

You know what… BOOKED. Leave me alone. I'm tired

Sara

I won't be happy if there are squirrels.

Hattie

Night Butt Chat

Priya

I'm going to go full on Disney Princess and force you to make friends with them

Sara

I *will* set traps

FOUR

The one where he hated our music

Four hours before I turned sixteen, Sam and I were jumping around his room like lunatics dancing to 'Untouched' by The Veronicas on full volume. The adults were downstairs doing their usual shmoozing and drinking until they could barely stand while we got buzzed off too much Diet Coke, jam doughnuts and Haribo. Earlier that day, we'd been to the cinema with a few school friends in a joint birthday celebration of sorts, but the Harrisons' house party that night was still very much for adults. It wasn't explicitly said so, but we knew we were to be seen and not heard. Except we'd decided to be heard and not seen.

We were in our emo era. It was all heavy eyeliner, dark clothes, messed-up hair and those black-and-white chequered belts. I even had a streak of pink hair for the Christmas holidays as it wasn't allowed at school.

Since we had become friends two years ago, we had been practically inseparable. Turns out Sam wasn't all that popular at school, so I was doing him a favour on my first day as much as he was me. We made a point of being introverted by slinking off to corners to listen to music, sharing earphones from one of our bashed-up iPods. There was a kind of melody to it. A friendship founded through our flaws rather than our strengths.

I lived a ten-minute drive away around that time, so Mum would drop me off outside the Harrisons' house so we could walk to school together. Dad had already been promoted, so he was no longer working for Sam's dad, which resolved any concerns I had about power dynamics.

One day, on our stroll in, Sam said, "You're my friend."

I snorted. "What? *No.* Haven't you worked out yet that we're mortal enemies? I'm just keeping you close."

"Obviously. But for the sake of appearances, we have to act like friends."

"Obviously."

"And if we're pretending to be friends, I have a rule."

"Rules are boring."

"It's important."

I tucked my thumbs under my backpack strap and shrugged. "Fine, I guess. What is it?"

Sam sighed. "You can't fancy my brother."

Heat pooled in my cheeks. "I thought we'd established he's an idiot? I'm not going to fancy an idiot."

Sam stepped ahead of me and blocked my path, his cool, blue gaze scrutinising my face as he flicked his head back to get the hair out of his eyes. I swallowed, trying to corral my features into blankness. I didn't even know his brother. I'd only seen glimpses at best. The problem was that the glimpses I had gotten had a way of making my tummy dip and my fingers tingle. The only other time I'd ever experienced that kind of sensation before was from watching the live-action *Peter Pan*.

If Sam could see that in my expression, he didn't let on. At the end of the day, I needed him as a friend, and he needed me. It wasn't as if I was ever going to have a chance with Freddie anyway, so I decided to continue to pretend.

Sam kept his narrowed eyes on me as he said, "It's important because he gets everything he wants and does whatever he wants, and I hate him. And if you like him then I can't like you. It's the way it has to be."

I nodded. "If you want me to hate him on your behalf then I will. Consider him hated."

"He's the worst," Sam reiterated, but he fell in step, satisfied with my declaration.

It wasn't until we changed the music to Panic! At The Disco and started to sing (well, scream and shout) the lyrics that the door to Sam's room opened so fast, we both jumped and flung ourselves onto his bed, squealing as if we were about to be murdered. I tried to hide under his pillow, but Sam snatched it off me to use as a shield.

A tall man stood in the door, looking at us with wild, kiwi-green eyes. His tawny hair was all mussed up as if he'd been sleeping or lying down. It took me a second to register that it was Freddie. I'd hardly seen him since he'd been at university. Especially as, when he was at home, he barely left his bedroom. There had been something stirring in the Harrison household that year. A shift in the mood. They patched it over whenever I was around but something was broken, the cracks hard to completely disguise. No one spoke much at dinner, sullen looks shared across the table, and everyone escaped to their rooms as soon as they were done with their food. The living room had become cold and lifeless.

When I'd arrived for the party, Sam's parents had been holding hands downstairs and smiling at each other. It occurred to me that it was strange to see them so close.

Sam never talked about it, though. The Harrisons were masters of sweeping things under the rug.

"Are you fucking taking the piss, Sam?" Freddie growled, taking two long strides across the room and grabbing the speakers.

Sam flung himself at Freddie, tackling his legs. "Don't... You fuck! That's mine!" He must've knocked Freddie's knees because he collapsed to the ground and rolled to kick Sam off. They scuffled like that briefly while I hugged my knees, out of reach.

"I have company, and they don't want to listen to this *shit* music," Freddie grunted between punches, both given and received.

I watched them grapple some more, thanking my lucky stars I was an only child. Sam was all claws and sharp angles, catching Freddie with elbows, knees and even his chin at one point. Meanwhile, Freddie was strong, able to keep Sam away from him for seconds at a time with only one arm.

"We're listening to that!" Sam wailed once he was finally pinned to the floor. "You're such a stupid fuck! It's my birthday! I'll listen to what I want to!"

Freddie hadn't noticed there was someone else in the room. He frowned when he looked up, his eyes connecting with mine in a way that could've melted me on the spot. Sam took this opportunity to kick him in the groin, which had Freddie rolling and coughing into the foetal position. Sam snatched the speaker back and kicked his brother once more for good measure.

"Get out!" Sam yelled.

Freddie slowly got himself together, climbing at first to a seated position before standing and giving Sam a deadly look. "You're lucky I'm too old to tell on you, you little shit."

"Idiot," Sam muttered back.

"Keep it down," Freddie replied, eyeing him with a warning stare.

"Whatever!"

Freddie looked at me again. Being in such close proximity to this handsome, grown man made me entirely incomprehensible. I could just smell a hint of mint and alcohol rolling off his breath. "Sorry you had to witness that, Hattie. But I'm even sorrier you have such terrible taste in friends. If you ever need rescuing, just bang on that wall three times, yeah?"

He left with a wink as a George R. R. Martin book from Sam's collection was flung towards the back of his head. I willed my imagination not to picture Freddie coming to my rescue but failed entirely.

"Stop it," Sam said to me, pointing a finger.

My eyes went wide. "What?!"

"You're such a girl," he said, rolling his eyes. "You know he has an *actual* woman next door, right? Like an adult female."

"Don't say female. It's icky."

"You promised not to fancy him."

I scoffed dramatically. "I don't! He's an idiot, remember!"

"Hmm..." was all Sam said before pushing his chest of drawers in front of his door and putting Enter Shikari on full volume to really piss Freddie off. My dancing afterwards was half-hearted, desperate to will away the heavy feeling from my legs.

FIVE

The next day, I hear a horn blare from the road. As per usual, I'm not as ready as I said I was, but it's the adrenaline kick I need to get out the door. I rush out of my room and into my small but clean kitchen space, grabbing my keys and a pink bobble hat from the table and squishing it down over my hair. I step up to the full-length mirror by the door and check for eye bogeys. I'm presentable, although I'm regretting my choice in jeans; these ones keep riding up a little high. I do the weird squat thing to set them right, pull on my brown suede boots and grab my black puffer coat.

I'm excited. Sam went all out, booking the place we chose until New Year's Day with late checkout to cater for hangovers.

I jog the short path from the flats to the long, black Volvo estate Sam's borrowed from Freddie. It's a great car – we've used it several times, including this summer, right after my break-up with Adam, when Sam insisted on a Cornish kayaking trip to cheer me up. And of course, the Harrisons own their own kayaks that can be attached to the roof of this estate. The windows are blacked out so I can't see his face as I slide my suitcase and the six bags of food into the huge boot, now full to the brim, before hopping into the front seat, which is always reserved for me since they've all been privy to my travel sickness horrors on our university road trips. The only way to avoid my queasiness is to sit up front and stare ahead.

"Sorry, I had to sort these jeans out. They're giving me a terrible wedgie." I turn to give Sam a hug across the centre console, but I pause in surprise, the car suddenly feeling extremely warm. "Oh!" I say instead, when I find those sharp, green eyes looking back at me. "Freddie."

"Hello, Hattie," he says, his face impassive as if he didn't hear what I just said. I swear my pulse beats in rhythm with the low timbre of his voice.

I twist in my seat, schooling my features into indifference to find Sam, Priya and Sara squished into the back seats. Sam does a stilted wave. "How's your wedgie now?"

Fuck. Why on earth did I say that? I'm a bit breathless so I focus on calming my senses. "Oh yeah. Fine, thanks."

Sam leans forward. "Freddie wanted to come so I'm making him drive."

"I *agreed* to drive," he corrects, his eyes unwavering from my face, as if he's counting freckles. It gives me shivers – and not the bad kind. The kind where I feel the need to cross my legs and bite my knuckles.

Why is Freddie here? This is *not* part of the plan.

"Oh, ok. Are there enough rooms then?" I ask.

"Eh," is Sam's reply. "We'll figure it out. Priya already said she doesn't mind sharing with Sara."

"I sort of wanted my own room…" Sara starts.

I spin round to get a read on her face. She's been distant recently which is very out of character. I almost want to shake her and demand she tell me what's wrong, but she's the kind of person who would shut down even quicker with the wrong kind of prompt, so I hold my tongue. Maybe there'll be time whilst we're away.

"Hey," I say softly to acknowledge my best friends. "I can share with Priya," I offer.

"I'll sleep on the floor if I have to," Freddie chimes in.

I message Butt Chat discreetly whilst Freddie fiddles with the satnav.

Hattie

WTF Sam. Thought you hated spending time with Freddie?

Sam

He wants to be friends again

Hattie

Ok so?! You just decided to invite him?

Sam

Didn't think you'd care tbh

Sara

Yeah, why do you care Hattie? xoxo

Oh, now she decides to chime in. Priya hasn't looked at her phone so she's oblivious. Freddie frowns, tapping on the car screen. "Sam, this doesn't seem right."

"What doesn't?"

"The postcode you gave me."

"It's what it says on the information pack."

"Yeah, but it's four hours away."

"It's *what*?" I ask but immediately regret when Freddie turns his intense gaze back on me. I shift in my seat, overly aware of his proximity.

Sam leans forward to look. "Oh, yeah." He sounds far too relaxed about this. "Well, it ticks all the boxes. Four bedrooms, hot tub and serial-killer-level rural."

"Why am I already regretting coming with you?" Freddie mutters, leaning back in his chair with a sigh.

I want to point out that this was *my* idea, and I didn't really invite him so he's welcome to leave, but he makes me nervous. Especially around Sam, who's always been very pointed about me not being nice to his brother. And because, more importantly, Sam is never very nice to him either.

The trip that I'd planned has already become weird. Why *is* Freddie here? Sam wouldn't normally invite him to anything. What does Sam mean by him wanting to be friends again? *Again*?! They were never friendly in the first place. Not really. At least that's how it's seemed in the fifteen years I've known them.

They've had a transactional relationship these past few years. The car, for example. But I haven't seen them have a proper conversation since before their parents' divorce and even then, it was fraught. But you know what, *no*, I'm not going to pass up on an adventure with my best friends. Besides, I can tell by the shadows under Priya's eyes, and the messy mum bun she's rocking, that she needs this more than anyone. She recently told me she hadn't slept for five days which took her towards the brink of a mental breakdown.

She looked me in the eye, during the worst of it, and said, "I googled whether you could die from sleep deprivation, Hattie. Do you know what it said? It said yes. *Yes*, I might die." If I can release her from that for even a few days, then I will.

And what's more, I need to find a way to get through to Sara. I have to understand what I've done to push her away.

In hindsight, I'm not sure we should've trusted Sam with booking a place. And Freddie being here is... I don't even know what it is, but I'm trying to remember *my* rules. I'm taking back the final year of my twenties and nothing, including a four-hour drive, is going to stop me.

"You know you guys signed off on this property so you can't blame me," Sam tries to defend himself.

"That's why you sent screenshots, isn't it? You knew where it was," Sara accuses.

"How dare you," Sam says back, deadpan.

She tuts. "You knew. You just wanted to go to bed so you gave up."

"In my defence..."

"I knew it."

"...it was an impossible mission to book somewhere with all your requirements in our puny budget this close to the New Year. So you'll excuse—"

"Does anyone want to bail?" I ask, interrupting.

"I need this," Sara mumbles quietly. I thought she'd be the first to jump out the car. She's not usually a fan of long drives.

Priya shakes her head, a grin taking up most of her cheery face. "Four hours to sleep in a big, comfy car? Count me in."

I look at Sam. "I'd go anywhere with you, my mad hatter," he says.

And without looking at Freddie, because I'm still squeezing my thighs too tight, I know he's in because he turns the engine on and puts the car into first gear.

I'm scanning the information pack Sam printed off. Apparently, we're going to a remote lodge in the Forest of Dean. I ignore the fact that it's meant to be freezing this week.

Freddie opts to use the built-in satnav for the first part of the journey as it's mainly motorways, but the instructions suggest we switch to Google Maps if we get lost nearer to our destination.

"You know, I can just connect my Google Maps now if that's easier?" I suggest.

"I can use mine."

"I've already got the postcode set up. It's no bother. I'll just connect the Bluetooth. Besides, then you'll have to listen to my music."

Freddie huffs a laugh. "Lucky me."

The feminine, robotic voice confirms the connection then starts reeling off instructions until we hit the motorway and it's pretty much 'go straight' for miles. I fold the printed info pack and hand it back to Sam, only to discover he's already dozed off, his head tipped back, with a lightly snoring Priya resting on his shoulder. Sara has her state-of-the-art headphones on, drowning us all out.

Freddie turns the volume down so as not to disrupt the others. Unfortunately, this also means I can't taunt him with some of my old-school emo classics.

I place the printout in the glovebox and check the time. We've only been driving for an hour and it's barely afternoon. So, somehow, I find myself in a car with the only other person awake, and the one I wasn't even expecting to be here. I peek across at him concentrating on the road. He's wearing a green t-shirt, his forearms all long lines with a smattering of light-brown hair, as he flexes his sturdy, large fingers around the steering wheel. I wonder what they'd feel like wrapped around...

Oh man.

I need to get a grip.

I look away quickly, leaning my elbow on the window. I fish my phone out of my pocket, texting Fliss.

SOS Freddie is driving and I'm in the passenger seat.

I twist my phone away subtly, so he can't see what I've written. Fliss will know what to do. She's sensible and switched on.

I slide my phone back in my pocket when I see she's offline, not expecting an immediate response, and wonder what I'm meant to say to my friend's brother whom I'm meant to hate. Do I ask him about himself or is that too friendly? Do I just ignore him? Will that make it awkward?

Has the silence already lingered on for too long? Is this weird?

Oh shit. I am not good at reading a social situation. I think it's because I've always had Adam or Sam to fill in for me in those skills. Or is this a panic specific to Freddie? I chew on my tongue, contemplating.

A prompt pops up on the car screen. Freddie reaches across to press *accept*.

The feminine, robotic voice says, "The hot one? The one you had a wet dream about at uni?"

I blink but I can't help giving Freddie a funny look. He too is frowning as if he's entirely mystified by these messages.

I roll my eyes. "A girlfriend?" I ask, which has him frowning even deeper.

"No. I don't have a bloody clue who that was."

Another message pops up. He hits *accept* again. How is he not wholly embarrassed? The robot says, "Don't ignore me. I can see you've read the message. Is he still hot?"

A sickening dread washes over me. I look at Freddie, whose expression says he's running through a million scenarios as to who these messages could be from, but my fears are *way* worse. I reach for my phone to confirm they are in fact from Fliss.

FUCK. The Bluetooth. *Ahhhhh!*

Heat flushes my face like someone's tipped a bucket of warm honey over my head. I scroll up to the top of my phone and turn Bluetooth off immediately. I hold my spare hand over my mouth, my breathing choppy.

I'm going to be sick. And this time, I can't blame it on travelling.

The stupid robot chimes in again. "Hattie's phone. Disconnected."

What a fucking bitch!

I'm frozen solid. Isn't that what Bambi would do? Play

dead if under threat? Am I under threat? It certainly feels like it.

"Do you have a thing for Sam?" Freddie whispers, leaning towards me.

I turn to look at him slowly. My face must be a picture. I'm sweating. *Why am I sweating*? How do I talk myself out of this?

"What? No! And I don't know what that was, but it wasn't my phone."

Freddie narrows his eyes. I swear I see the corner of his mouth drift up but then it's gone so quickly, you'd never know. "What a strange coincidence. There must be another Hattie driving nearby."

I nod. "Very weird."

He signals to overtake a middle-lane-hogger, and that's the perfect distraction for me to stare out at the lowering amber sun. The inside of my cheek is going to be so blistered by the time we reach the lodge from all the biting. I make a desperate plan to persuade Sara to switch seats with me when we stop off at the services. Anything to escape this embarrassment.

He must know it was about him. But he's so cool, so schooled, he knows exactly how to play it and that terrifies me. I'm not on his level. He's expert. I'm a bumbling beginner. I don't dare reply to Fliss just in case.

I jump when he clears his throat. "So, how've you been since I saw you last?"

"Erm, remind me, when was that?"

He scratches his chin. "Probably in hospital... When Sam..."

I save Freddie from having to remind me of the details. "Oh yeah. That was what... Two, three years ago?"

"It was three years ago," he confirms. "You were living miserably in London if I remember."

"That's right." I swallow, thinking of the flat I lived in with Adam briefly and the reasons we decided to live apart. Was that when the relationship started to crack?

"Sam mentioned that you're working at the Budes' gallery down on the seafront now," he says, changing the subject, the perfect segway from thoughts of my ex.

"Yes, that's right. It's the best job I've ever had, actually. Wouldn't trade it for the world."

"Great," he says, then adds, "and I heard about Adam." He frowns and wipes a hand over his face as if he's flustered. It's a look I've only seen on him once before. "Sorry, that was insensitive. You probably don't want to talk about that."

"No, it's ok. I'm over it," I say, which grants me an impressed nod. "Well, I'm over *him*. I'm not over *it*, if you know what I mean?"

"I think so?"

I'm not sure I'm quite ready to explain to Freddie how it all went down with Adam, so I stare ahead. "What about you? Still enjoying city life?" I ask, changing the subject as smoothly as I can.

He shrugs, his gaze focused on the road ahead. "I don't mind it. The money is great." I nod, unsure where to take it from there. But Freddie starts talking again before I can worry whether I've let the silence linger too long. "Do you ever feel like you've somehow managed to cram yourself into a box you can't escape from?"

"Like a cardboard box? Did Sam tell you I did that?" I throw a frown over my shoulder at my blabber of a best friend.

Freddie's eyebrows knot together. "Huh?"

"I was drunk. It was one time. Sam had to cut me out."

He blinks. "I was talking metaphorically."

I bite my lip. "Mmm. Yeah, I know." *Stupid*.

He laughs. "How big was the box?"

"What box?"

"The box you got stuck in."

"What?"

"Ok, we'll add that to the pretend-it-didn't-happen list, yeah?"

Ah, crap. My eyes go wide, which makes Freddie chuckle deeply. Is it normal to be able to feel your pulse in your wrist?

Sexy, stupid man with stupid sexy, deep laugh.

"Tell me about the metaphorical box then. Sounds like you're having a crisis and I'm hoping it's worse than mine."

Freddie snorts. "I just feel that because I've been promoted so many times now..."

"Hate that for you."

"...that I'm stuck in a big, important, pointless role I don't even really like. I have to drag myself into the office these days and all I do is talk about toplines and budgets all day, every day. It's... I don't know." He shrugs.

"Sorry, but are you seriously sitting there complaining about being *too* well off and successful to someone who barely earns minimum wage running a tiny gallery?"

"You love it, though," he points out. "I feel like that's worth a lot more."

"No. It literally isn't. That's how money works. How did you get promoted again?"

Freddie shakes his head, his green eyes sharp as he laughs.

"I forgot how gobby you get." He finds Sam in the rearview mirror. "You two were always so alike. It was like he'd recruited you to join his army against me."

"That is exactly what happened. We were mortal enemies, brought together to ruin your life."

Freddie's expression goes taut again as he signals to overtake, and I wonder if I've touched a nerve when Sara startles me by tapping me on the shoulder. "When's the first stop? I need to go."

Freddie takes over, saying he'll make a stop at the next services. Which, thank God, because I was in very real danger of getting along with the man I'm contractually bound to hate.

SIX

The one where he dobbed us in

A week before Christmas, ahead of our eighteenth birthdays, Sam cycled over to mine in a hurry and explained he had his mum's house to himself for New Year while she was abroad in Sydney. And even better, Freddie was going back to university early so literally nobody would even find out.

Sam's dad had moved out that summer and things were rough in the Harrison household. Despite being Sam's best friend, we rarely discussed his family life. So, although I was there for him and we hung out even more than usual, he never really told me much about it. Or, I suppose more importantly, how he *felt* about it. He just wasn't that kind of person.

But I was aware of two key things. Firstly, Sam no longer spoke to his dad. And secondly, Freddie *was* talking to their dad and this made him even more despicable than before.

"Why are you telling me this?" I asked, busy finishing off an art project due in for my assignment the very next day.

I couldn't see beyond this canvas, let alone a fortnight away. My head was in crafting mode – not party mode.

Sam positioned himself next to me, facing the opposite way so I literally couldn't help but look at him. "What?!" I demanded. I was stressed. My paints weren't doing what I wanted them to. Before moving to Seaford, my art had been all about city animals, squirrels and pigeons and urban foxes. Now all I could get inspired by was the sea. And I was trying out different techniques to capture its beauty. But something about mixing art and exams and qualifications stole the joy from me and all I really felt right in that moment was frustration.

Frustration, because the colours weren't coming through in the way I was hoping for.

Frustration, because I wanted to do a collage, but my art teacher pushed me to do paints.

Frustration with Sam, because he was distracting me and I only had one sleepless night left before this was due.

And did I need to start it again from scratch!?

Sam took the paint brush out of my hand, dipping it into the wrong water pot, and that was the last straw. I stared at him as I burst into tears.

"What the hell?" he said, blanching at first but then tentatively taking me into his arms and squishing me in that way he did. It was so unromantic, it would make me laugh.

I sighed. "I'm just so tired."

"Perfect. This is a great opportunity to let your hair down and go a little a wild."

"I'm always wild."

Sam stepped back to look me up and down. "Right now, you're a bit uptight and I'm frightened."

"I'm just trying to get this done."

"But hello, *party*? For our *eighteenth* birthday? Yeah? Go on, you know you want to."

"You could do it without me," I pointed out.

"I can't, though; it breaks tradition. And besides, you're the one who has all the friends. They only hang out with me because of you."

"You have *some* friends."

"Yeah, but they're lame, and you know it."

I snorted. "Oh, I see. You want me to invite girls."

"Whaaaat?" Sam objected half-heartedly. "I mean it would be good if there were girls there as well as lads, but I think you're missing the key point here."

"And that is?"

"We have the house to ourselves on our birthdays!"

I faux-gasped. "How could I resist?"

"Exactly. So, yes, you're in?"

I groaned. "Yeah, yeah, I'll be there."

And so, we set about organising the house party of the century, or at least, that's what we called it. It was an open house for everyone in the sixth form who wanted to let their hair down, and to celebrate our birthdays *and* see the New Year in in style.

We made some mistakes.

We'd put the event as an open invite on Facebook. Need I say more?

The event invite was shared between friends, and friends and more friends, and cousins, brothers, sisters... eventually getting way out of hand. And we didn't cotton on to how insanely popular the party would become until around eleven at night, when the house was so full, we could barely move.

Then there was the startling sound of glass smashing.

Sam's alarmed eyes found mine from across the living room. He was sporting shorter hair then, styling it to look messier than its natural state, which was saying a lot. There must've been at least 300 people at the party by that point. Waves of faces and voices and music. All in this massive sensory overload.

Pip, a friend from art class, pushed through the crowd to reach me just as Sam did the same. "Someone's smashed the back doors in," she said.

I laughed. "Pardon?"

"The back doors!" she screeched. "There's glass everywhere!"

Sam looked at me with terror. "Do you think we fucked up?" he asked.

I didn't have time to answer; instead, I pushed through the crowd, Sam hot on my heels, towards the kitchen at the back of the house. There was sick on the stairs, blue liquid (I assume some kind of alcopop) thrown all up one wall and a boy curled up on the floor by the downstairs loo. I leant down to check his pulse and...

"Oh, for crying out loud!" I yelled.

"What now?" Pip asked. I hadn't even notice her follow us. Her mousey features were pinched with worry as she ran her hands through her sleek, dark hair. She was too much of a goody two-shoes for all of this. I could almost hear her vibrating with anxiety.

Sam leant over my shoulder to get a good look as I took

my phone out. "No! You can't call your parents! If they come round and see this, we're toast."

"But Dylan's fucked. Look at him." *Stupid baby cousin.* When had he even arrived?

"Why did you invite him? Isn't he sixteen?"

I scoffed. "Why the hell would I have invited him?"

"He's here, isn't he?"

"I didn't invite him, dickhead."

"We should watch our language," Pip said as if me swearing and calling Sam names was going to add more bad luck to this whole scenario.

I leant down again to double check Dylan's pulse and thanked our lucky stars that he was alive. Sam was right. Better to sober the kid up and take care of him than call the parents.

"Can you watch him for a bit? Maybe try get some water down him while we deal with the other emergencies?" I pleaded with Pip. She nodded, ever the good Samaritan, as Sam carried on past, grabbing my hand and hauling me through the people milling in the hallway.

When we reached the kitchen, our eyes bulged.

"Sam… We've really fucked up," I yelled over the noise. A few school friends we went to gigs with had moved the furniture against a wall and were reenacting an intense mosh pit. Clearly, someone had thrown something through the French doors.

Sam waded his way through the crowd. There was glass everywhere, crunching under our shoes. He tried to open the door that was most broken, and it shattered completely.

"Ah shit balls," he said.

"We should call someone!" I shouted but Sam shook his head.

"Mum will fucking kill me!"

I waved my arms at the smashed doors, a deranged laugh escaping me at the ridiculousness of it all. I looked around at all the chaos and felt my stomach turn. How the fuck had we managed this? "You're already dead, you turnip. The house is completely ruined."

Sam ran a hand through his hair. "How do I get rid of everyone?"

"Turn the electricity off!" I shouted. It was what I'd seen in a soap one time. Probably *Hollyoaks*. They always had parties that got out of hand.

Sam nodded, storming back through to the hall and stopping at the cupboard under the stairs. Once he'd flicked the switches off at the main switchboard, there was a moment of screaming throughout the house.

Silence followed, before the long, collective groan.

"PARTY'S OVER!" Sam bellowed.

It took a good twenty minutes to clear everyone out. I spent extra time making sure the drunkest strays were accompanied out the door with a promise of a walk home. Sam locked the front door, and we collapsed onto the sofa, popcorn and crisps scattered about us. He popped the electricity back on as people were leaving but made a point of turning all the music off and the big lights on.

Nobody stays at a house party with the big lights on.

Pip was still nursing Dylan in the hallway, but he was conscious again and sipping on the water she was giving him.

"Oh!" Sam said, bouncing up again. "We have fireworks."

I scrunched my face. "I don't know if we should do that now. We've got about twenty hours of cleaning to do here. And I've got to figure out how to get my annoying cousin home."

He leant forward so he was eye height with me. "Hatter, we're too drunk right now to do any of that sensibly. We have ten minutes until midnight. You'll be eighteen! The last year before you're officially old!"

"I don't know if that's strictly true."

"FIREWORKS! FIREWORKS! FIREWORKS!"

"Finneeee," I said, hopping up and following him out to the back garden. The sky was a hazy, icy mist and if it wasn't for the alcohol thick in my veins, I'd probably have felt the chill.

Sam jogged the few steps down the garden where he'd already set up a bucket of sand to plant the fireworks in. Once he'd lit the rocket, he came back and sat on the garden bench with me as we watched it fly up into the mist, exploding and turning the night a soft red.

I snorted. "Well, that was shit."

The neighbour's back door opened and slammed. We both looked to our left to see a man in a dressing gown on the phone, yelling.

"Ah crap, Tony's getting involved," Sam muttered.

"Fireworks were a really shit idea."

Sam checked his watch. "Midnight. Happy birthday, my mad hatter." He placed his warm, bare arm around my neck and squeezed me into him and we sat like that for a while. It wasn't until I could finally feel the chill creeping its way over my skin that I looked up at him to find his gaze already on me.

"What's that look for?"

He semi-shrugged. "You ever wonder if maybe we're more than friends?"

It had occurred to me, yes. Specifically as I found it so difficult to relate and have fun with any of the guys who looked at me like I was a meal. I'd not had any luck with boys really and I was worried about going to university without any 'experience'. I wondered if Sam hanging around put boys off, or if I was too tall or if my hair was too frizzy. I wondered if it was my personality. Or because I was freckly and wore ugly glasses when I needed to read anything. I could be reserved when I wasn't drunk and too loud when I was.

So, there I was, eighteen and still a virgin with a male best friend who was maybe, just maybe, the answer. Right there all along. He was good looking and sweet and funny and...

"I don't know. Maybe?" I said.

Sam's hand found my chin and squeezed lightly, lifting my face towards him. Nervous jitters brushed through me. And as his lips pressed down over mine, we both paused, statue like, right there in his mum's back garden, freezing our tits off.

He leant back first, a grimace on his face which made me burst out giggling. His gurgled laugh followed next before he was mock gagging and pretending to fall away from me.

"Yeah, we're not... Whatever the fuck that was," I said, rising from the bench and striding back towards the house, relieved I could keep my best friend as exactly that.

I stepped into the kitchen and was about to flick the kettle on when a dark, tall figure rounded through the door. My scream was so shrill, I felt it before I heard it.

"What the fuck now?!" Sam yelled, stumbling into the kitchen, glass clattering across the floor.

I held a hand over my heart as the intruder turned the main light on. His green eyes were alight on me, looking me up and down like he was surprised to see me in a short skirt and crop top. My tummy dipped. It was him. It was Freddie and he was ever as good looking as before. He blinked, shaking his head, speechless, before turning to his brother.

"What the fuck is right. Mum got a call from next door saying there was a party."

"Well, he's lying," Sam spat back, still out of breath. "Why do you care anyway? Surprised you even picked up."

"Sam, I'm not a stupid prick. Don't treat me like one."

"Are you going to tell on us?" I asked, my voice pitchy, panicked.

Freddie's eyes flicked to mine and I swear I recognised something that resembled pity before he turned around and, without another word, placed his phone to his ear.

SEVEN

He could've helped us clean. He could've covered for us. He could've given us a break, but he chose not to. I know Sam didn't forgive him for that for a while, but I was surprised to find that I also hated him for it. Because who did he think he was? The opportunity to become the supportive older brother was right there at his fingertips but he chose to rat on Sam instead. Surely he could've told them it was all a big misunderstanding, that the neighbour was being over the top.

It could have been so easy to secretly like Freddie. And yet, he made it impossible.

I stare at the back of his head as he strides into the service station, his short, tawny hair rustling in the breeze, and I think about the call that cost Sam and me hundreds of pounds in repair and cleaning costs. Not to mention the fight with my parents. I wonder if he even remembers it.

Sara stormed off on her own the second we parked, ever

Miss Independent, and so I join the queue for the ladies with Priya.

"How's Ollie?" I ask. Her nine-month-old baby has quite literally ripped a hole through her entire life. She isn't going back to work now, since the cost of childcare is insane, and Izzy earns more than her. Priya is a chef. A damn good one too. That said, she never has many happy words to say about the hospitality industry; despite her love for food, the long hours, the toxic environments and low wages are likely not missed. And yet, I know she had ambitions and I'm sure she'll get back to it when she's ready. I wish I could help her but, honestly, I'm terrible with babies.

"Ollie's good, thanks."

Her short response tells me that I've asked the wrong question. I press my lips together briefly then say, "And you?"

This makes her laugh, a crazy look behind her eyes. "Me? Am I a person?"

"Of course you are! Priya, how are you? Are you ok? Talk to me."

She waves a dismissive hand but then huffs out a breath. "I just feel like I'm only alive to be a mum these days. Who am I beyond Ollie? Don't get me wrong, I'd die for him. I'm obsessed. He's perfection in every possible way. But I don't have a career anymore. My boobs are always sore, and I have no energy for anything fun. I'm barely alive. I give him everything." She startles at her own words as I peek behind her to the next woman in the queue who seems totally unfazed. "Shit. I should go home. What am I doing leaving my baby?"

"*What?* No. Priya. You said Ollie is with Izzy and her mum. They're fine! This trip away is for *you*."

She gives me a look. "Is it?"

"Well, and me a little bit. And Sam. It's for *everyone*. We need to let our hair down and enjoy New Years again. Properly."

She nods, but her dark eyes don't seem convinced. "What about you?"

"What about *me*?"

"How are you doing since… everything that went down? I haven't had time to ask you, and I've felt so guilty about that, really, but then Ollie is sick, or I need to pump and I just…"

I touch her shoulder as we move forward in the queue. "It's ok. *I'm* ok. I'm better. I'm going to be so much better."

She frowns. "Are you convincing me or yourself?"

"Me, mostly. Are you convinced?"

"If you want me to be."

I laugh, but I can't help feeling a little whiplashed. I change the conversation. "Hey, do you know what's up with Sara?"

Priya looks distraught. "Something's up with Sara too?"

I shake my head. "No. I'm probably just being overly worried about nothing. You know what I'm like."

Priya nods, relieved. "You do overthink everything," she confirms casually like that doesn't make me think, *Do I? Is that annoying for you? Do you hate me because I worry too much?*

She changes the subject, pulling out her phone to show

me recent photos of Ollie, who is growing at a wild rate. She occasionally scrolls over a photo of her pumping, her boob on full show. For me, it's a jump scare, but Priya doesn't acknowledge it.

I know something is up with Sara because I've known her too long not to, but I get the impression Priya isn't in the headspace to take on any more emotional baggage, so I'll keep this one to myself.

Once we've navigated the services and the sun is almost entirely over the horizon, we settle back into the car. I'm dismayed when I offer Sara the front seat, but she shrugs me off, saying she prefers to sit in the back.

Nobody prefers to sit in the back.

That isn't a thing.

I climb into the front again anyway and buckle in as Priya says, "Ok, two hours to go. I need a distraction. I say we play car rules. I bought some classics from WH Smith."

My brain sticks on the word 'classics' like she's about to hand me a Jane Austen novel, except she waves a bottle of liquor in the rear-view mirror instead.

"I'm not car drinking, Priya. I'm nearly thirty."

Priya scoffs. "You wanted a party, right? We play car rules."

"What are car rules?" Freddie asks as he climbs in too. I shift closer to the passenger door in hopes of escaping his hot-man energy. I don't even know if that's a thing but I'm certainly feeling it.

"You can't play, sorry. You're the designated driver," Priya points out. "But as a reminder to the rest of you, and for your info Freddie, this is something we invented for car trips in our third year of uni."

"I'll play," Sara says, and it almost sounds like she's agreeing to it because I'm not, and so I twist in my seat again to look at her, but she's staring away at the rows of parked cars.

"And me," Sam says.

"Fine, I'm in too," I say.

Freddie drives us back onto the motorway whilst Priya takes us through the rules again. "Ok, so we each get a bottle of drink. I found WKD and Smirnoff Ice in the shop. Honestly, what a throwback."

"You say that like we could afford WKD at uni. We just drank the fake shit," Sam says.

"Yeah, until we became immune to it and needed the stronger stuff," Priya adds.

"Oh, don't get me started on the absinthe nights. The hangovers were shocking," Sara mutters. I hear a clinking behind me as bottles are passed around. Priya taps me on my shoulder and hands me mine.

"Why does it look like dirty dishwater?" I ask.

"It probably is," Freddie says, giving me a quick grin before turning back to the wheel with a scowl. Whiplash. These people are giving me emotional whiplash. "Did *you* do absinthe?" he asks.

"Me?" I ask. Why am I squeaky? He obviously means me. "Yeah. Once or twice."

There's a collective snort in the back row. Ok, so it was a few more times than that. I turn a glare on Sam, who gives me a strange look in return, because, yeah, why am I downplaying it to Freddie? Why is there heat coursing through my body? Why can't I just be cool around his older brother?

"We sip when there's a lorry," Priya says. "We sip when

66

there's a yellow car. If we see cows, we sip. If someone says, "What?" because they weren't listening, we drink also."

Freddie makes a face. "What?!"

"DRINK!" Priya says.

I unscrew the lid and take a sip. "Christ, this stuff is shite. Like murky lemonade."

"LORRY!" Priya shouts.

"We can't drink for every lorry, Priya. We're on the M4. It needs to be more specific, or we'll be stopping at every service station to buy more bottles."

Priya refuses to add specifics and so our bottles are drained within the hour. Sam feels sick. Sara is sleeping, and Priya is smiling like she's on cloud nine. I, on the other hand, am surprised this stuff has made me feel tipsy. I was convinced it was mostly sugar and E numbers.

As the navigation takes us off the M4 and into the forest, Freddie connects his phone to use Google Maps without commenting on my earlier embarrassment. I feel it nonetheless, cringing internally.

It's completely dark in the car except for the lights on the dashboard.

I take my phone out and notice the long string of messages from Fliss demanding to know if I'm ok. I quickly reply to get her off my back, eyeing Freddie to make sure he can't see my screen.

The motorway was rapidly thinning of vehicles as we closed in on the Forest of Dean, but now we've driven off the slip road, it feels deserted and even darker under the cover of trees. We drive for at least another twenty minutes down tight, winding lanes with high hedgerows and half-crumbled tarmac before we reach a steep hill and a lane that breaks into two. One goes down to the left, the other carries on up and looks so narrow, the car might struggle to squeeze itself between the trees and the wall.

"Wait," I say to Freddie as he signals left. "Google Maps says to go up."

He stares in concentration at the slope, the lights from the dashboard highlighting the small wrinkles at the corners of his eyes. "Why would Sam book this place? It's in the middle of nowhere."

"In his defence, I did ask for rural."

"I can hear you," Sam mutters. "And I'm going to be sick."

"Yeah, we heard you the first time," Freddie says, ever the sympathetic older brother.

I turn to Sam, the red glow of the brake lights catching on his face enough for me to see his outline. "You want to swap? Sit in the front?"

"I just want to get to the lodge."

Freddie leans forward to get a proper look at the road going up the edge of the hill. There's a crumbled wall to one side. The first fifty metres or so are so steep, I reckon I'd struggle to walk up it, but it evens out.

"You sure it's up there?" he says.

"No. I'm just telling you what the directions say."

"Alright, well, let's give it a go." He puts the car in first gear and revs it up the steep incline. The car thankfully makes easy work of it and Freddie's casual and relaxed driving style has me fidgeting but at least we're in the clear.

When did I become attracted to competent, sensible driving?

"This is *really* rural, Sam," I mutter, staring out into the darkness. I haven't seen a house or any lights in a while.

"That's what you wanted," he says, his voice low like he's fighting a wave of nausea.

"What's that?" Freddie asks.

I look at him in alarm. "What's what?"

"That up ahead."

I blink as far as the headlights allow me to see. Something is blocking the road but it's hard to tell what. We drive closer until Freddie slows the car to a stop, pulling the handbrake up.

"I'm going to check it out," he says, opening the door his side. I don't know what possesses me, but I reach for his arm. I could scream at myself as my fingers latch onto his rock-solid bicep. Not only is it stupidly firm, it's also toasty warm and I snatch my fingers back as if they've been scalded.

He turns to look at me with a quizzical brow. "Your fingers are cold."

"Be careful," I say at the same time.

"Of what?" he asks with a smirk.

"I don't know. We're in middle of the forest in the dark."

"Get a grip, Hatter," Sam grumbles, stumbling out his side too.

"Ooh, are we here?" Priya bounces awake, followed by Sara, who both climb out of the car too. The doors slam shut and then I'm left alone, which somehow feels worse. I join them outside, sucking in a breath of the cold, night air.

"Where's the house?" Sara asks, her voice sleep drunk.

"There's something blocking the road," I tell her. "We're not there yet."

"Oh," is her sullen response before she goes back to the car and leans against it, waiting.

Freddie is right up ahead. "It's a fallen tree," he calls back.

Sam joins him and they talk together quiet enough that I can't hear them. I pause to watch this scenario play out. They seem brotherly and respectful of each other for once which I find incredibly disconcerting. Why don't they hate each other?

Priya touches my arm, making me jump. "Can you hear that sound?" she whispers.

Shivers rack through my body. "Don't say shit like that in the dark."

"No, but listen," she says, her arms wrapping round mine. I go quiet and hear a rustling too. The headlights cast our bodies into long shadows that stretch right out to where the boys are inspecting the tree.

"Probably just an animal…"

"Yeah. Definitely. Not a bear, though. They don't have bears roaming free in the UK. Do they?"

"No. Don't be ridiculous. It can't be a bear."

"But it sounds quite loud."

More rustling occurs. It sounds closer. We both peer into the forest to our left where it's coming from. A shadow moves and I tense all over.

"Boys!" I yell. "Something is over here!"

Footsteps head our way with haste and Priya ditches me to jog back to the car. Sara sees her coming and they barrel through the door. "Hattie! Come on," Priya shouts, waving me over but I'm frozen still.

70

I can't move as the shadow gets closer.

Whatever it is, it's big. A dog? An escaped animal from the zoo? It sounds lion sized.

I can't move my legs.

I can't do anything.

I'm the girl everyone screams at in a horror movie for being totally and completely incapable of survival.

An awful squealing, screeching sound calls out in the darkness as the shadow takes form of a hideous beast and barrels straight towards me.

My heart feels like it's in my throat.

This is it.

I'm going to die.

Except a large, firm body encloses itself around my waist and suddenly I'm perched on the bonnet of the car instead. I blink and there's Freddie, watching me, his face so close, I can feel his breath on my cheeks, green eyes ablaze in the loom of the headlights. He squeezes my thigh. One short, sharp squeeze.

"Are you…" he asks before the screeching intensifies and his legs are taken out from underneath him.

I scream again. Sam tries to run back towards the tree.

"Fucking stupid pig," Freddie yells.

The short run has Sam doubling over. He must throw up the entire bottle of WKD followed by his Burger King lunch. I lift my knees to my chest, waiting for the chaos to unravel.

Freddie scrambles back to his feet, his hair dishevelled. "Fucking wild bacon," he grumbles, his gaze drifting over me like he's checking for something, before finding his brother's outline up ahead. "Sam, you alright, man?"

"Yeah," he says, but he doesn't sound ok. He sounds miserable.

"I'm regretting this whole plan," I announce.

"Are you ok?" Freddie asks, stepping up to stand beside me. I blink at him. I can still feel where his fingers squeezed me just moments ago. Little warm imprints branded there for keeping.

"Me? I'm fine. I'm not the one who just got attacked."

"I wouldn't call it an *attack*," he quips. "It just knocked me over."

"How big was it?" I ask, since I hadn't seen it as it barrelled past.

"Massive."

"Ok, but where did it go?"

Freddie looks behind him, unbothered. "Somewhere over there. I guess we disturbed it."

Sam rises to a standing position again and slowly makes his way back towards us just as the horrible, high-pitched sound blares again. He tries to outrun it. He almost makes it, but he's just been sick. He's too slow. Stumbling. It knocks him down too before screeching back in between the trees. Freddie runs to his brother's aid, grabbing him by the arm and hauling him along. Sam flings himself into the passenger seat and slams the door.

Freddie returns to where I'm now hugging my knees on the bonnet. He stands his ground, refusing to move again for the horrible creature, eyes searching the darkness for its return. But the boar clearly reads his energy, as we hear him trotting off into the forest, the distant cracking of twigs.

"Well, looks like we're going to have to walk the rest of the way," he says.

I laugh at his joke, but he doesn't even flinch.

Because he's dead serious.

EIGHT

The one where he watched me murder a song

It wasn't that we actively picked the same university. It was just that Sam wanted to go to Brighton, and I wanted to do an art degree which the same university offered and so it was a convenient thing for us both.

Was there a degree of separation anxiety at play? Maybe. We did have a wider group of friends by this point, but Sam and I were inseparable in a way that was more like family than friendship.

At least it felt like that for me.

The first term had been a whirlwind of growing up. Sam and I hadn't shared halls, so we lived at least some of our lives apart, making new friends and learning to be independent in the beautiful, messy way you do during those first weeks at university.

Boys had become a new hobby of mine and, although I was still very much a virgin thanks largely to being irritatingly shy when it came to making the next step, I'd dabbled in the game, kissed plenty of frogs. I was a different girl. I dressed more risqué, making more of a habit of wearing tank tops instead of oversized band t-shirts. I tried miniskirts over jeans. Not to mention getting contact lenses so I didn't need to drag my glasses around the clubs.

That's why when Sam suggested we got a few friends together for New Year's Eve, I was excited to show off the new Hattie.

To me, it felt like it had been years, not months.

After the previous house party, which cost us hundreds each in repairs, we were on strict instructions *not* to have a party.

What we did manage to negotiate with Mandy was having a few friends round for dinner and karaoke. It was very much *not* an open invitation. Priya and Sara visited and stayed at mine just so they could celebrate our birthdays.

After a few drinking games, I fled to the kitchen to grab a glass of wine. I helped myself to the open bottle instead, already chilled in the fridge, and was just about to walk off with it when I closed the door and stepped straight into a large body.

"Shit," I stammered, stumbling back a step until I could feel the cool granite worktop against my bare lower back. Freddie set his sharp gaze on mine, a slight twist in his lips.

"Where you going with my wine, Hattie?"

"Erm…"

"Can I have it back, please?" he practically purred, putting his hand out like I would simply give it to him. Something about the interaction made me want to challenge him. It felt feral, wild even, considering Sam was next door and Freddie was a grown man.

But I felt grown-up too. Empowered. A dangerous flint flaring in my core.

"What you going to do if I don't?" I said, holding his eye contact bravely as I took a sip direct from the bottle.

Freddie watched the way my lips fastened around the stem and locked his gaze there for an earth-shatteringly long time. I wavered slightly.

He stepped in closer, folding his arms across his chest, his baggy, grey t-shirt bunching around his smooth muscles. I gulped.

"What will you give me in exchange for it?" he asked.

My lips parted. His eyes caught that too. He was too experienced for me. I was playing with fire, and he knew it. And yet, something in the way my tummy dipped told me I should keep going. I liked how it felt to taunt him.

"What do you want?"

He smirked, shaking his head like he was having fun.

Unfortunately, the game ended as Sam's voice echoed down the hall. "Hatter! Hurry up! We're getting started, for fuck's sake."

I gave Freddie one last challenging stare, stepping past him with the bottle to see if he'd snatch it or say anything else. He watched me the whole way as if he was seeing someone or something new.

"Fine. Have it," he said; the low rumble of his voice seemed to have some kind of control over my pulse. "Be a good girl, Hattie."

A good girl? Fuck!

Heat rushed through me as I skittered away, joining Priya on the sofa and sipping straight from the bottle until I felt the energy Freddie had riled up in me ebb away. Of course, this meant I was suitably drunk when Sam, the current birthday boy, set the karaoke machine up, starting us all off with the classic 'Sweet Caroline'.

"Hattie, you next," Sara yelled, her long, blonde hair falling flat across her shoulder in silky drapes.

I scoffed. "Why me?"

"Because you're the birthday girl."

"That should work *for* me, not against me. Especially at my own party. Besides, it's Sam's birthday right now. I have a few hours yet," I pointed out.

"Oh, come on," she goaded. "Look at your cheeks. You're perfectly drunk enough for this."

"I've been on the wine," I said proudly, displaying my empty bottle to the room.

"*Ooh someone's doing well,*" Priya joked. "How can you afford wine?"

I shrugged. "Stole it from the fridge."

Sam heard this. "That was Freddie's, I think."

"Was it?" I asked innocently.

"Come on, you have to go next," Sara pushed again.

Priya gave me a shove, so I took the bait, stepping up to the small space by the bay window which was pretending to be the stage. Sara took me through the options.

"Not Taylor Swift. Priya will critique my performance. And can you really karaoke to LMFAO? I don't feel like you can."

"Sure, you can," Sara said. "You just have to have fun with it."

"Oh wait," I said, pointing to the track I wanted to try.

Sara blew out a breath. "Ok, you're absolutely bloody wasted. You really think you can sing this?"

"*You really think you can sing this?*" I mimicked.

"It's really high pitched."

"I'm doing it. Sod it."

"Fine. But I'm already embarrassed on your behalf." She set it up on the machine then went to sit next to Priya. And as it started to play, the room broke into a round of laughs and humoured groans. Sara and Priya had the giggles, holding onto each other as I got into the early beats of 'Thunderstruck' by AC/DC.

Challenging? Yes.

A party starter? Absolutely.

Something I was vocally capable of pulling off? *Fuck* no.

And yes, I was suitably drunk as it turned out. Thank fuck for that or I would have definitely bottled it during the first chorus. Sam jumped up beside me, playing his air guitar like a pro while Brandon from school sat on the windowsill behind to play the pretend drums.

I was having so much fun, I almost missed the tall, broad-shouldered body taking up most of the doorway. Freddie leant on the frame; his lips quirked into an impressed grin. Whatever it was that impressed him, I knew it wasn't my pitchy voice.

At one point, I was so screechy, Sara was covering her ears. But it didn't matter, because most of the room were dancing and laughing and isn't that what parties are all about anyway?

Freddie watched the whole way through. Even when the

pretty, dark-haired girl appeared at his side, hanging onto his arm. I was unnervingly aware of his presence but carried on proudly. If he wanted to watch, so be it.

I could be his forbidden muse.

NINE

Navigating rural forest lanes in the dark, with nothing but a phone torch each, is not something I'd recommend. There are thousands of unidentified sounds. Scuffling. Twig-snapping. The random screams of what can only be described as some kind of demented demon (Sam promises me it's just fox cubs). I never knew the forest was so loud. It's eerie, unsettling. I keep jumping when branches move above me. It's bad enough we were just chased by a wild boar then had to climb over a slippery fallen tree but now we have a mile to walk to the lodge.

Priya is up front with Sam, holding onto his coat sleeves. Freddie strides ahead, enough to lead the way and confront any issues before the rest of us, but not so far that we are left behind. This means, whether by accident or not, Sara has found herself stepping along with me. I seize the opportunity to work her out.

"So, how's wedding planning going?" I ask.

She does this strange, breathy thing that isn't quite a sigh. "Fine."

"Did you sort the flowers?"

"Actually no. I have quite a lot to do still." She blows on her hands, rubbing them together. She's wearing a flimsy, teddy bear coat, not designed for the countryside at all. But I'm not dressed much better either. These wedgie jeans are not made for walking.

I wait for her to carry on, but she stalls. So, I try again to stoke the conversation, "But you have a few months, don't you? That's not so bad."

"Five months."

I know her wedding is mid-May. I have an invite with a plus one for shits and giggles. I don't think she thought about it when she sent them but who the hell am I supposed to bring? I was kind of hoping I'd have been picked as maid of honour or at least a bridesmaid so I could act busy, pretending to be running after the bride all day. But, so far, she has chosen not to have bridesmaids. I suspect, sensitive soul at heart, she doesn't want to be the one causing drama in her family. She has too many cousins and high-maintenance little sisters who will all be expecting a slot. If she has one, she has to invite them all and I know this is true because I've seen the photos from her cousin's wedding last summer – there must've been twenty bridesmaids. At least 80 per cent of them had the same silky, blonde hair as Sara.

"How's Mike feeling about it all?"

"Fine, I guess. Why?"

"I don't know. I'm just surprised you didn't invite him."

"Do we have to do *everything* together now?" She pauses

as if she realises her tone is too sharp. "Sometimes, it feels like you lot prefer him to me. Is it so bad to just want a few days to myself?"

"Ok. You have to know you're being weird though, right?"

"I'm not being *weird*. I'm being... I don't know."

I stop walking, hoping she'll stop too but instead, she glances at me before speeding up, seizing her opportunity to escape the discussion. I jog to catch her.

"Sara!" I hiss. "What the hell?"

"Just leave it, Hattie. Please."

"Are you guys ok?"

She shrugs but I can see the apprehension in her eyes. "We're fine."

"Then, what's going on? I feel like you're being..."

"I'm *fine*," she insists, waving her hands at me, playing with a smile I can just about make out in the dark. It looks strained. "This is fine. Me and you are *fine*."

"It doesn't feel like..."

She sighs, her breathing faster now she's upped the pace. "You need to stop worrying."

"Right," I say. It's not the first time I've heard that.

Stop worrying, Hattie. Why do you care what other people think so much? Stop saying I look grumpy. Stop trying to read me. Stop trying to make this into something.

Adam hated that about me. But in my defence, he'd switch moods so fast, it would leave me wondering where I stood with him. How was I meant to react, when he'd be happy and smiling one moment, then moody and frowny the next?

And so, forgive me if I'm a little bit worried about Sara's

change in mood. She's always been so strong-willed and brutally honest, but I lived with her long enough to know she feels deeply yet privately, her outward sharpness is her big sister protective layering It's why, to most people, she comes across as a sharp, confident businesswoman. Afraid of nobody. So in control of herself. Now I have no idea what this is. I'm not sure how I'm supposed to not care.

"Does Mike speak to Adam still?" I find myself asking. I've wondered a few times. They were good friends, after all.

"They've been for drinks a few times. I didn't go."

"Were you invited?"

She's quiet for a moment. "I'm nodding, by the way."

I snort. "I'm rolling my eyes."

"I didn't go. I don't want to be around someone who'd treat my friend like he treated you. And I didn't want to hear about it from Mike either."

"Ok, well, I wouldn't care if you did."

"Liar," she accuses gently.

I shake my head. "I'm shaking my head, by the way."

For the first time in weeks, I hear her laugh. I feel it in my chest like some kind of triumph. *My friend is back. I got her back.* But then we've caught the rest of the group and her guard flies up again, back to barely speaking.

We walk quietly for most of the way after that. It's hilly and a few of us are feeling out of breath, not to mention freezing. An owl hoots from barely metres above us; shivers and tingles run up and down my spine. The fact that we can't see it makes it worse.

As if he can sense my fear, Freddie drops back to stand beside me as Sara takes Sam's other arm. He hauls them up the incline, fallen twigs and mulchy leaves crunching under their shoes.

I'm not sure why being in Freddie's presence makes me so nervous but I have a hunch. It's the forbidden-fruit thing: I'm not allowed to fancy him, and he's also three years older than me. There's something about the age gap that meant Freddie never gave me so much as a glance when I was taking whole eyefuls.

And then there's the Adam thing. I'm twenty-nine in a few days and I've only ever been with one man. We met at university on a night out. We started flirty texting which developed into more and more and steadily, we became an item.

The same question rattles around my head that has done since Adam and I split: *What if I'm no good between the sheets?*

I haven't vocalised this to anyone because it feels somewhat embarrassing and desperate to even think. Besides, what would they even say to that?

Adam rarely had complaints about our… situation, but he did have a few and they lingered, crushed my confidence and eventually, made me want to push him away rather than pull him towards me. I'd be lying if I said I didn't think that was one of the reasons he left me. He was tired of being… Not rejected per se, but not pursued either.

I have no strategy for escaping that lingering worry.

I think back to that time I challenged Freddie over a bottle of wine, and it feels almost surreal that I could've been so confident with so little experience. And now, experience in hand, I have nothing. Pathetic.

I trip on something, thankfully finding my feet before

I face plant. Freddie's big hand holds my elbow, propping me up.

"You ok?" he asks.

"Yeah," I reply, breathless. "Thanks."

He releases me and we walk on. The lane has started to crumble away; it's wide enough to get a car down but is more like a path than a road. I hope this means we're getting close. I need lights. And electricity. Just a hint we are in the twenty-first century would do. Besides, my phone battery is on 15 per cent, and I do not want to try and find my way in the pitch black without the torch.

We all jump out of our skin when a security light flashes on, blindingly bright. It's up a short bank, surrounded by trees and attached to a big, oak-timbered lodge. It's creepier than the pictures advertised, but I suppose there's no surprise there. We are arriving in the dark, after all.

Sam fishes the paperwork out of his pocket, so he can enter the key code, whilst we wait patiently.

Once inside, we're all pleasantly surprised. The lodge is clean and modern. The downstairs has a big, open-plan living space, with a kitchen along one wall, and a massive island with tall stalls tucked underneath it. We find a games room in the basement and four bedrooms, two downstairs attached to the living space and two upstairs, one a twin which is ideal considering our new, higher numbers.

We'd crammed as much of the food from the car into our bags as we could but didn't bother with our suitcases just yet. Sam tries to call the owners to sort the tree and get the car up to the lodge for ease but can't get through.

Priya is already out on the balcony, having opened the sliding doors, which take up nearly one whole wall.

"The hot tub is hot guys!" she calls back in. "I'm going to get straight in."

"Read the pamphlet first," Sara says. "I think you're meant to shower."

But Priya is already climbing the steps and dipping her toes in.

"I'll make a quick pasta for everyone or something," I say as Sara stalks off to check out the bedrooms upstairs, no doubt aiming to score the best one.

I fly around the kitchen trying to find a big enough saucepan and cutting board and get to work dicing onions. Freddie and Sam decide to walk down to the car again to grab as many suitcases as they can and haul them back up. I lock the front door as they leave. Arriving here in the dark has given me the jitters.

Once everyone is back and fed, we all go about getting showered, cleaned and settled, not feeling much like socialising after the long drive here. I decide to grab my bikini from the twin room where me and Priya have set up camp, our suitcases open and contents spread everywhere. Sara would hate the mess so maybe it is best she has her own space.

I'm ghostly pale at this time of year and don't try to hide it. Mum swears I was born fully ginger but as I grew up, it turned blonde and that's why I have such a red tint. I don't buy it. Although my freckly skin and almost translucent thighs does throw some truth behind the theory. But, even knowing all this, I still jump at my reflection in the mirror behind the wardrobe door.

The pink bikini only makes it worse. I think about Freddie being downstairs. Why does he make me so nervous?

What kind of chemicals does he emit that I'm so reactive to?

I shake out my limbs. *Get a grip, Hattie.*

I throw on one of my long jumpers for warmth and wrap a towel around my middle.

Luckily, Freddie is nowhere to be seen as I trot down the stairs and out onto the balcony.

Priya holds up her arms. "WHEY! Finally, a friend cometh to join moi!"

I laugh. "Are you drinking?"

"Yeah. Do you want some?" she passes me a bottle of fizz and a plastic glass. "I read the instructions, see. No glass in the hot tub."

I take them from her, pouring myself one and sitting back. The water is hot. The bubbles tingling around my neck. Yep. A hot-tub getaway was exactly what I needed. This is lush. I allow myself to close my eyes for one moment before a thought occurs to me.

"Are you allowed to drink when you're breastfeeding?" I ask, then pause, worried I've said something stupid. "Oh shit. Sorry. I hope that's not rude."

Priya waves me off. "Not rude. I don't care. And no, none of the Boobleys will make it to Ollie."

I snort up prosecco bubbles. "Sorry, what? Boobleys?"

"Yeah, boozy milk. Like Baileys, but Boobleys."

I can't help cracking up right in front of her. "I don't know if that's really gross or sort of sweet. What happens to the Boobleys once you've pumped?"

Priya eyes me. "Don't ask questions you don't want the answers to, Hattie."

I make a face. "Ok, you're right, don't tell me."

"Hey, do me a favour?"

"What's that?"

"I'm going to rest my eyes for a bit because they're sore. Like sore, sore. It feels like I've been on that SAS show and they've kept me awake with loud music, uncomfortable chairs and bright lights for a few days. I need to just close them. But don't let me drown. That's what it's come to. I'm asking a dear old friend to protect me from falling asleep in a hot tub."

"I'd never let you drown. I hope you know that," I say, meaning to be silly with it but instead sounding deeply sincere.

Priya doesn't open her eyes. "Hattie, it's why you're the chosen one. That, and you're the only person who joined me."

"Why don't you go to bed? Get an early night?"

"I am not leaving this hot tub."

"You read the rules, Priya. Thirty minutes max and you need to get out."

"I'm using plastic champagne glasses. Isn't that enough rule-following for you?"

I sniff a laugh but let her settle. Her 'resting eyes' are soon accompanied by gentle snoring. I keep my eyes firmly on her face to make sure she doesn't drop below the water. I've been trusted. I will not fail her.

Sam walks out onto the balcony, hugging his arms to his chest. "Brr. It's cold out here."

"You can't tell once you're in," I say. "Keep your voice down, though."

Sam quirks his head at Priya and raises his eyebrows. "She ok?"

"No. None of us are."

He nods. "Well, isn't that the truth. More prosecco?"

I nod and he darts back into the house to grab another bottle. I spot Freddie set up with his laptop, his back to us. They share another brotherly exchange and that won't be an easy sight to adjust to. It's so unlike them. I wonder when it was that they started getting along.

TEN

The one where he brought me a gift

Imet Adam in those early months of the year when the rain is thick, the winter grey and endless. He felt like a beam of light pushing through it all. This handsome, funny man with longish, dark hair, tanned skin and light eyes, who liked me. *Me*. He liked me. And I was a sucker for that. He chased me down, always asking about me, messaging to meet up for coffee or breakfast and never just as a hook-up.

He felt like mine right away.

That's what the romance books I was obsessed with trained me to believe. They trained me to look for the knight waving me down. The one who would fight for me. To run away with the one who is kind and caring and wants to be part of your life.

At nineteen, that's all I had to go with, and so I did.

Sometimes, I wonder if he knew I was green. I wonder if I wore it around like a stamp on my head. Could they all tell? Did it put some boys off and entice others? I was all legs and long cardigans that year. I gave up trying to train my hair to be something it wasn't and enjoyed wearing it down. Loose and wild.

After a few weeks, I was so swept up in Adam, we made it official. He became part of my world, and I his. But I never lost touch with Sam. Our friendship never really became a problem because we were so casual with it.

Sam grew into himself at university. He didn't have Freddie's height, but he had the glint in his eye and the humour that drew girls towards him. Sam, much like Freddie, has never been one for a long-term relationship. He feels suffocated by them and retreats before they do. I suspect much of that is to do with his own parents' strained relationship.

That year, for our twentieth birthdays, we threw our party at the student house on Butt Lane. We all decided to go back to university a few days early to celebrate in style without the fear of parents shutting us down. We started off in the city for drinks then towed our arses home to finish the evening, mostly due to budgets and the fact all the clubs charged a small fortune to get in on New Year's Eve.

A little before eleven in the evening, I was surprised when there was a knock on the door. I thought it might be a neighbour yelling at us to keep it down, but our neighbours knew this was a student house and mostly let these sorts of things go.

I opened the door, a whisk of icy sea air brushing across my face, to find Freddie leant against the porch wall.

"Oh," I said. "I mean, hey," I added, remembering I was cool now. I'd had a boyfriend for eight months. I'd had sex. Lots of sex! I was a woman. And he was just my best friend's older brother. No need to panic.

And yet my body still experienced that familiar surge of heat whenever I was near him.

He was taller than Adam and it showed in the way he took up most of the doorframe. Just looming there with all his sexy, green-eyed energy.

He grinned. "Hello, Harriet."

"Why you calling me that?"

He frowned. "Because that's your name."

"It's not, though."

"Harriet isn't your birth name?"

I shook my head. "No, it's *just* Hattie."

Freddie shifted, quirking his head. "No, seriously? Your parents actually registered you as *Hattie* at birth."

I nodded. "Yes. Is that a problem?"

"No. I suppose not. I'll call you Hattie then, I guess."

"I don't actually care what you call me." *Why were we discussing my name?!*

I think I just liked picking fights with him. Sometimes, I disguised it as sticking up for Sam, but this hadn't been about Sam at all. I paused, still holding the door open. Why was he here? What did he want? I blinked at him.

He looked over my shoulder to the bustling kitchen at the back of the house. "Can I come in?"

I considered him. "Why are you here?"

"To see my baby brother and wish him a happy birthday."

"Does he know you're coming?"

Freddie shrugged. "I don't know."

"Have you at least bought him a present?" I asked, feeling protective.

"Of course, I have. I've got you one too." There was that glint in his eye again that made me want to cross my thighs.

"Fuck off. You haven't!" I tried to lean around him to see what was in the bag he was hiding but he dodged me.

"I'll give it to you if you let me in."

"I'm not letting you in until you prove it. Also, it might be a shit present and then I wouldn't want to let you in."

"Hattie, if you don't let me in, I will be forced to call my brother, and I was really hoping to surprise him. So, if you don't mind."

I fidgeted on my feet. He really was gorgeous. Since he'd moved into his long, double-breasted trench coat era, he seemed even more grown-up. Even more untouchable. So why did it always feel like he was flirting with me? Or at least having fun with me?

Which reminded me. "I have a boyfriend, by the way."

Freddie frowned, then looked around mockingly as if there was someone else I was talking to. "Why you telling me that?"

Good question. "I'm just saying."

"It's not Sam, is it? That would be weird."

I choked out a laugh. "Oh, yeah, *no*, don't be gross."

"Sounds like you've put that one to the test…"

"His name's Adam," I said, changing that subject. "He's here."

Now that news made Freddie smile. "Oh, well now you *have* to let me in. I need to see this man in the flesh. To have won the heart of Hattie Tycer, he must be a true phenomenon."

I narrowed my eyes at his strange reaction but quickly moved aside to let him in. It felt sort of like I was a little piggy and had forgotten the tale of the big bad wolf. He had a natural sort of swagger about him, like when he walked into parties, he knew he'd catch people's gazes. He took his coat off and hung it on the stairs, heading back towards the kitchen. I tried to grab at the bag he brought with him, but he was too quick, holding it out of reach, smirking.

He tutted. "Come on now, Hattie. We don't want to ruin the surprise, do we?"

"You're hyping it up, so it better be good."

He just winked, turning my core to liquid silver.

I followed him into the kitchen. To my surprise, hardly anyone flinched that he'd joined the party. In fact, the only person who'd noticed was Adam; he flicked his grey eyes from Freddie to me and then back again as if he was making a calculation.

"Hey, everyone. This is Freddie, Sam's brother," I said, but again, everyone was too drunk to really care.

Sam finally looked up, his eyes wide. They had their usual stunted brotherly style of half-hug, half-handshake. I took a seat next to Sara.

"Is that really Sam's brother?" she asked, eyeing him from top to bottom. She clearly hadn't seen him the previous year, because she wouldn't have forgotten.

I wondered if Freddie's girlfriend, from last year, was still in the picture. Silly thought. Why did I care?

"Yes. It really is."

"Wow."

I gave her a sharp look. Was she into Freddie?

Something about my reaction made Sara laugh, but she didn't have time to dwell on it because Adam had joined us at the dining table, taking my spare hand that wasn't wrapped around a bottle of beer, and started to fidget with

94

my fingers. It wasn't unusual for him to be affectionate, but it was a random, very obvious, sign of ownership.

Part of me liked it.

I wanted to be someone's. I wanted to be wanted.

Sam introduced Freddie to everyone for a second time, like he hadn't heard me do it thirty seconds ago, before they went for a chat in the hall. I watched the door, wondering if I should referee. Why did I feel like that was my responsibility? Especially considering they were both adults by this point. It was something about knowing them since children that made me feel involved. I'd seen enough of their fights.

The voices in the hall started to rise, albeit muffled by the door. I looked at Sara, who had noticed too. She gave me a *'what the fuck?'* look, like I should do something about it.

When there was a bang, I jumped to my feet, shaking Adam off my arm and stepping into the hall.

"What the hell was that?" I demanded.

Sam was red-faced, Freddie the picture of calm as he said, "It's nothing, don't worry."

I tried to shut the door, but Adam squeezed through to join me. I frowned at him, but he didn't look my way, too busy staring Freddie down.

"This is a party, mate," he said, direct to Freddie. "Maybe you should leave if you only want to bring the mood down."

Freddie smirked, before rubbing his chin. "Maybe mind your own business, bud. What was your name again?"

"Ok, I think we should all just de-escalate," I said, trying to cool the mood. Because if Freddie had come in here like an earthquake, looking for trouble, Adam was a volcano already boiling over with lava.

"You should go," Adam said again, his jaw ticking.

I watched Sam for a moment; he was biting his lip as if holding back tears. He needed space. I could tell. This wasn't like him at all, and he didn't need Adam stirring up shit from the sidelines. "Adam, it's fine. I've got this," I told him.

He didn't budge. "I'm not leaving you with *him*," he said without looking at me.

"Do you mean *me*?" Freddie almost choked. "You think I'd hurt Hattie?"

"I don't know you. But you've come in here, hit a wall and caused a problem. So forgive me for thinking you should go."

Freddie laughed bitterly. "Hattie, please can you tell your boyfriend to butt out? I'm having a conversation with my brother." He looked at me, the softer version of him pressing the button on my heart. "Please. Can we just have a moment?"

Something was wrong; I could taste it. I knew Sam well enough to know him not saying anything was a very bad sign. Was it about their dad? Freddie was calm though, his eyes sincere as he implored me to leave them.

"No hitting walls though, yeah?"

"Tell him to leave!" Adam interrupted, his tone irritable. "It's your birthday in like an hour. Why do you want him here causing trouble?"

Sam still hadn't said anything. I couldn't read him. I looked at Freddie. "Maybe you could take this outside?"

Freddie's shoulders drooped. He gave Adam another hard glance. "You know what, I'll just go."

"*Wait*," Sam muttered, his voice thick with emotion.

Freddie paused. "Hattie's *boyfriend* is making a scene. It's better if I go."

"You hit a wall! And I'm the one making a scene?" Adam spluttered.

"Adam!" I reprimanded. Besides, no one had witnessed what or where the bang had come from. "Just leave it, please."

"No. It's fine. I'll call. I should've called," Freddie said. He stepped towards me, handing me the bag he'd had with him since he'd arrived. "Give this to Sam when he's ready, yeah? And look after him."

He didn't pay any attention to Adam, who tried to move between us. Then he grabbed his coat again and was out the door, slamming it behind him.

Adam laughed and muttered something unhelpful before turning back into the kitchen. I frowned after him.

I felt like something much bigger just happened than a brotherly disagreement. I put the bag on the stairs to look at later.

Sam was dead still, staring at the wall, his features blank. I tried to wave him back to me. He startled like he'd forgotten I was there.

"Are you ok?" I asked.

He held up his hand and frowned at his bloody knuckles. I knew Freddie was too calm to have hit a wall. But it was so unlike my best friend to react with any kind of thuggery, it made my heart hurt. What had Freddie told him?

I blew out a breath. "Maybe don't tell Adam it was you. He'll kick you out of your own party."

Sam snorted. "Sorry. I shouldn't've done that."

"What happened?"

"Freddie told me something… But don't worry. I'm ok. It just upset me, that's all."

"I've never seen you do anything like punch a wall."

He shrugged. "I surprised myself, to be honest."

I looked back to the kitchen where all our guests were now mingling again, clinking glasses and picking at splayed-open packets of crisps. Checking the time, we had thirty minutes before we counted in the New Year.

"Hey, want to do something stupid?" I asked.

Sam shrugged. "Fuck, yes. Get me out of my head, Hatter."

"I have fireworks in my room."

"I don't know if you should keep them in your room…"

"Let's go let them off at the park," I said.

"Ugh. People will be so mad."

I laughed. "Exactly. Then we'll run away. It'll be funny."

He nodded towards the kitchen. "Do we bring that lot?"

"Absolutely! The more the merrier."

The park was only a few hundred metres from our house. We bundled ourselves up in coats and strolled down together. It turned out nobody even cared about us letting off fireworks in the dark public spaces as loads went off all around us, filling the sky with bright colours.

I hugged Sam. I kissed Adam. But I couldn't stop thinking about Freddie and what he'd told Sam to rile him up so much. Every now and again, I'd turn and half-expect him to appear in his dark coat and brooding gaze.

A few people sang 'Happy Birthday' to me as we walked arm in arm back to Butt Lane. Some kind of event was going on down by the seafront; we could see the lights and hear the rumble of music drifting up the hill on the calm, coastal winds.

Once we were back, I finally snuck off to grab the bag Freddie left. I took it upstairs to my room and pulled out two presents. So, he *had* bought me something.

I checked the tags. Yes, he had. One was addressed to me.

I frowned, wondering why he'd handed me the bag and not Sam. Was I meant to tell Sam he'd given this to me? Or was he trying to be sly about it?

It was a small, wrapped box. I opened it quickly, tearing at the paper to find a delicate bracelet with a storm-cloud charm attached to it.

All I could think about was how he'd watched me sing 'Thunderstruck' last New Year's Eve. But it couldn't be that…

There were loud footsteps on the stairs, so I quickly crammed the paper and bracelet under my pillow. Sam knocked, then poked his head round the door. "You ok, birthday girl?"

"Yes!" I squeaked, then proceeded to distract him with his present from Freddie: a Lynx deodorant giftbox. He put it aside straight away.

"Shall we exchange gifts now?" he asked, a pleased grin on his face. Considering we'd been spending our birthdays together since we were turning fourteen, it was remarkable that this was the first year we'd decided to exchange presents. I leant across to my bedside table and took out Sam's present from the bottom drawer.

I'd wrapped it in Christmas paper because that was all I had.

"Really?" he said. "Are you not sick of Christmas yet?"

"I am. But I also didn't have time to buy birthday paper and gift wrapping is stupid anyway."

"How is wrapping stupid?"

"It's a waste of paper. And most of the time, adults already know what they're getting anyway. Why wrap it?"

Sam shrugged. "It looks nice? It makes it more fun?"

"Does it though? Really?"

"Shut up and open your present," he said, handing me the gift he'd been hiding behind his back.

"See. This proves my point, entirely. This is clearly a weapon of some sort."

"It's not a fucking weapon," he sputtered, his eyes bright with humour.

It turns out to be worse than a weapon. The moron thinks he's funny and has wrapped a rounders bat.

"I'm well glad I got you something shit too," I said.

"How is that shit? You said last summer that you wanted to play rounders."

"No, I never!"

"You so did."

I scoffed. "Ok, so let's pretend that did happen... Last summer, Sam?"

"You're so ungrateful. And what do you mean you got me a shit present?" He ripped the paper and snorted as he took out the shittest socks I could find in Brighton Mall. They looked like meat.

"Now you have meat socks," I said with a grin.

"You know, I'm not even disappointed. This would've taken you time to find."

"It did. It was between them and the sharks that make it look like they're eating your ankles."

"Sexy."

I smiled, chewing on my bottom lip. I slapped the end of the bat into my hand a few times. "Thanks for the weapon."

"Again, it's for rounders."

ELEVEN

The first night at the lodge is a quiet one. We're all pretty tired from the four-hour drive, and the unexpected hike in unsuitable clothing. Freddie is distracted by something on his laptop. And Sam is already hungover. So, after a short stint in the hot tub, we made our way to bed.

Priya snores all night and I end up sleeping with the pillow over my ears, desperate to get some shut eye. I wake in the morning feeling less fresh than I'd like. It's as if Priya has passed her exhaustion onto me like there's some kind of equilibrium to be had. Instead of coffee, I decide the best way to wake up is to go for a nice run in the forest. Get my bearings.

I've always been a morning person. There's nothing I love more than the satisfaction of having been for a jog down the seafront before I start work.

I slide into my running gear, peeking out of the window at the freezing fog icing the tops of the trees and add a warm, softshell jacket to layer up. Considering I plan to run alone in the forest, I decide to leave my headphones in my suitcase and take my GPS sports watch.

I head out onto the front steps with my trainers in hand and am shocked to find Freddie there, tying his laces. I freeze, blinking.

But he's heard the door so now stares up at me too, either surprised or confused. It's hard to be sure. His expressions mostly all blur into some form of grumpy. Even when he laughed or smiled yesterday, there was still a touch of a frown there.

"Good morning," he croaks.

I rub my eyes with my spare hand. I must be seeing things. But no, he's still there, staring at me. "What you doing?" I ask.

"I'm going for a jog."

"Oh." Fucking obviously.

I pause, wondering if I can somehow backtrack and sneak to bed, making it look like I wasn't about to do exactly the same thing. However, I am very clearly holding running trainers. It would be an obvious lie if I said I was just out here for the fun of it. What is the etiquette here? Do I leave him to run alone, or do I offer for him to join me? And if he offers, should I say no because it's only a polite offer anyway and not really a real one, or do I say yes because it's rude to refuse?

The biggest issue for me is that Freddie is sublimely underdressed for this weather. Honestly, it's indecent.

I wasn't hot before. I was actually worried about how cold it would be. The weather app said below freezing.

But he's in just a skintight base layer and shorts. He's dressed kind of provocatively.

I don't know if you're allowed to say that.

I shouldn't be judging him for his running gear.

It would be sexist the other way round.

I'm probably overthinking it.

As if he's heard me and to prove he's dressed sensibly, he pulls a thin, black beanie over his head to cover his ears. It brings out the green in his eyes and it doesn't help that he's currently scanning my own outfit of skintight leggings and a snug-fitting, bright-yellow running softshell. I have a headband to keep my ears warm and my hair has been tied up into an explosive ponytail.

Maybe I'm dressed provocatively too.

Hypocrite.

"You running?" he asks. I can't tell if he's surprised, impressed or annoyed.

"Is that ok?"

"Why wouldn't it be?"

I shake my head. I'm so confused. It's too early to engage my brain. "I have no idea."

"Well, do you want to join me?"

I bite my bottom lip, his eyes following the movement before lifting again. I perch on the top step, leaving enough room between us, to casually tie my laces. "You want *me* to run with *you*?"

"I asked, didn't I?"

"I'm probably not as fast."

He nods at my legs. "You're built like an antelope. I bet you'll be leaving me in the dust."

"Ha! I'm a slow runner. I like to enjoy the scenery."

Freddie nods at this, finally the ghost of a smile on his lips. "I can admire the scenery."

I nod ahead at the forest before us. "It's beautiful here."

Freddie doesn't say anything, his eyes still watching me carefully, but he jumps to his feet instead, doing little heel hops to warm himself up. I try very hard to keep my eyes on his top and not the bouncing in his shorts.

I pat my legs to motivate myself, my heartrate already higher than it should be considering I'm yet to start running. I shake out my legs, then with the adrenaline kick I need, I run right past Freddie and head down a path I'm hoping loops back at some point. He sprints to catch up, then joins beside me.

We jog the first kilometre, which is mostly downhill on forest tracks. Freddie is barely out of breath at all, whereas I'm definitely noticing it a bit.

I didn't lie about wanting to enjoy the scenery, but here is different. The forest encloses you in its clutches. The proximity of the trees is almost claustrophobic. Add in the ceiling of fog layering itself between the branches and it's like existing in a kind of fairytale.

There are no people around this part of the forest. It could be because it's before eight in the morning, or maybe Sam really did take my brief of being private and found us the most rural spot he could.

A puddle has frozen over ahead of me, so I make a point of hopping it.

"You run much?" I say, after I realise we've not said anything this whole time. To be honest, it didn't feel uncomfortable being silent with Freddie. But damn, I need to disguise my puffing better.

"Most days. Then gym in the evening."

Why isn't he even slightly out of breath?

"Figures," I say. And shit. "Not because you're like…
What I mean is…"

Freddie laughs, unbothered. Not even a blush. "We'll add
that to the list of things that didn't happen if you like?" he
says, and I almost sputter.

All I can do is try to shake it off.

Luckily, he rescues me from my clumsiness once again,
changing the subject. "What about you? Run often?"

I nod. "Three or four times a week. I go with running club
one night if I can. It's full of older women and I've learnt a
lot of very wise things from them these last few months."

"Go on then, impart this wisdom on me."

"It's just about how to be happy really. How to live
for yourself. How to be self-serving without being selfish.
Finding a balance."

"I could do with some of that. What do they advise?"

I glance at his face. I wonder if he's worried about the
same thing as me, on top of the work stuff.

"They say to find enjoyment in the smaller things. Like
right now, I'm enjoying the fog immensely. I've never seen it
like that before and the air is so fresh, you know?"

Freddie slows a touch. "Ok."

He isn't convinced, I can tell. "And they eat a ton of cake,
so there's that. I swear every week they design the running
route around stopping at a café."

"They eat cake mid-run?"

"Oh, yeah. But this is on the longer runs and we stop for
a good break then run back. They're happy, though. It's like
the secret, I think. Eat more cake."

"Eat more cake," he mutters under his breath. "I'm not
sure I buy it."

Rude. What does this guy have against cake? "No? You have a different theory?"

He's quiet for so long, I worry I was too blunt. I focus on putting one foot in front of the other, especially as there are more hurdles: a fallen branch here, a muddy section there, the occasional crumbled path.

"I think happiness is finding a way to lean on yourself. Knowing if all else fails, you've got your own back."

Interesting.

There's a steep incline now. I push forward into the hill, enjoying the burn in my thighs and calves. My toes are so cold, they've gone numb, and I can see my breath in front of my face, puffing out in little clouds. When I look at Freddie, he's surrounded by his own aura of steam too. His eyes catch on mine. There's a vulnerability there that I've never noticed before. He's always so sure, so steady and confident.

I realise he's waiting for my response. It's like he needs my approval or feedback on his statement which, in a way, rejects his hypothesis. "That makes sense," I manage to huff out. "I don't know if I'm quite there yet. But I'm trying to be."

"Yeah?"

"Yeah. I'm taking..." I sigh, barely able to get the next word out. "You know what? Let's talk up there," I say, nodding ahead to what looks like a clearing.

We finally reach it, both of us out of breath. I take a seat on a carved-out log that's been left here as a bench. I rest my elbows on my thighs and cup my face in my palms as I look out at the forest below us. We're higher than the mist now so it just looks like one big, fluffy, white blanket for as far as the eye can see.

It's freezing but it's also damn refreshing. I look up and breathe it in.

Freddie comes to join me on the log, leaving a bit of space so we're not touching. He smells so masculine: sweat and forest and mud. It draws me away from the clean air and I find myself wanting to move closer towards him.

"You were saying you're not quite there yet…" he nudges me back to before.

"Oh yeah." I nod. "I've decided to take the final year of my twenties back. So, I kind of hope the time with myself will do me good."

"What do you mean? Take it back from what?"

"I gave up pretty much my whole twenties for Adam. I have one year left. And I need to make it my own. I'm doing this house party with my best friends. I'm going to do some travelling. And I need to live by myself."

He sucks in a breath. "Sounds very mature of you."

I sit taller. "I think so."

"Why only a year?"

"Well, no. It's more of a year minimum. I couldn't think of anything worse than hopping straight into something new when I've only just escaped the last one…"

Freddie rubs a hand down his face. "Escaped? That's…" He shakes his head as if correcting himself. "That sounds like a great plan. I didn't realise that you left Adam. I thought Sam said…"

"Yes, he left me," I confirm, fairly confident that was the question he didn't want to ask. "But I'm grateful for it now. I would never have broken up with him myself. I was too busy trying to keep him happy in the hope that it would make *me* happy. So it's still a lucky escape, I'd say."

Which is an overshare. It's the running. I always overshare with the club runners. I thought it was because they seemed so wise but maybe it's the endorphins.

Freddie is frowning while I tell him this.

"Are you grumpy with me? Have I done something?" I ask.

He frowns even more. So confusing.

He shakes his head. "Why do you ask that?"

"You're always frowning at me."

The wrinkles in his forehead deepen further. He looks down at his hands in contemplation. "I'm definitely not grumpy with you. Why would I be grumpy?"

"I have no idea. I just don't know how to read you. And this back and forth we have. It feels kind of…"

"Flirty?"

"What! *Is it?* Am I?" My eyes go round. I fist my hands, feeling vulnerable.

Freddie stares at me. "I just thought that was our thing. I didn't…" He shakes his head. "Well, ok, I literally cannot stop frowning. And now you've brought it up, I feel like I've forgotten how to do anything else."

Something about this makes me snort. "Try a smile."

"How do you smile?"

"You use the muscles around your cheeks, apparently."

"I don't know if I have those."

"Everyone has them. Maybe you should add smiling into your gym routine."

He barks out a laugh. "Ten reps of grinning, building up to full blown smiling in three weeks."

"That sounds like a *Men's Health* article."

"I'm sorry, Hattie," he says. "I don't want you to think

I have a problem with you. I definitely don't. If anything, it's the opposite."

I make a disbelieving sound.

"No, seriously. I'm grateful for how you've been there for Sam these past few years. It's not been easy on any of us, and it would've been a smoother path for you if you had just left him to it. But you never did. You were always there when I wasn't."

"I don't see it that way. And it wasn't like you didn't want to be there... I'm sure. I don't really know the ins and outs of yours and Sam's relationship. I think it's better if I keep my nose out of it all, really."

Freddie nods. We sit in silence for a bit, our breathing almost back to normal. I did hope this trail would turn into a loop of some kind, but it didn't. So, I guess it's an out and back.

I jump to my feet, clapping my hands. The cool air on my sweaty skin is sharp. I need to get going. Freddie doesn't move for a moment. He looks like he's assessing my expression for something but whatever it is, he doesn't push for more conversation.

"Right, well..." He starts jogging, flying past me. "Race you back!"

I sprint after him, never one to shrug off a challenge.

TWELVE

Later that afternoon, after a relaxing day of hot tubbing and strolling around the forest, I'm in the kitchen helping Priya cook a curry she's very excited about. We're drinking wine like it's going out of fashion. Sara is sitting on one of the stools opposite, eyeing up the whole venture while topping up our glasses without us knowing. So, honestly, I have no clue how much I've had to drink.

Sara is a proud anti-chef. If she ever invites me over for food, I know it's going to be a takeaway. She once said that there is nothing worse than reading instructions for an hour on how to make a dish that will take five minutes to eat. I sort of get it. But I've always enjoyed the accomplishment of cooking.

Same with running. I enjoy the moment at the end when you can look back at what you've just achieved.

It's about the input, not the output.

"How many bottles have you guys drunk?" Sam asks, walking across the living space where there's a big central log burner with a chimney. As usual, he's dressed like he does sport – gym shorts and an Adidas t-shirt – but I've never seen him exercise.

Sara shrugs. "Three or four."

"Three *or* four?" I sputter. "You're in charge of the bottles. How drunk am I going to be in ten minutes? One bottle drunk, or two? There's a major difference."

It's the difference between fun Hattie and loose-lipped, occasionally lairy Hattie.

She eyes me. "You've not been complaining, have you? This is a party! Drink up, it's fine."

I go back to stirring the sauce, which is simmering slowly, and watch her curiously – noting that she too is drinking plenty. I will get to the bottom of whatever is going on with her eventually. I'm just conscious of any confrontation ruining the getaway for the rest of the group. It has to be the right time and place.

And I don't want to be marked as the difficult one.

After dinner, we all make it to the hot tub, except Freddie, who is once again staring at his laptop. We reminisce about university, particularly about Sara's ex boyfriends. Maybe it's because she's such an independent and strong woman that she would always pick the ones who needed babying. Or imprisoning, in some cases.

She shrugs it all off good-humouredly until we reach Mike, the man who finally stood tall and strong enough for her to lean on instead. She changes the subject and leaves the hot tub before the conversation can venture back that way. I frown at her damp, golden hair as she wraps a towel around herself and hot foots it back to the lodge. I'm sure I see her swallow nervously just as she closes the door. And so there it is – Mike must be the issue. I'm tempted to follow her, but the conversation drags my attention back to my friends in the tub.

It's almost midnight when Priya starts snoring beside me. I nudge her awake and she calls it a night. Then it's just Sam and me left.

"You went running with Freddie this morning," he says, and it isn't a question, just a statement.

I startle inwardly. Was I not allowed? Should I have shunned him on account of not crossing a line with Sam? "Yeah. But it wasn't planned. We were just both running in the morning."

Sam doesn't seem bothered. "Yeah, he said."

Did he? Why did Freddie feel the need to tell Sam?

I nod, taking another sip of my prosecco. Ok, I'm extremely tipsy now. I think if I tried to get out of the hot tub without assistance, I'd probably fall. I like a glass of wine here and there. A few cocktails with Fliss. But really, I'm not much of a drinker.

My tongue feels loose.

"What's going on with you two anyway? I thought you hated him?" My words are all drawn-out and sleepy.

Sam grins at me. "You're such a lightweight these days."

But I'm warm and giddy and I don't care. "Bite me."

He laughs. "We're good. We're trying to not let our parents divide us. It's not easy, I'll admit." He rubs his face. "It was Freddie, actually. He's trying to fix things between us. Says our relationship is more important than anything else."

I nod to show I'm impressed but I spill some prosecco in the process.

Sam snorts at me.

"Oh shit, this is glass. I'm not allowed glass in here."

"It also says not to tub drunk, but here you are."

"What? That's bullshit."

"You're so drunk," he says, shaking his head.

"I'm not drunk. You're just blurry."

"Right. Well, I just wanted to make sure Freddie was nice to you this morning. I know he can be blunt at times."

"Oh, he's always nice to me. Just frowny."

Sam tilts his head. "Frowny?"

"Always frowning. You must've taken all the smiling genes."

"Uh huh," he nods. "That is exactly how genetics work."

I raise my glass to him. "To DNA and clever things."

"To random shit that comes out of your mouth," he toasts back.

"Thanks for coming with me. I needed this."

"Hatter, I'll always follow you on any adventure." Sam starts to rub his eyes. "Although I might head to bed, to be honest. I'm no spring chicken anymore."

"Nooo, I'm not done!" I point to the bottle balancing precariously on the balcony rail beside us. "There's still half a bottle to be drunk. Sara bought so much! And oh shit! Is it midnight now? Happy birthday, Sammy. You're so old."

"Ok, thank you. Maybe you should leave that for tomorrow."

"It'll lose its fizziness."

Sam tips his head back with a laugh. "I'm so tired, Hatter. I've been working mad hours." And I know that's true. Sam becoming a secondary-school teacher was never on my bingo card for him. Partly because I don't trust Sam with his own safety most of the time, let alone a bunch of teenagers, but it seems to be giving him purpose and drive I didn't know he had. "We'll celebrate my birthday in the morning, yeah?"

A new, deeper voice interrupts before I can complain further. "I'll sit with her," Freddie says. And I guess this is where I discover Sam was just being polite. I was being babysat out here. Well, that's embarrassing.

I twist around to find a topless Freddie climbing into the hot tub. I bite my lip then release it immediately, turning to see if Sam noticed my reaction, because *holy hell!* My cheeks feel hot. So do my thighs, come to think of it.

Freddie is all shoulders and lean muscle. I catch a glimpse of his chest as he takes a seat below the bubbling water. He leans back, lifting his arms out and resting them on the edge.

To my surprise Sam smiles at his brother, nodding and leaning across to kiss me on the head. "Goodnight, trouble," he says, before climbing out and grabbing his towel hanging on the back of the chair. He's not quite as lean as Freddie but you can definitely see the resemblance. He's shorter and cuter, whereas Freddie is all tall and sharp. Sam points to his brother. "Don't leave her out here. And be nice."

"I'm always nice."

"You're working on it," Sam says, winking at me before heading to the door. He slides it closed then I'm alone with Freddie and the forest and the hum of the tub. I finish off the rest of the prosecco in my glass and offer him some.

He grabs Sam's empty glass and holds it across to me. I have to lift my top half out of the tub in order to fill his glass. He doesn't let his focus drop to my bikini top, which shows how practised he is.

Too practised.

Or maybe he's really not interested and I've just been fawning over him all these years.

Doubly embarrassing.

I spill more fizz into the tub.

Once I finally sit down again, letting the bubbles close in like a scarf around my neck, I allow myself a moment of eye contact. His green gaze surges against mine in a way that has my heart racing. He takes a sip of his drink then places it down, leaning back again, his gorgeously toned arms, all ripples and curves of muscles, stretching out beside him.

"You ok?" he asks.

"Me?" I squeak.

He nods. "You're determined to stay out here. Even if it means enduring my company. So, what's up?"

"I don't mind your company. I'm not sure why you don't join us more often. You seem to prefer your laptop, I suppose."

He rubs his chin. I notice he has a light smattering of stubble, whereas he was always clean-shaven before. I want to run my knuckles over it gently, feel the scrape against my skin. I wonder how it would feel in other places too.

I drop my head a little into the water, covering my mouth to hide the colour building in my face.

"It's work," he says, and I can tell by his tone that isn't a good thing.

"What do they want? Didn't you take annual leave?"

"Yeah. They don't really operate like that, though. I'm always expected to be on. I need to check on things regularly or the whole team could be screwed."

I pout. "Sounds stressful."

He looks at me again and this time, my tummy dips. I squirm under the water, praying he can't see.

"It pays well."

"Does it make you happy?"

"Sometimes, my pay cheque makes me smile."

I laugh. "Oh, mine doesn't do that. So, I guess that's nice."

He grins and it brings that glint to his eyes, the one he always used to have whenever we sparred in our younger years.

I gasp, pointing at his face. "Oh, you smiled!"

He goes back to frowning but it's forced, I can tell. He's having fun. "I just realised you expertly dodged my question. I asked if *you* were ok. How did we end up talking about me?"

I touch my nose. "It's all about misdirection."

"You're not getting away with that this time. Come on, spill the beans. What's up with you?"

"Why do you care about me?"

"I've always cared about you."

I pull a face. "No, you haven't!"

"Hattie…" he says, before dipping under the water enough to grab my foot. He runs a rough finger up the middle which does something unholy to my core muscles.

I gasp, kicking him off. "Dick."

"Come on, talk. Or I'll tickle your other foot."

I narrow my eyes at him, but I can't help ruining the image with a nervous laugh. "Fine. I'm fine. Well, no." I take big sip of my drink. "I'm actually a bit scared, to be honest."

"Scared?" He leans back as if I might be scared of him.

I'm scared of what I want to do to him, if that counts.

"Yeah. I'm scared of where my life is leading me next, you know? I was on a path. I had plans. I was organised. I was going to marry Adam, when he finally bloody proposed. I was going to have, like, maybe two kids. We were going to buy one of those big, terraced houses a few blocks from the sea. It was all planned."

I'm so fucking drunk. My loose tongue is feral.

Freddie doesn't say anything but takes another sip, which says more than any words could. He thinks I'm pathetic.

"And I guess, in some ways, thank God he broke it off, right? Because whatever was going on in here," I point to my head, "was pretty tragic. Why was I settling for someone who was never happy with me? Or *for* me. He complained all the time. The only thing he ever looked forward to was a fucking skiing trip. I should never have been jealous of snow. And you know what, he never fucking invited me. Not once. Not even to just watch. He liked leaving me behind. He liked me feeling small. I'm so sure of it now. He liked me feeling dumb and useless.

"When he complained about my lack of career, I don't think he'd have been happier if I suddenly took up a big, fancy job like him. No. I don't think that was what any of that was about. I think he liked pushing me down. He liked me always trying to kiss his feet and worship the ground he walked on. He liked leaving me behind and being better than me.

"But now he's actually gone and done it. He fucking left, Freddie. He actually fucking left. And the worst part, I think, is that was his plan all along. He never planned marriage and babies with me. He didn't want a nice, terraced house. He wants a mansion with his imaginary, hot, model wife who falls at his feet the second he walks through the door.

"He never wanted me." I gasp at the realisation of saying it out loud. It's fucking shit. But it's true. I was never enough for him and there was nothing I could've done to change that.

And I'm not even sad now.

No. I'm angry.

I'm fuming he let it get that far.

I'm angry he took so much time from me, knowing that was always likely to happen.

"He never wanted me and now I've wasted my twenties on him. I'm supposed to just pick myself up and do it all again? I don't understand it. I feel so lost. So unprepared."

I take another big gulp of prosecco and find myself holding an empty glass. I don't top this one up, though. I'm woozy to say the least. I place it on the side of the tub, but it falls in and floats there before slowly sinking.

My companion is watching me warily like I'm a danger to myself, as he fishes the glass out and places it on the side.

I'm fine. I'm just pissed – in both meanings of the word.

"I've only ever had sex with *one* guy, Freddie," I whisper before dipping my whole head under the water. I'm embarrassed. Tortured.

I hate saying this out loud, but out of all the people in this lodge, I get the impression he's the least likely to judge. I mean, I know Priya and Sara are aware of this. They knew Adam was my first, but I don't think it's crossed their mind since. Or maybe they don't think it's this whole big thing.

It's not embarrassing to them. And they're so absorbed in their own stuff, why would they even think of it?

I stay under for a few seconds before two large hands are on my waist, lifting me. The pressure from his fingers feels incredible. When I surface and open my eyes, Freddie's so close, I can make out the amber flecks in his irises. He moves one hand up to my cheek, his thumb squeezing gently.

"Please don't do that," he says, his voice serious. His breath fans across my face, hot and minty with just a touch of alcohol.

"I was going to have to come back up eventually."

He chews on his bottom lip, and I copy because I'm jealous of his teeth.

He's so handsome. It's even worse this close up. The way his firm jawline ticks, the small wrinkles at the corners of his eyes, his clear yet rugged skin. *Agonising.* His tawny hair is short but probably just long enough to run my fingers through and tug.

I want to tug on his hair.

"Hattie," he admonishes, pushing himself backwards.

"What?" I blink, bereft at losing his proximity.

He just shakes his head. "You. Just... you."

"Adam made me feel like I wasn't any fun."

"*You*? He made *you* feel like you weren't fun? Hattie, you have to know he was wrong." He says 'he' with a touch of spite and I love that. I shouldn't. But I do. It feels good for someone else to hate Adam. Not that I hate him. But maybe I should. Maybe that would help me get over this hurdle.

Heat surges through me. He doesn't know what I mean. I need to say it directly. And I don't know why it has to be him to hear it, but I probably won't see him again for a year after this getaway and I don't think he'd tell anyone else. He's too private for gossip. Too stoic.

And besides, all logic went out the window after my fourth or fifth glass of prosecco.

"No, like in bed," I whisper.

I stare at Freddie for a second, but his face does nothing. He definitely heard and now he doesn't know how to respond.

Shit.

I dip back under again, submerging my entire head.

This time, Freddie's hand gently encircles my wrist, pulling me not only upwards but towards him. I take a big breath of night air, looking up at the stars poking through the branches. Anything not to give him eye contact.

His hand around my wrist doesn't move but his spare hand gently takes hold of my waist. I'm brazenly aware of the heat in his fingertips. I float in the middle of the tub, waiting for him to clear the air. But instead, my lips are moving again. Loose. So loose. I say, "You know what you're doing. I heard all the stories. You could help me."

"Fuck, Hattie," is his deep response, sending shivers down my spine.

"Yes. Exactly. *Fuck Hattie*. Just once. Once and then I'll never bother you again," I say, finally looking at him.

His mouth is slightly parted. His eyes aren't filled with pity like I thought they would be. No, it's something worse. It's frustration or disappointment. Whatever it is, I recoil.

"I'm so fucking drunk," I say, forcing a laugh. "I'm sorry. Oh my God. Please add that to the list… I'm just… I need to prove him wrong. I am fun. I know I am. I just—"

"Hattie…" he interrupts, his voice low like he's trying to prevent the others from hearing it. I've put him in an awkward position. I'm terrible. I hate me.

I turn to face the steps to escape the tub. I'm desperate to find my bed and pretend this never happened, but his hand is still enclosed around my wrist, and he squeezes me to stay. Something about the way he does it, so gently, yet firm, makes my insides fizz.

THIRTEEN

The time he found my daytime knickers

Mandy, Sam's mum, had decided to stick around for most of the day on Sam's twenty-first birthday. We'd gone for lunch during the day and to a late-afternoon comedy show at the theatre. But she kept promising to hide in her room once our friends arrived. Freddie, although staying with his mum over Christmas and New Year, like every year, despite the tensions, opted out of joining us. I mean, Sam also didn't invite him.

"Mum, you don't have to do that," Sam said. "You can hang out. We're not embarrassed by you anymore."

"I was never embarrassed by you, Mandy," I pointed out.

"Suck up," Sam muttered.

Mandy waved her hands as she finished filling the dishwasher, before ringing a cloth to wipe down the sides. "I won't be able to stay up until midnight anyway. If I need something, I'll pop down, but I haven't got the energy for you lot."

Sam foraged through the cupboards for the big bowls

so he could put out our carefully thought-out party buffet for the evening which consisted of six different flavours of crisps, breadsticks and one crappy selection of dips.

I was carefully taking out the champagne glasses from the top cupboard and placing them on the side.

Mandy paused in the doorway to watch us. I could tell she wanted to say something. I had to look away so as not to smile.

"Mum you're staring," Sam said, not even looking up from the table as he emptied a bag into a bowl with zero finesse.

"I was just thinking…"

"Oh God. *Save our souls.*"

"Sam…" I mumbled. I could never get away with mocking my mum like he did. He just rolled his eyes in response.

"Your brother is still here…"

"Ugh. *No.* Freddie isn't joining us. I thought he was going back to his flat tonight anyway. Doesn't he usually go and watch the fireworks in the city?"

Mandy sighed. "He decided to stay another night."

"How's that my problem?"

"You could have a drink with him."

"Mum…"

She raised her hands in resignation. "I just think, despite everything, you boys should be brothers. You should stick together."

"He blew that though when he spoke to Dad again, didn't he?"

"Forget I asked," she said, waving her hands.

I was so awkward whenever there was something family-related going on in the Harrisons. For the most part, my presence alone would be enough to put a stop to any big row, but this didn't feel like my business. I found a clean, dry cloth and pretended to polish the glasses. Not that anyone who was invited tonight gave a toss about how sparkly they'd be.

I think the issue with Mandy was that she liked having Freddie there for Christmas and New Year, but in the same breath, she hadn't fully forgiven him for speaking to his dad as much as he did. I'd heard he'd even funded a deposit on a city flat for Freddie. Sam was livid as he'd never get the same – especially now he'd gone full non-contact with his dad.

There was too much resentment for them to all coexist for that length of time and yet they did it anyway.

I, for one, was not sure how I felt about Freddie joining us. Adam would be here shortly, having cut his ski trip short to spend my twenty-first birthday with me. His flight had landed two hours prior, and his brothers were giving him a lift to Sam's. And yet the mention of Freddie was what was giving me nervous flutters in my stomach. I wasn't prepared.

Prepared for what? Why did I feel the need to prepare?

Sam groaned. "Fine. Whatever. If he joins us, I'll just pretend he's not here."

Lucky him. I'd never had that skill in my repertoire.

Mandy slunk off to her room with copious amounts of wine and snacks for what she described as her 'cosy lock-in'. I went to Sam's room to get ready. I prepared the black, shimmery playsuit I was going to wear and hung it up on the back of his wardrobe then grabbed the towel Mandy left out for me and shot across the hall to use the shower.

Once I was done, I contemplated pulling my clothes back

on but there was no window in the main bathroom which meant it was extra steamy. It would've been a pain to haul my jeans back on over my damp skin. Instead, I wrapped the towel around myself and peeked into the hall. The main light was on, and I could hear the TV in Mandy's room.

I was safe.

Wrong.

The second I closed the bathroom door, Freddie's opened.

"Sam, what have I told you about showering until you're a fucking prune… Oh." Freddie paused. His eyes latched onto my bare legs. He blinked away. "Er. Sorry."

"Why are you sorry?"

"I… am not sure…"

"What did you do wrong?"

Freddie fixed his eyes firmly on the ceiling. "I thought you were Sam."

"Rude."

He pursed his lips to prevent a laugh. "Like I said, I'm sorry. Terrible mistake. I was just hopping in the shower."

"Good. I'm just going to get some clothes on."

"*Good.*"

"Good."

I stepped sideways, carefully, my damp hair dripping down my neck. I was impressed with my performance, sensationally so. I'd done very well. Performed calmly under intense pressure. I was so proud of how I quipped at Freddie like it was no challenge at all. Like I hadn't been telling myself to act cool the whole time in the shower. Preparing conversations I could have with him tonight to show how unbothered I was around him.

Go me.

Wrong again.

I was so distracted, I crashed straight into Sam's bedroom door, the towel becoming loose and half-falling around my ankles. The bundle of clothing I was hanging onto fell to the floor. I managed to keep hold of one end but there was definitely some side boob on show. "Fuck," I muttered, trying and failing to get a grasp on the damn round doorknob. I was flailing. A pathetic mess, honestly.

"Let me get that for you," Freddie muttered, somehow knowing exactly the predicament I was in while also keeping his eyes on the ceiling.

"It's ok, I can…"

"Here," he said, his voice right by my ear, low and husky, as he carefully twisted the handle. The door swung open, and I clambered to get the towel back around my damp, naked body.

It could've been a second. Maybe even a nanosecond. But I found myself searching for his gaze, those wild, green eyes that made my tummy flip. And he seemed to do the same thing. A perfect friction hung between us, a long, delicious pang of awareness swept through me, fizzing from my ears to my toes.

I watched him swallow a lump, his throat at eye level.

And then he was gone.

I whirled into Sam's room, closing the door behind me, hovering for a moment, my hand covering my mouth as I let out a nervous giggle. I heard the bathroom door close on the other side of the hall and took a calming breath.

Thirty minutes later, after I'd dried my hair and begun applying make-up, now in my playsuit, Sam's girlfriend, Alice, knocked at the door. "Hey, Hattie. You decent?"

"I am now."

She came in, a pair of my comfy day knickers hanging from her finger. Alice was cool for the most part. She'd known Sam and I for years through school, so she was well aware of how little a threat I was to their relationship. She was also a good fucking laugh. Which is a critical requirement if you're dating the biggest goofball in town, AKA Sam Harrison. "Are these yours or Sam's?" she asked.

"Oh my God," I spluttered, snatching them from her hand. "Where did you find them?"

"Hanging on the door. I thought you were using it like a sock for privacy."

"No. Oh my God!" I sniggered. "Who uses knickers for that?"

She smiled, her hazel eyes wide with humour. "I thought you were."

"Nooo! Gross."

"Can you explain why your knickers are hanging on my boyfriend's door then?" She was joking but trying to play it off as a serious question. "Because, I'm not going to lie, this is suspicious."

Oh hell. "I must've dropped them in the bathroom…"

Alice snorted. "And someone hung it there?"

"Probably Mandy," I added quickly but my heartrate was racing. Only one other person had been in the bathroom… He wouldn't. He wouldn't have found my knickers and then just hung them on his brother's door. If I had been a braver woman, I would've marched across the hall to demand his reasoning. Except I wasn't.

I was more of a sweep it under the rug and hope it goes

away kind of person. Alice watched me squirm, raising her eyebrows. "Good?" she asked.

"Totally."

"Great. Can you help me with my dress?" she asked. I was grateful for the change in conversation.

An hour later and people were arriving. Sara introduced me to her new boyfriend who initially seemed fairly normal until he opened his mouth and turned out to be one of those manically posh *Made in Chelsea* types.

"He buys good gifts," she explained before waltzing off to the kitchen with the magnum of champagne he'd insisted on bringing with him.

Adam was chatting with Sam and Alice in the kitchen as the evening went on, and I went from living room to kitchen and back again to make sure I was talking to everyone. The thought of turning twenty-one was hanging over me in this weird, uncomfortable way. I'd tried to explain it to Adam before. How turning eighteen was fun. Sure, you're an adult now, but not really. You're still in your teens and everyone refers to you as a child. Nobody expects you to be sensible or make good decisions.

But at twenty-one? There're no age restrictions left. You're expected to be a grown-up and get your life on track. Which, at that point, I did not. I had no plans after university, and it was making me skittish. Adam had a job lined up. He had plans to move to London. I still wasn't sure what I wanted to do at all. Painting my canvasses full-time certainly wasn't a career option when I had no customers.

At around twenty to midnight, a wrench of panic rolled through me. I often wondered if other people saw their birthdays in like I did, or if this was particularly unique. Counting down to being another year older felt somewhat intense whilst others just went to bed and woke up a new age.

I tried to shake out my limbs. Take another sip of my drink. Nothing helped me rid of the sensation.

I crept out of the kitchen, leaving Adam chewing the ear off one of Sam's friends about the economic climate, and decided to use the downstairs office for a moment's calmness. Nobody used it since their dad left. It was at the front of the house and Mandy had started hanging clothes in there to dry.

I opened the door and flicked the light on, only to realise I'd walked in on a private moment. A looming figure curved over a petite, brunette, his hands in her hair, her leg hitched over his hip.

The girl gasped, shifting away from him and turning her back on me. Whilst the man peeled himself off her to glare in my direction.

"Do you mind?" the girl hissed, not evening looking my way, as I latched eyes with him.

Freddie...

It was like a shot to the heart. Fuck, I mean I had *zero* claim on this man. He was Sam's older brother. I didn't even want him. My boyfriend was literally next door, but I gasped nonetheless and stumbled back out of the room.

"Hattie..." His voice sounded from behind the door. I'd left the light on, so he was probably annoyed. I flitted back through the hall and into the kitchen, taking my seat beside Adam.

"Hey, you," he said, wrapping an arm around my waist. Sam caught my expression and frowned at me.

He mouthed, "You ok?"

I nodded but he continued to frown which meant I was completely unconvincing, and my pale skin was giving me away.

Sara leant across to confirm this. "You're wearing it on your sleeve."

"What's on your sleeve?" Adam asked, inspecting.

I shrugged. "Nothing. Ignore her."

"One minute, Hattie," Sam said, pointing to the clock on the kitchen wall.

Ugh. My heart would not settle. What on earth had gotten into me?

"Thirty seconds!"

I took a deep breath as Sara topped my glass up from the magnum, spilling it all over the table. I used paper napkins to mop it up.

"Ten! Nine!"

Just as the countdown begun, Freddie appeared in the doorframe to the kitchen, his eyes grazing over me as I forced a smile and a laugh. What was even wrong with me? Why was I so bothered about catching him kissing another girl? And where the hell had she gone?

"Four! Three! Two! One! HAPPY NEW YEAR!" Sam yelled, throwing his arms in the air for a big round of cheers. "And now for the most important part! Happy birthday to you…"

I cringed as I always did when they all sung to me. I both hated it with every fibre of my being and couldn't live without it. Once they'd finished singing, Adam kissed me in front of the whole room to more cheering. Freddie hadn't moved an inch. He wasn't really taking part in the merriment, but he was there all the same.

"Hattie, here," Sam said, passing me a small, wrapped box. "Where's mine?"

"Ok, rude." I laughed but fished his tiny present out of my back pocket.

Sam had gotten me an AC/DC tape to go in my ancient little car.

Whereas I'd gotten Sam a bright-pink and furry thong with *Alice* embroidered along the back. He nearly fell over laughing.

"PUT IT ON! PUT IT ON!" Sara began to chant as Alice helped Sam pull down his trousers.

"NO! Oh my God! My eyes," I squealed. Adam squeezed me into him, pretending to hide me from the horrors of Sam's naked butt. "It wasn't for show and tell!"

But Sam danced around in it anyway with Alice proudly snapping photos of his goofy arse.

An hour later, as sleepiness came over the guests in that way it does on New Year, people started to leave. I grabbed the duvet from the cupboard upstairs that Mandy had prepared for me and Adam, so we could sleep on the sofa, when Freddie stuck his head out of his bedroom door.

"Hey, happy birthday," he said, his expression cautious. "Sorry about earlier."

"Which part?"

He pressed his lips together. "Erm. The office…"

"I don't know why you're apologising. You've not done anything wrong."

"Well… You seemed pretty startled."

"Yeah. Sorry I interrupted. I didn't expect anyone to be in there." I swear my heart was beating loud enough to hear.

He shook his head. "I'm sorry too, but not for the reason you're thinking."

I hugged the duvet to my chest, taking a step towards the stairs. "What am I thinking?"

He shrugged, his eyes watching me warily. "You're probably thinking I'm annoyed. But really, I'm pretty sure it's the same thing I think whenever the tables are turned."

I swallowed, unsure what to say. Did he mean when I kissed Adam?

But he never expanded on it. And I wasn't ready to ask.

"Goodnight, Hattie," he said, before turning back into his dark room. From what I could tell, there was nobody else in there with him.

FOURTEEN

I close my eyes as I drop back into the warmth of the tub. Freddie moves away, using his spare hand to turn the bubbles on again. I hadn't even realised they'd stopped. We sit down.

"Hattie, look at me," he says, his voice soft but commanding.

"No," I whisper.

I feel my foot being lifted like before. He runs a finger up the middle again, forcing me to squirm. I finally open my eyes but only to glare at him. "You know what that does to me, don't you?"

He sighs, shaking his head. "It gets a reaction."

I give him a look. He knows. I know he knows. I feel the sensation all the way up to my ears. It makes me crave pressure in places he's making it very clear I can't have. I feel wanton and needy, and I hate it.

God, I'm so embarrassing.

"You do know if a guy says a girl is no good in bed, it means he doesn't know how to press her buttons right.

Please tell me you know that. No one is bad in bed. He was just being cruel," he says, still holding my foot, his finger poised as if he will tickle me again if I don't pay attention.

"Well, he said it anyway," I say.

"Then he was being cruel."

"I *know*. So, I want to prove him wrong."

Freddie nods, his eyes still on me.

"I shouldn't have told you any of that."

"Hattie, it can't be me," he whispers.

I drop my head again. This is mortifying.

"I can't do that to Sam. You know how it was. I can't take you from him."

I balk at this. "I'm not *his*, though. And I didn't ask you to do anything that would cause a problem between you two. I'd never purposefully hurt Sam. He wouldn't know." I shake my head. "It was a childish agreement we made. You don't really think he'd hold it against me now?"

He exhales sharply. "I think he'd hold it against me, though, and I can't take the risk. Not with you. And besides, I'm really not that guy anymore."

I frown at him. "What guy?"

"I've been a fling for women for a long time. You know that. I'm not trying to hide it. And I enjoyed that time in my life but that's not who I want to be anymore."

I swallow a lump in my throat. I can feel tears building, the familiar, unwelcome sting behind my eyes.

I'm being rejected. This hasn't happened since I was a teenager.

He quickly lifts a hand to my cheek like he knows I'm about to cry and brushes his thumb there. If he's trying to soften the blow, I can't tell if this is sweet or fucking brutal.

I lean into it anyway because it feels nice to be touched. Even if only platonic.

"You don't know this but I was broken up with this year too. A few months before you."

I part my lips, eyes wide. "I didn't know you were even dating."

"I didn't tell anyone."

"I'm sorry..."

He shakes his head. "I needed it. I needed to be hurt for it all to sink in. For me to see what the world looked like for me right in that moment. I had no one. No one who really cared about me. I'd leant on Dad's support for years, his pressure to pursue success, to better myself, always thinking about the next step. As soon as I achieved something, it was time to look forward, never ok to just settle there.

"And when Mia left, I didn't realise how fucking lonely my existence was, because you know what? Dad didn't even want to know that I was feeling down. It was all, "Get up, Son. Keep pushing on." There was no time for me to wallow. No patience for it at all. So, I reached out to Sam. And you know what?"

I nod. Because I know exactly what my best friend in the whole wide world would do.

"He listened," I say.

He half-smiles. "And I didn't deserve that from him, I know I didn't."

"You did. You just..."

"I didn't. I did not deserve it. And now I have a second chance to be his brother. I have a chance to make it right between us."

He pauses, waiting for me to catch up on his point, but

I already know it. I push back to release my face from his hand. He lets go as I float backwards. "I'm so sorry I made that awkward," I mutter.

He shakes his head as if to say I didn't as he rises out of the tub. I try not to look at his perfect, wet body as he climbs out, guilty I ever took the time to look at him at all, when he's only here to get closer to Sam again. Of course, that makes sense now. Sam is *so* forgiving. So, kind. To even think about touching his brother, after all these years, sends a shot of guilt right through me.

"Hattie," Freddie mutters. I look up to find him holding his hand out for me, my towel already in his other, ready to wrap me in while he stands in the freezing night air, not even shivering.

I step up, taking his hand to help me out, but only because I'm drunk and the chances of me falling and slipping to my death right now are high. I take the towel and wrap it quickly, hating the bite of air against my wet skin.

"Thanks, and I'm sorry," I whisper, before trotting off to the doors.

"Hattie," he says again. I pause briefly at the door. "We can add that to the list. Nobody has to know. And don't apologise; I understand. And I'm sorry too. Trust me. I am really sorry it can't be me."

Mortifying.

I smile but it feels more like a grimace. Then I disappear inside the toasty lodge, sprinting to the shower on the first floor to warm myself up before I go to sleep.

FIFTEEN

The next morning, I wake up late. I feel like shit, as if there are splinters in my brain. Unfortunately, I wasn't drunk enough to forget what happened. Freddie's response to my stupid question is imprinted on my brain. It will be one of those memories that wakes me up in the middle of the night to obsess over for the rest of my life. I'll be in my care home staring at the ceiling at two in the morning, desperate to go back and delete it.

Oh, but it's worse than that, isn't it? Because he is *here*. In this very lodge. And I have to face him this morning. There's no hiding from it.

It doesn't really matter that I don't think he'd tell anyone. I know it happened. And he knows it happened.

Horrific, really.

I sit up, sliding my legs out from under the duvet. Someone has turned the heating up because it's baking in here. I throw a hoodie on anyway and some fluffy socks over my pyjamas and check myself in the mirror before strolling downstairs. I look hungover. You know, blotchy eyes, messy hair and dry lips.

Priya is making a coffee, her eyes drawn and her lips flat. It raises my heckles. "What's up, Pri?" I ask softly, walking round the kitchen island to place my hand on her arm. She turns away from me, sniffing.

"Priya. Seriously, what's up?"

She turns back, flicking her dark hair behind her back. "I'm a bad mother, aren't I?" she whispers before smacking a hand over her face on a sob.

"Oh my God, no! You're an amazing mum."

"But I'm here and my baby is not here," she sniffs. "I was just so delirious; I didn't know what to do with myself. You said about getting away. I just needed a break. But that makes me *terrible*. I'm an *awful* mum."

"No! No, that's not true at all."

I pull her into my shoulder, and she goes limp, resting her head right in the crook. I can feel her sobbing silently against my neck. Sam walks into the main living space from his room across the other side of the lodge. He notices the interaction and freezes. He's a great friend. Very emotive and caring when he wants to be. But, like most men, he has an irrational fear of crying women.

I glare at him as he steps silently back towards his room, running his hands through his soft, golden hair.

Stroking Priya on the back, I say, "I don't know much about these things. But I listened to a podcast recently by this girl who has babies, and she pointed out that needing rest when you're a mum isn't the same thing as wanting to be away from them. And I hope that resonates with you because I have no idea what I'm talking about but I have nothing else helpful to say."

"I just feel so rotten and guilty. Izzy sent me a picture of him having toast soldiers this morning and I burst into tears because that's my morning routine. I'm the one who does his toast."

I squeeze her again. "But you're so much less tired, right? You'll return to Ollie ten times the mum because you'll be rested and raring to go. You can even let Izzy take a break."

Priya steps back, wiping her eyes, as Sara joins us. She blinks at the situation, then turns on her eldest sister energy. She comes round and asks Priya the same questions, offering a hug before working the art of distraction and asking her to help with the coffee machine.

Priya gets to it, demonstrating how to use it with her old barista skills.

While they do that, I rifle through the fridge. My eyes feel heavy, and my muscles all have that familiar post-drinking ache. Every now and again, I remind myself Freddie is in the building and have a minor panic attack, my heart rate spiking as adrenaline flows through my veins.

I need something to distract myself with, so I say, "I'm making breakfast for everyone."

I grill bacon, eggs and halloumi, while Sara peels the avocados to mush them and Priya does the dishwasher, laying out warm, clean plates to serve on. Sam smells the bacon and finally returns with a hop in his step. He eyes Priya nervously before giving me a look as if for confirmation that the tears are over. I roll my eyes at him.

"Can I help?" another deeper voice asks.

My heart lurches. I look up as if I've been spooked to find him stood there dressed in black running gear like before. He's watching me cautiously, clearly having been out again, his hair ruffled with sweat and wind.

I wonder if he waited for me on the step. Or whether he knew I'd be too hungover for jogging.

"No, thanks," I say, dropping his eye contact and busying myself flipping the bread in the toaster. My face feels warm. When I look to Sara to check whether she's got onto plating the vine tomatoes, I find her watching me with that knowing expression.

She leans across and whispers, "You're wearing it on your sleeve."

I glare because Freddie is still within hearing range and also because it's something she used to tell me before. And it's never not been annoying.

Ok, so I was drawn to Sara because of her outward strength and ability to stand up for herself. I've never not felt safe in her presence. I have no doubt she would help me hide a body. That's who Sara is. She's the friend who can be mean and blunt but will be the first one at your side ready for battle if you needed her to be.

It's very hard right now not to channel some of her energy and point out that whatever's going on with her hasn't only been on her sleeves these past few days; it's been right there on her face.

Freddie clears his throat again. I think he's trying to get my attention, but I skilfully ignore him, turning to butter the toast on the other side so I can keep my back to him. It feels unjust considering I'm the one who caused this awkwardness in the first place, but I'm not ready to face it yet.

Or ever.

Probably never.

"Have you guys seen the weather? It's threatening snow," he says.

Sara leaves a gap in the silence for me to reply but when I don't, she takes the hint. "Oh, snow! That'll be nice."

"Not if we get snowed in."

"Breakfast is ready," I chime in, interrupting. "Can you guys set up? Freddie, do you like bacon?"

He too, lets the silence linger a second too long. It's a simple question. I don't need to look at him for the answer. But after a beat, I can't help myself; my eyes drift to his. He's frowning but crooks his head when I stare back as if to tell me I'm overthinking it. At least, that's what I think he's doing.

"Well?" I ask. "Bacon?"

He shakes his head. "I don't eat bacon, thanks. Eggs, halloumi and avocado would be nice."

"No toast?"

"I'll take toast. And tomatoes."

I nod, then busy myself again serving up as Sam walks over. "I feel like there was something I was meant to tell you, but I can't remember," he says, leaning on the counter.

"Wow. That's super helpful."

He scratches his chin. "It'll come back to me," he says, before strolling back to the table where the others are seated.

Freddie hovers by the sink, filling his glass incredibly slowly. I'm just trying to make my own plate up and I know it's on purpose. I speed up my process, hoping to escape the moment.

"Hattie," he whispers. I pause, the sound of his voice sending shivers down my spine in the most splendid way. He's closer now, placing one hand beside me, enclosing me against the kitchen side without touching. I could step back now, and I'd feel what it would be like to have his whole body pressed against mine from behind.

Get a grip, Hattie.

"Would you walk with me to check on the car in a bit? See if the log has been moved? Grab some more supplies?"

"I think we can leave the prosecco," I say. Currently of the mindset that I'll never drink it again despite knowing that's not really true.

"I think we should talk."

Checking the table to see they're all focused on their breakfasts, I turn quickly. His face is right there. I could lean up on my heels and seal my lips with his. My eyes trace the line of them. He steps back to give me space, but I know he's aware of the closeness of our bodies as I watch his Adam's apple bob in his throat.

"I don't know if there's any more to say," I murmur.

"*I* have more to say. I have things to get off my chest. Last night didn't feel like the right time. Besides, I'd like to move the car in case it does snow."

"Ok, fine," I say, brushing it off and grabbing my plate.

SIXTEEN

The one where he carried me home

After university, Sara and I lived together for a few years in a shabby flat in Brighton City Centre. I worked a retail job in the shopping mall, trying to figure out what I was going to do with my art degree. Sara was practically a genius and was back at university studying business economics. And so that little place was all we could afford. When the wallpaper would peel from the damp walls, we'd use gorilla glue to put it back up because our landlord, practically unaware of our existence, rarely responded to our pleas for help. The positive was that he didn't care if we threw a New Year's Eve party.

That New Year's Eve, Sam was mixing a punch bowl on the kitchen side which had very limited prep space, whilst Sara set up the speakers on the windowsill. I had been trying to reach Adam all day to wish him a lovely evening, but he'd been missing my calls. He was invited out to the slopes in the French Alps by one of his new colleagues on the graduate scheme.

I wasn't bitter about it… Ugh. Ok, I was.

But I also wanted him to succeed, and he convinced me these excursions were basically networking. It was all about who your friends were in his industry.

There was just something about not being invited that made me feel hollow and I couldn't work out why.

I'd seen a lot less of Adam since he'd ventured into London to start his career for one of the top banking firms. And that was ok. We had to be independent. We were still too young to be in each other's pockets all the time. I trusted him and he trusted me. I chose not to follow him to the city right away, knowing that the seaside towns were where I felt at home. Besides, he promised to visit every weekend which he mostly did.

But not prioritising my birthday that year stung.

To make matters worse, Sam had a new girlfriend who didn't like me. Sara was busy chewing (literally) on a male stripper's ear she'd met one night out clubbing. And Priya was in Thailand for a beach party, so wouldn't be coming. I felt lonely and miserable.

I started to drink faster, washing back whole glasses of punch in one. At just before midnight, the flat felt too small, I was insensibly drunk, and a weird friend of Sam's was hitting on me.

"Do you like *COD*?" he asked.

"With chips?"

"No. Like the game."

"I think cod is fish, not game," I pointed out, to which he pulled a face.

I knew he meant the actual game, but I didn't want him to feel like we were connecting. Then he put his hand on my thigh.

"I have a boyfriend," I said, nudging him off me.

"So? He isn't here, is he?"

"He will be in a bit," I said, smirking. And the horrible knobhead decided to respect the man he didn't know, who wasn't even here, instead of the woman who clearly wasn't interested.

The next thing I knew, I latched eyes on my cousin who was necking shots with some other random guy I'd never met. Was this even my party anymore?

"Dylan!" I said, marching over. "What're you doing?"

"I'm drinking."

I leant on the wall beside him, crossing my arms. "I don't remember inviting you."

"I just assumed you'd be having a party. And I wanted to wish you a happy birthday."

"No, you didn't. You haven't even spoken to me."

"Ok. But I was going to."

"No, you weren't. You just wanted free booze."

"Ok. Fine. I want some free booze. But I'm *family*, Hattie, so you have to be nice to me."

"That's not a thing you can use against me. You can't just rock up to my flat, uninvited, with random strangers."

Tanned stranger scoffed. "Who is this diva?"

"This *diva* lives here. This is my flat."

Dylan made an irritated sound. "Can you just chill please? We *were* having fun."

"Wow," I said.

That was my cue to leave. I made my way down to the seafront, only two blocks away, to watch the fireworks light up the city. Not the smartest move for a girl to go out drunk on her own. But I wasn't feeling very smart.

145

I was moody and irritable. My New Year's Eve wasn't going the way I'd envisioned it for the past few weeks.

The night sky was clear enough that the stars were shining bright as I took a seat on an icy bench down on the seafront. As the clock struck midnight, I wondered if anyone at the flat had even noticed I was gone. After another ten minutes into my birthday, I realised they didn't care.

Nobody walking by paid me any notice in my glimmering dress and bare legs. I probably looked like a stray from one of the clubs down below on the beach in the converted boat storage buildings.

I grabbed my keys in my pocket and held tight. A weapon of sorts. If anyone tried to bother me, you bet I was going to key them to death. I took them in my hands and examined the little storm cloud charm Freddie had given me two years before. I didn't really wear bracelets, so I repurposed it into a keyring.

Something about being in the cold night air was sobering in a dull and miserable way, so I made my way down the steps to the beach. A few hundred metres further and I was at our favourite club, Dices. Mark, one of my day shifters at the store, worked the doors during the night, so I ran to him to bypass the queues and see if he'd let me in.

"All alone?" he asked, looking over my shoulder.

"Friends are inside," I lied.

He nodded and gave me another suspicious glance like he didn't believe me. I was definitely swaying. "Alright, hang on. I'll see if I can get you in. It's meant to be tickets only, though."

With that, he strode into the building, leaving one guy on the door, fielding a long, shivering queue of people who stared at me with disdain. I didn't care. I could hear the buzz from inside and wanted to let loose.

Mark popped his head out the door and waved me in.

"Can you see them?" he asked, as someone stamped my hand.

"Who?"

He frowned. "Your friends?"

"Oh." I made a face. "Yeah, totally. They're over there. Thanks, Mark!" I said before darting away to the bar where I paid well over the odds for shots.

I was fine.

I was a grown woman.

I didn't need taking care of.

Besides, the one man who was meant to give a shit about me on my birthday clearly didn't. So, I yelled, "FUCK IT!" and necked them all before running to the dancefloor and just bloody going for it. Rage dancing.

I felt queasy pretty quick and made for the ladies, except I don't remember making it at all. I do remember being placed on a long red leather sofa. I remember someone attending to me like I was a child. And I really remember the face that crouched down to my level, with sharp, green eyes that made me want to squirm and that deep voice that said, "Happy birthday, storm cloud. What the hell are you doing? Where's Sam?"

I shrugged. "His girlfriend hates me."

"Right… And Sara?"

"Stripper guy," I slurred.

"Ok… I've forgotten your other friend's name. The one with the black hair."

"Thailand."

"Boyfriend?"

"Alps."

He muttered an expletive. "So, you're here *alone*?"

"What you going to do with her?" another voice asked. Much more feminine, much more impatient and annoyed.

"I guess I'll take her back to the hotel. Sober her up," Freddie replied.

"Why? She got herself like this. It's hardly your problem."

"Trust me, she's my problem."

"I'll walk home; I'm fine," is what I think I said but Freddie just frowned in response.

"You'll what?"

"Walk home."

"Wa hun?"

"Yeah!" I tried to stand and push past him, not wanting to cause a rift between him and this – *wow*, beautiful – woman he was with, but Freddie was holding my arms and had a hand wrapped around my waist.

"Ok. Not happening. I'm taking her back to my room."

"Are you kidding?" the woman said, eyes wide in disbelief.

"She clearly needs to be looked after. I don't know what's gotten into her, but this isn't normal. She can barely stand."

Mark popped up out of nowhere. "Oh, are you Hattie's friends? Good thing she found you; I'm afraid this one's a bit too drunk."

"Yeah, I can see that." Freddie frowned. "And yeah, I'm her best friend's brother. I'll take her home."

"Sam's brother?"

"That's me. I'm Freddie. You can call him if you need to."

Mark waved him off. "Nah, mate. You're good. I've got three more drunks to get home. Have a good night."

"I'm not drunk," I argued but whatever slurred words Freddie heard just made him laugh, exasperated. He stopped briefly at the closet booth to grab his coat, propping me against the wall as the woman he was with left with another group of people, giving me one final, disappointed look.

I mean, I had just ruined her night with Freddie Harrison, so I couldn't blame her.

She must've hated my guts.

Freddie returned to me, placing his rigid, long, dark coat over my shoulders before encouraging me to wrap one arm around his neck so he could help me back outside. I was drunk but I could still feel the warmth of his fingers against the soft skin at my hip and the tiny flames that flickered there.

As soon as the fresh sea air hit my face and the icy mist glazed my skin, I felt my insides rising. I fell to my knees on the pebbles and watched all the alcohol empty from me. Freddie managed to save most of my hair from getting covered.

I vaguely remember staring up at a clear, starry night sky and listening to the chop of waves crashing and retreating while Freddie hovered over me, running a hand through his hair.

The next thing I knew, I was in a bright hotel room. I held a hand over my eyes, groaning. My body was in tatters. Had I been run over?

I groaned. The sun was pushing through the thin blinds, the seagulls cawing into the wind in a way that rattled my brain. I rolled over, pulling the duvet over my head and hoping I would just fall asleep again.

But instead, I realised this couldn't be my bed because the sheets were all white and mine were pink. I looked up, panicked, peering at my surroundings. There was no one else next to me. No one in the room. But it sounded like the shower was on in the bathroom. I squinted, trying to remember where I was.

I sat up. The material I had on was softer than my dress. It smelt different, masculine.

I knew the smell right away. The sweet, saltiness of it.

I was in Freddie's bed. I was in one of Freddie's t-shirts.

Fuck! I leapt up, searching for my things but I couldn't see them laid out anywhere, so I rifled through a pile of clothing the other side. It was all massive. I decided to grab a pair of joggers and just accepted I'd have to hold them up as I ran back home.

Oh, hell, I'd never done a walk of shame before.

Was I doing a walk of shame? Oh God! No. Surely not. I had a boyfriend.

It was just as I grabbed my phone and started heading for the exit that I noticed a messy sketchpad, with pieces of paper spilling out of it, left beside the mirror. I paused, eyeing the bathroom door. The shower was still on. I chanced it, my eyes heavy as I carefully opened the dark-red, leather cover.

Small, detailed sketches covered the pages. Little, insignificant objects were drawn neatly. A post box, a well-used trainer, a metal grooved bin, the start of a squirrel, a seagull. On the next page was a large drawing of the old Brighton pier. You could tell it wasn't finished, the shading undefined. But it was almost professional level skill.

Were these Freddie's?

I kept flipping the pages to see what else there could be. Just sketch after sketch after sketch of random things, all unfinished, all just halfway done.

Then I happened upon a more refined sketch of a girl laughing. This was the only person he had sketched. Her eyes were open and bright despite it being in black and white, her smile lit up. It wasn't until I took in the freckles, the softly sloping nose and the start of the light, wispy hair that I gasped.

It was me. This was a sketch of *me*.

Just then the shower in the bathroom squeaked off. I panicked, quickly shutting the book, cramming one of the loose pieces back in and hoping it wasn't noticeable. My heart was thundering. I could feel a pulse in my fingertips.

Did Freddie draw me?

And when was that? Had he taken a photo to work from? Or was it just a made-up sketch of me?

I darted for the exit. But the bathroom door opened, blocking my escape.

I stopped in my tracks, speechless. Freddie appeared with only a short towel around his waist. When he noticed me, he paused too, one arm leaning on the doorframe. A lush covering of light-brown hair ran up his stomach to his broad shoulders, and…

"Are you trying to sneak out?" he asked, his voice genuinely surprised, a drop of water from his wet fringe dripping down his nose.

I relaxed my shoulders and glared at him. "*Did we…?!*" I looked behind me at the bed, the sheets ruffled. This man had drawn me. What the hell did that mean? Maybe those sketches weren't his. I didn't have him down as an artist. He was sporty and focused on his career. He wasn't an arty type.

Freddie frowned. "No! You collapsed down on the beach covered in sick."

"Oh. So…"

"I carried you here, Hattie. You were in a state. You were singing all the way home, don't you remember? Honestly, what does Sam tell you about me?"

"Not much these days. I was singing?"

"Yes. 'The Black Parade'. You thought it was hilarious."

I snorted. The thought of singing that song drunk while Freddie, who hated emo music, tried to haul me back to the hotel was actually quite funny. He rubbed his chin, clearly annoyed by my unserious response.

"Can I go?" I said, nodding behind him to the door.

"You want to leave here like that?" he asked, raising an eyebrow at the stolen joggers I had on.

I sighed. "Well, I don't know where you put my clothes. *Oh!* Did you undress me?"

He didn't even have the decency to look embarrassed as he shrugged, like it wasn't a big deal and said, "I wasn't going to let you sleep in sick."

"Fuck," I hissed, covering my face. "I have a boyfriend. This looks *bad*."

"It could've been worse. There were plenty of dickheads swarming. Your clothes are in the bin. Like I said, they're covered in sick, and they stunk. You can wear something of mine. I didn't touch your underwear."

Oh, but he saw it!

"Has my dumbass brother tried to call you yet?"

I took my phone out and groaned. "Hmm. Only like 100 times."

"Seriously?"

I waved my phone at him to prove it then quickly called Sam back to tell him I was alive and that he could call off the search. I did, however, retain some of the truths regarding my whereabouts.

"Want me to drive you back?" Freddie offered.

I cringed, holding a hand to my head which was now beating like it had its own heart. "Only if you promise to drop me off a street away."

"I want to see you in the door. You're still drunk."

I scoffed. "I'm fine, honestly."

"If nothing happened, why does it matter if Sam knows you're with me?"

"You know why," I said, giving him a look. "And besides, I think Adam would feel…"

"Where the fuck *is* Adam? It's your birthday."

I scoffed at him. "How about you mind your own business? Why you in Brighton anyway? Thought you lived in London now."

He nodded, raising his eyebrows at me. "I do. Except I was seeing someone…"

I cringed again. "Oh yeah. I bet she hates me."

He shrugged this off. "Don't worry about it. I wasn't going to abandon you, and she had friends to go home with." He paused, watching my face like he was hoping to read something there. I dropped my eyes, too afraid to maintain eye contact while he was practically naked.

153

"Can you put some clothes on, please?"

Freddie looked down. "Right. Yeah. Go in the bathroom. I have a spare toothbrush in packaging in my washbag. I'll knock when I'm dressed, and we'll make a move."

It didn't take long to realise why Freddie would carry spare toothbrushes in his washbag. Hopefully, the woman from last night didn't harbour the ability to use voodoo dolls or I was in for a rough couple of years.

Ten minutes later and Freddie was driving me out of the hotel's underground car park, his hair still damp. He smelt divine, musky and clean. I rolled my head back and closed my eyes, willing my brain to behave around him.

"Ahem," he said. I must've fallen asleep in the five minutes it took for him to drive me back. He'd ignored my request and parked right outside the flat. I looked up at the window to see the curtain twitch. *Shit*.

"Thanks, I guess," I said, taking my keys out. He'd leant me his bomber jacket as it was all he had that didn't look excessively long on me.

As I reached for the door, I felt a tug from the keyring. Freddie had grabbed the storm cloud charm, holding it between his forefinger and thumb.

I swallowed, blinking at his stern expression.

"You kept it," he said.

"Yeah."

His eyes flicked to mine. My tummy dipped.

"Why?" he asked.

"You gave it to me." I bit my lip.

He nodded and looked away. "Guess I'll see you around then, storm cloud."

I didn't have any comeback. I was hideously hungover

and about to get the third degree from Sara, hoping and praying Sam wasn't there so I could change out of his brother's clothes without him ever knowing.

"See you around."

SEVENTEEN

I wrap up in as many layers as I can, silently wishing I'd bought my long, winter coat and not this cropped puffer. My butt's going to get cold. The thermostat nailed to a beam outside the lodge says it's -4 degrees outside. My hands already feel it, so I stuff them in my pockets. Freddie is perched on the bottom step, ready to go. He has a thicker beanie on than his running one and his long, dark coat sits perfectly over his broad shoulders.

I've worn that coat before. I can almost feel the weight of it, like some kind of muscle memory.

"Ready to go?" he asks. I look behind me, wondering if Sam has noticed we're walking together and whether he'll have something to say about it. But he's already in the hot tub with Sara, so I nod.

We stroll in silence for at least 100 metres. I become extremely interested in a squirrel shooting through the icy overgrowth before darting up a tree.

"About last night…" Freddie starts.

I blanch. "No, no. It's all on me. I'm sorry. I'm the one who made it weird. It won't happen again. I was really, stupendously drunk and as you know, that is *never* a good look on me."

Freddie sniffs a laugh. "I feel like I didn't get a chance to fully explain myself," he says anyway. "And besides, I don't even think you did embarrass yourself last night."

"Oh, come on, Fred. You know that's not true."

"You were vulnerable. That's not the same thing."

"In my world, it is."

He shrugs. "Well, not in mine and I don't know… Can I say I'm flattered I was the one you picked?" he jokes. I can hear the humour in his voice, neatly disguised in his dry tone.

I laugh, short and sharp. "You were just the guy in the hot tub. I really wouldn't be flattered if I were you. Could've been anyone." I cringe and look away. That was mean. And not true.

I almost go to take it back but he's smiling. "Good thing I have such a huge ego."

"I'm sorry. I'm just saying…"

"That I was just a 'body' to you?"

"No! Not *just* a body, a body I *trusted*. That means something."

I finally turn to look at him but regret it immediately. He's watching me, his face passive but his eyes anything but.

"Can I explain myself?" he asks.

I open my mouth to respond, but I'm unsure what to say, so I close it and nod. I think I want to say he doesn't need to explain himself. What is there to say? But I'm intrigued that he feels like there's something that needs to be said.

And maybe I'm nosy.

157

"I'm sure you remember much of what went down with my parents. Or... I don't know, they were so private, it probably wasn't that noticeable right away." He looks at me for confirmation.

It takes me back to the weeks when Sam would come to ours instead of me going to his, which was weird. Whatever my mum did or didn't know about the situation, she took Sam under her wing. Freddie was hardly around because he was at university. I don't remember there being any talking about it and there was certainly never an explanation. Besides, it didn't feel like something I was supposed to ask.

"I remember the time. I don't know what happened," I say. "Other than the eventual separation."

Freddie nods, like that confirms his thought process. "I wasn't there for Sam. I was at university, barely an adult myself and their break-up was uglier than it looked from the outside. My dad used to get angry. He threw things. Broke things. Drank until he passed out and blamed my mum for a whole ton of shit. He was a crappy dad.

"At university, I was trying to reset my life, finally free of him. I sort of forgot about it all. I learnt a lot about myself, and I was doing ok in my course. It just felt like things made sense away from home. But I'll honestly always regret that Sam had to take those years on, on his own. I don't know if he'd have kept his head above the water if it wasn't for you. You meant the world to him back then. Still do."

I swallow, digging my hands deeper into my pockets. "I don't think you're giving Sam enough credit. He always seemed so unbothered by it all. And once your dad moved out, he was happy as anything living with Mandy."

"Yeah, I know. I'm glad him and Mum get on so well."

"Even though you didn't? Or don't?"

I'm sure Freddie flinches but he covers it up by rubbing his chin. "Mum thinks I chose Dad. It's been a difficult few years trying to get back in with her and Sam."

I don't feel like it's my place to pry so I stay quiet. I can't work out what this has to do with last night.

As if he can read my mind, he continues. "Dad needed me. He wasn't well. And all of a sudden, he was on his own. I'm not saying he particularly deserved my company, and I regret losing touch with Mum for a time. I was like his own personal hobby for a while and I don't know why, but I let him guide me, assist in my career and get me set up in London.

"I have trouble figuring out some of my decisions sometimes. I want to be the good guy, but I resoundingly end up being the villain. I tried to get Sam to not take sides that year when you kicked me out of your party…"

I gasp. "Oh, the night Sam punched the wall! But, hang on, I didn't kick you out!" But when I look at him, he's smirking. For once, it's not a fucking frown. Trust him to finally try out a smile while talking about the darker stuff in life.

"I know. That idiot ex of yours did." He chews on his bottom lip for a beat, then adds, "I just couldn't abandon Dad. He lost a lot in that divorce. Even if it was self-inflicted. And I understand why Sam cut him off. I do. As much as I'd have liked to have seen him set up too… I'd never ask him to try out that relationship again."

"Do you still talk to him?" I ask. "Your dad?"

Freddie takes a deep breath. "I do. But it's more strained than it used to be. He doesn't want to talk about anything except my career."

"The career that you hate."

He rubs the back of his neck. "I don't love it."

"Well, what you going to do about it?"

He smiles, tugging on my beanie. "What would you do, storm cloud?"

It's out before he's even realised he's said it. He pauses in his step, looking out at the forest on his side. It's been three years since he called me that last.

"Do you need your own list of things that didn't happen?" I joke.

"Nah. That doesn't count because I'm not embarrassed."

My core feels like warm honey despite it being freezing outside.

Distraction. Think of a distraction…

"What I would do, if I was in your situation," I say, "is I would reevaluate what it meant to *me* to be happy. What it is that makes me smile and how I can manifest that even if only for ten minutes every single day."

"Damn. That was profound." He ponders for a moment as if trying to work out what that single thing could be each day. Then asks, "Do you have that at the gallery?"

"I do. Especially when we get new art in." I can't even fight the smile. "Like last week, for example, this local landscapist brought in the most simplistic oil painting of the sea during winter. It was incredibly minimalistic. So real. It was just varying layers of grey and the slightest amount of drab blue." I look across at Freddie to see him scowling again in thought. "I'm not selling it very well. But it's beautiful. It does so little but makes me feel so much. I just sat there all afternoon smiling at it."

"It sounds very you," he says.

"What? Grey?"

"Not grey but plain."

Well, ouch. "You think I'm plain?" I choke out. "No wonder you didn't want to sleep with me…"

"Hattie… No. I mean you're beautiful without even trying."

"Oh, well." I bite my lip as a stroke of warmth rolls right through me. Head to fucking toe.

Freddie thinks I'm beautiful.

Not fucking grey. Not plain.

Beautiful.

I think about that sketch. I think about the last time we spoke…

I'm tongue-tied. Literally not a single clue how to respond.

Thankfully, his car is in sight. As is the fallen tree, which has been dismantled and stacked to the side of the road. Freddie does a quick walk round to check there's no damage while I jump in and try to reengage my brain. Somehow, it's colder inside the car than outside and the windows are so iced up, you can't see out of them at all.

I realise, to my horror, that this means we'll have to wait for it to defrost first before driving back up to the lodge. My adrenaline spikes again. I need to do something to set this right. It's my fault it's awkward. It's my own fault I'm panicking. There's no one else to blame.

I tap my fingers against my thighs, trying to get myself together and to warm up.

Freddie hops in and cranks the engine, blasting the heating

on the window screen. The fans are so loud, I can barely hear myself think. I roll my head back on the seat whilst we wait.

"I'm trying to work out what decision makes me the good guy in our situation," he says, his voice just loud enough over the hum of the heater.

I blink at him. "What do you mean?"

"You asked for my help last night and I said no. And now I can't help but wonder if that makes me the bad guy in your eyes. But if something ever happened between us, I have no doubt Sam would be..." He blows out a breath, struggling for the word.

"Apocalyptic?" I offer.

"That bad? Do you think?"

I'm trying to grasp that he's thought about something happening between us and I wonder just how much thought went into it. "I didn't think he'd find out, so..."

"And so, in Sam's eyes, I'd be the bad guy for helping you which, by extension, would make me the bad guy in Mum's eyes too. And if we *did* do something and you wanted more, but we couldn't without hurting people..." Freddie laughs. He fucking smiles again. "I have no idea what path I'm supposed to pick to avoid being the villain. Does that mean I'm the bad guy by default? I never seem to get it right."

I puff out a visible breath. It's so cold in here. "Well, I can make that decision super easy for you." I feel so stupid. I feel responsible. I feel like some kind of homewrecker. Even if it is between brothers, not husband and wife. (Hell, I'd never do that!) But I should never have put Freddie in this position where he's questioning his fucking morality. I force a smile as I say, "I'm taking helping me off the cards."

Freddie's lips fall flat as he leans back. "You are?"

"Yeah. I'm surprised you're even humouring it," I laugh, incredulous now. "It was never a good idea, Fred. I was drunk."

"Right." He runs his fingers over the steering wheel. "Good."

"I can't believe I was going to trust the villain of the Harrison household," I say.

Freddie laughs but it's stunted. "I was never a villain to you, was I?"

"Only when you dobbed us in after that party and were mean about my music choices."

He chuckles, throwing his head back. "Christ. Your taste in music was terrible."

"I take extreme offence at that statement."

"And I had to dob you in, sadly. The alternative was lying to Mum again."

"Again?"

"Yes. There were things I kept from her about Dad. I regretted it. So, a few days later when your disaster party happened…" He sighs and it's a ragged sound. "Believe it or not, I really didn't want to dob you guys in. I would've helped you out had the circumstances been different. But I was used to being the evil older brother then and I think I just assumed my role."

"Ugh. I didn't know all that was going on."

The windows are clearing up. Freddie straps himself in and puts the car in gear. We roll slowly up to the lodge, the tyres crunching on the icy, ragged surface. Once he parks outside, he turns to me as if to say something but just stares at my face.

"What?" I demand, wondering if there's a splat of mud on it or something.

"Do you still have it?"

I know what he's referring to, but I don't want him to know that. "What?"

He's onto me. "You *know* what."

"Maybe," I say, taking my keys out of my pocket.

He eyes it in my hand, reaching over to squeeze it between forefinger and thumb. There's a vulnerability to it and it makes my heart swell. I watch his face, a few of his tawny hairs escaping the edge of his beanie, the small wrinkles on his forehead scrunched together. His lips pink from the cold.

I tell myself I *do not* want to climb across the car and feel them against my own. But I'm lying.

The moment stretches, then he laughs. "Fuck, your rendition of 'Thunderstruck' burst one of my eardrums."

I tip my head back on a laugh, snatching the charm away from him and jumping out of the door. "Get stuffed, villain boy."

EIGHTEEN

The one where he wanted to feel at home

"Shit," Sam hissed.

I spun round to find that he'd cut himself on a bottle opener. "How the fuck did you manage that?"

There wasn't a ton of blood but there was enough to ruin a tea towel. I helped him patch up the cut whilst the music and chatter carried on in the living room. Our parties were still lively but somewhat more sophisticated than before. No smashing windows. At least, I hoped not.

We were in Mandy's kitchen, where he'd been staying for the last few months. His most recent girlfriend, the one who hated me, had split up with him that past summer, citing his immaturity as the reason. Which is ridiculous because he was only twenty-three. *I thought you were meant to be immature at twenty-three.* But unfortunately, it did mean he was back to sleeping in his childhood bedroom, *Teenage Mutant Ninja Turtles* stickers all over his bed, and feeling like bit of a mug.

"When's Adam getting here?" Sam asked, eyeing me.

I didn't look at him for fear of giving away how I felt about his absence. Adam had been promising to help set up and stay the whole party in retribution for having missed the previous year due to his skiing escapades. But that had already gone to pot, since he hadn't arrived yet. "He said around ten."

We both checked the clock. It was half-ten. Sam didn't need to point that out.

"Why didn't he just arrive with you?"

I shrugged. "His brothers wanted to grab a drink at the pub."

"You didn't fancy going with them?"

I gave Sam a disappointed pout. "This is our thing. I'm always going to choose to spend New Year with you."

"And he isn't skiing this year?"

"No. The least he can do is show up to my birthday."

Sam nodded and I swear he threw in an eye roll, but I couldn't be sure. I had a growing suspicion that Sam was weary of Adam. That past summer, we'd all been to Ibiza and stayed in a villa, and I really hoped they'd find some common ground. I loved Adam because he was kind and gentle. He was the sort of guy to take care of things in many ways. I'd never had to figure out how to pay the energy bill, for example.

And that was great because it sounded really fucking boring.

Then there was this weight that came with our relationship that made me feel anchored to him. Sometimes, I wondered if it was because we'd made so much effort to get to where we were. Navigating the period of being long-distance, exhausting careers and university dramas – I couldn't give up on everything we'd been through for something as harmless as being late for parties. We were Hattie and Adam. People used us as an example of a couple that survived it all, how could I let them down? Let us down?

"So, he'll be here soon then?" he asked for confirmation.

"He said so."

"Right, ok then."

One hour later, with thirty minutes to go until my birthday, the house brimming with people, music and the clinking of glasses, Adam strolled through the front door with two of his brothers. They weren't invited but I could hardly say no to them joining. I popped another bottle of fizz to prepare for the fireworks and handed it to Sara to top up glasses.

Her newest boyfriend adventure was a Greek man who didn't speak a word of English. She'd picked him up while she was working the clubs in Malia during the summer. But it was ok, she'd explained, because they mostly communicated carnally anyway. Which... gross.

Adam gave me a hug and then him and his brothers leant against opposite walls in the hallway. I hovered between them, unsure why they didn't make a move to come into the house some more.

"So, Sam still lives with his mum?" Adam's oldest brother asked, peering around the space like he was planning to buy it.

"For a bit, yeah," I said, my heckles up. Sam was paying rent and stuff. He wasn't just living with his mum for free and racking up the benefits.

Adam's other brother, Dom, laughed.

"Is that a problem?" I sniped.

Adam rested a hand on my lower back as if to simmer me down. I'd been careful not to drink too much that night. There was no deadly punch this year. I wasn't mixing. And I even had a glass of water around for sipping intermittently. Even so, I was tipsy enough to get lairy.

Dom folded his arms. "Yeah, come on, Hattie. It's a bit pathetic. All of us Suarez brothers were out of the house on our own, set up, with careers by twenty-one. You don't move back to your parents' home under any circumstances. It's tragic."

I shook my head. "You're wrong. You don't know anything about Sam."

"He doesn't even have a job right now," Adam added, a smirk in his voice.

I twisted to glare at him, surprised he'd dip so low.

"He had to move back from Brighton and is looking for work. It's not like he's *choosing* to be unemployed."

Adam looked at his shoes, the smirk on his lips not fully retreating. I ground my jaw. To change topics, I reluctantly offered to get them another round of drinks and slunk off the kitchen. When I returned with three open bottles in my hand, Adam's brothers had put their coats back on and were hovering by the door. My smile dropped.

They were leaving. I could feel it.

"Why's your coat on?" I asked Adam, who was fidgeting with his sleeves, a sheepish expression on his face.

He grimaced. "This party is a bit shit," he said.

I opened my mouth and stammered for a few seconds. "But it's *my* party. It's my birthday!"

"I know, babe..."

"Don't *babe* me! Adam, why do you do this every year?"

"It's New Year's Eve. I want to be with my brothers. I've hardly seen them this year."

"Then tell them to stay," I said, staring him down.

But I could tell by the way he was glancing between us that he was never planning to do that. "It's not my fault your birthday is New Year's Day, is it?"

"What?"

"I just... Look, they want to hang out at the pub. It's a great atmosphere over there. I showed up, didn't I? I'll see you tomorrow. We'll have lunch."

"But I'm seeing my parents tomorrow."

"I'll join you," he offered, splaying his hands as if that answers this predicament.

I scoffed. "Fine. Whatever."

Sam appeared, jogging down the stairs and slowing to a stop. His cautious expression told me he could tell something was up. His eyes didn't stray from my face. "Everything ok?"

"You must be the party boy?" Dom said, a horrible grin on his face. I wanted to punch him. If my hands hadn't been full, I'd have done it.

Well, probably.

Instead, I waved them off, accepted a kiss on my cheek from Adam and watched them leave. Sam didn't say anything, but again, he didn't need to.

This was the thing with Adam. I really did believe that he loved me, but there was always a better offer. Even if that offer was the pub.

At five minutes to midnight, Sam set up the fireworks in the garden. A new girl that was just his type, short and quirky, was hovering around him and, as always with being his female best friend, I didn't feel like cramping his style, so I retreated.

Once all the festivities were done, people slowly started to leave and I wasn't in the mood for farewells. I stayed in the garden, wrapped in my coat as more fireworks in the local area went off, littering the sky with sparks of reds and blues and golds. I leant on the wall of the house and hugged myself to stay warm in the icy chill.

A tear rolled down my frozen cheek.

"Hello, storm cloud," a familiar, deep voice murmured.

I jumped, peeking around the dark garden, spotting his large, dark figure at the back gate. He'd obviously decided to avoid being seen via the front door. I frowned, quickly wiping my cheeks dry and sniffing. "What are you doing here?" I asked.

"Nice to see you too."

His features were difficult to make out, but I could tell he was in his long coat again, hands in his pockets, as he came to stand beside me, leaning one shoulder on the wall to stare at my face.

I had to get it together or he'd notice.

"Happy birthday," he said. "Sorry I didn't bring a gift."

I shrugged. "I don't even know when your birthday is."

"Fifth of March."

"How dull."

"Terribly. You going to tell me why you're out here crying in the dark at your own birthday party? Do I need to have a word with someone?" he asked, peering over my shoulder at the kitchen, still filled to the brim with chatty people.

I swallowed, my tummy squeezing. "I'm not crying."

"What happened?"

"I don't want to tell you."

"Are you ok?"

I sniffed back tears. What is it about a line of questioning when you're right on the edge to push you over? "Yes, I'm ok," I squeaked.

"Right." He nodded but didn't seem fully satisfied. "Did someone hurt you? Try it on?"

I shook my head. "No. Honestly, I'm fine.

"Does Sam know you're crying?"

I changed the subject. "Why are you even here?"

He didn't respond for a long moment, but I welcomed the silence. At least it meant I had time to breathe and collect myself. He shifted so his back was flush with the wall and rolled his head back. I could hear the scrape of the red bricks against his coat. "I was supposed to be back at my flat tonight but… I wanted to feel at home," he murmured. "So, I guess I'll just stay out here with you."

NINETEEN

"**G**uys!" Sam strides into the living room where Priya, Sara and I are huddling with sandwiches and watching *How I Met Your Mother* on E4 because this TV isn't set up with the streaming sites. "It's snowing."

We all turn to look out of the main doors. There's the lightest drift of snow, like frozen dust falling from the sky. It's hardly worth getting off the sofa for. But Sam is hopping at the window like a golden retriever who wants to go out and play in it.

"Is it settling?" I ask.

Sam stares at the ground and pouts. "A little."

Sara is not impressed. "It looks cold."

"How weird," I say.

She mock-scowls in response, and for the briefest of seconds, I see my old friend. There's hope yet. Maybe she isn't totally lost.

"We should go for a walk!" Sam says, his enthusiasm bursting in each word.

Priya snorts. "No, thank you. My toes do not agree with the cold. There are not enough socks in the world."

"Hattie?" he asks, noting he doesn't even bother trying to persuade Sara to join.

I shrug. The fire is on and there's a bowl of sour cream and onion crisps in front of me. My toes are warm in my fluffy socks. Going out in the cold right now doesn't feel super enticing. "Maybe in a bit, Sammy."

I briefly wonder where Freddie is. Probably working again.

An hour later and the snow is coming down in thicker chunks. There's a light layer of frosting covering the decking and hot tub. The thin branches of the nearby tree are starting to wilt under the weight. Sam hasn't been able to take his eyes off it, having moved a chair right up to the window.

Priya went off to take a call from Izzy, but she returns now. "Hey, guys... It says there's a snowstorm coming. Apparently, this is just the start."

"They always say that," I say, brushing her off. "And then it will be a shitty layer of snow that will melt within hours. It's not that bad."

"What if it does get bad though and we're stranded?" Priya asks.

"We have two more nights," I remind them. "It will be melted by then."

"The lanes around here did seem pretty treacherous," Sara adds, just to stoke the fire. I can hear the humour in her voice. I turn to give her an admonishing look, but she holds her hands up innocently.

"Honestly, it's fine, guys. It's just snow. It's not a big deal."

Sam stares at me, his mouth agape. "I'm definitely forgetting something."

I groan. "This is why I tell you to write things down. Or message me so you don't forget."

"I feel like I was meant to do something…"

"I'm sure it was nothing," I say. "Guys, let's just relax. You know what snow is like in this country. At best, it will be a light inconvenience. We'll be fine!"

An hour flies past and I'm chewing on my nails. The snow is bucketing it down now. It's only two in the afternoon but the thick clouds have shrouded the forest into darkness. I've moved to stand at the window.

Sam is in the kitchen, and I hear him shout, "I've definitely forgotten something!"

"Oh my God!" I shout back. "Why are you like this?"

"What was it?"

I throw my hands up. "How am I supposed to know?"

Priya strides over to stand beside me, wrapping her arms around mine and resting her head on my shoulder. She's so much smaller than me and Sara. I want to apologise and tell her I was wrong. I never trust the weather reports. Especially living by the coast. Things change so fast, and they get it so wrong all the time, but this one time, they might be right and now I've potentially screwed her over and we'll be stuck in the lodge for longer than she expected. And she's already so worried about being away from Ollie.

I bite my lip as I spot Freddie's reflection a few feet behind me, his hands in his jean pockets, a thoughtful expression etched across his face.

I can see Sara too, snuggled under a fleece blanket, drinking probably her tenth coffee of the day. Caffeine doesn't make Sara buzzy. It makes her mean and agitated. Like feeding coal to a dragon.

Priya squeezes my arm. "I'm going to call Izzy again. Just in case."

I nod and hope my expression portrays how sorry I am for not getting this right. She could've left before it got too bad.

When I check Freddie's reflection again, I find him looking at mine too, our eyes connecting through the glass; the corners of his lips quirk. Knowing he's on my side feels like I'm a small boat being anchored to a ship during a storm. It's as if he can see me trying to keep all my friends together for a just a few days and already flailing.

I turn away, giving him a shy smile as I pass and go to sit with Sara. She immediately shuffles as I settle.

I take a deep breath, suddenly emboldened. "You know what?" I whisper. "I know you wear invisible armour, and I know you don't like to get into feelings and vulnerabilities, but I want you to know that I'm ready to listen to you if you need it. I'll always listen. And I'll believe you too."

Sara blinks but still doesn't look at me. "There's nothing to say."

I know that's not true. I think about asking her a direct question about Mike. Target one of my suspicions that it's to do with him. Because why wouldn't she invite her fiancé to a New Year's Eve party when we said he could come? The question of whether she's spoken to him since we left is right on my tongue, but I choose a different strategy.

"Ok," I say, using every fibre in my body to leave it at that. I stuff my face with crisps to prevent myself from slipping up and saying something else.

"I'm serious," she adds. "There's nothing wrong." Now she's staring at me but I'm refusing to look back.

"I know. I believe you."

She huffs, whipping her hair behind her shoulder. "Fine. Whatever." She looks around to check nobody is in hearing distance. "You and Adam breaking up has properly messed with my head."

I stop crunching and gape at her. "What?"

She nods. "I wasn't meant to be the first person in this group getting married. It doesn't sit right with me."

"Ok? And this is my fault?"

"No…" She doesn't sound very convincing.

I lean back to get an even better read on her face. Her cheeks are red in a way I've never seen them before. She's finding this discussion very difficult. And now so am I!

"Obviously, it's not *your* fault. It's just… You guys were so good together. So solid. You had a future planned. He was a good man. And then he just…"

"Left me," I finish for her. "He left me because he didn't *love* me – crucially."

"But how can that happen to *you*," she says, waving her hands at me. "You're so good. You were such a great girlfriend to him. You did everything right. You were always there for him. You made his life better. I saw it so many times! When he was sick, you would cater to his every need. He didn't deserve you!"

I don't know what to say to that, but I can feel myself welling up. There's a lump in my throat and it's expanding. I swallow it down.

"I don't do any of those things, Hattie," she adds. "I'm not a good fiancée. I don't deserve Mike. He's too sweet. He's so wonderful and I just know it's going to end. I work too hard. I'll always be there for him, you know? But I can't always be sweet and kind and gentle. That's not me. And recently…" She pauses, playing with her hands.

"Recently what?"

She huffs a breath. "Recently, he seems to be getting tired of me, you know? Like when my work gets crazy, he doesn't fight it like he used to. He doesn't remind me to put it down, put it away and spend time with him. He seems almost… resigned."

I shake my head. "What do you mean? He loves you. He knows all of that about you and he proposed anyway!"

"Adam loved you too," she points out.

"You can't compare our situations." I take a deep breath. God, this is harder than I thought it would be, dredging up feelings about Adam which have somehow changed in the last few weeks from heartbreak to anger. Now I feel sorry for myself. Sorry that I didn't stand up for *me* when I had the chance, because I could've saved myself from wasting a ton of years.

Sara runs a hand through her hair, looking behind to find Freddie and Sam cleaning the kitchen. Which is highly suspect, come to think of it. The glass in Freddie's hand has already been cleaned.

Never let it be said that men mind their own business.

"And now I'm upsetting you," she says. "See, I'm the fucking worst! I have this horrible feeling building up inside of me. I'm finding it hard to ignore, Hattie."

"Sara, you're a good person."

"Don't," she says, shaking her head. "I'm uptight. You've told me as much on many occasions. And I have three younger sisters who remind me daily."

"But people who know you, know that's only your outer shell. You're the one we turn to when shit gets real!"

She sniffs, biting her lip. "I would hide the body with you," she whispers.

I nod. "Likewise. Without question. Oh, Sara. I hope you know that you're smart and independent and beautiful in a way most men would be incredibly lucky to have. Mike is batting way above his average, and he knows that. You know that too."

She laughs, wiping a tear from her eye. "He's well above average in the bedroom."

"Ok."

"And has the biggest…"

"Personality?"

"Sure."

I snigger. "Your wedding is going to be ace and I'm here to help if you ever decide you need it. It would be an honour. I'm almost offended you haven't asked, to be honest. Like, I'm literally in the art industry… I could make it so beautiful."

"I didn't want to bother you with it. I thought you'd be too sad after your break-up."

I stare at her for a long second. "So, you're telling me you were doing this all on your own because you didn't want to dredge up my feelings?"

"Well, obviously. In theory, you should be my maid of honour. You know, if it goes to my favourite female friend. Don't tell Priya." She whispers the last part.

"Am I not your overall favourite friend?"

"It's a close tie."

"I'm offended."

She rolls her eyes because we both know she has no other friends than the ones in this house. "Do you want to be my maid of honour or not?"

I gasp. "Can I throw you a wild hen do?"

She cringes, lacing her fingers together on her lap. "As long as it's classy. I don't want dick straws."

"Oh, well, in that case," I say, twisting my lips, "I'm out."

She scoffs. "Are you freaking kidding me?"

"I'm not going to a hen do without dick straws, Sara."

She relents, shaking her head. "Ok fine, but only because I can tell my sisters to back off. They won't shut up about doing something. Are you prepared for the number of people I'm ambivalent about that need to attend this bloody thing for family reasons?"

"It can't be that bad."

"Twenty-seven."

"Well, fuck."

She nods, her expression sober but with a hint of a smile. "And you'll have to throw it in less than four months. Do you accept the challenge?"

"You know what? Yes, I bloody do. Because you'd do the same for me, even if you think you wouldn't."

"Sure. But I wouldn't inflict dick straws on you."

"Sara, dearest, the dick straws are just the start. I heard you can get dick-shaped jelly shots."

"I'm not doing those," she says with certainty.

"We'll see. I know the effects tequila has on your inhibitions."

She's about to reply when there's a loud knocking at the door. We all freeze before turning in that direction. I can see from the windows surrounding it that it's now completely dark outside.

Freddie is the first to move, striding bravely towards the knocking.

Sam gasps dramatically from the kitchen. "Oh fuck!" he says. "I know what I forgot!"

Freddie swings the door open, and I feel the chill from across the room. It's practically Baltic outside. There's a man in the doorway; he collapses to his knees, his lips blue.

TWENTY

It's not until I see his curly hair, much like mine, that I work out who it is. "What the… *Dylan?!*" I say, hopping off the sofa and running across to him where he's collapsed on the floor. I help pull his body in so Freddie can close the door.

"I forgot Dylan was coming," Sam says. He looks almost pleased he's remembered the thing he forgot.

I stare at him, aghast. "I don't understand what's happening," I say. "Sara, can you run a tepid bath for Dyl, please?"

There's a flurry of action. Sam helps Freddie lift Dylan onto the sofa, wrapping a blanket over him. The kettle is boiling in the kitchen and Priya has come back to help get the fireplace roaring again. Dylan's teeth are chattering as he stares at me with a guilty expression. His cheeks are so red, he looks like he's added blush to them, but I guess that might be the frostbite.

"Care to explain?" I ask, rubbing his arms to help warm him.

"S-s-urp-ris-ss-ee!"

"What's the surprise? You arriving at our party uninvited? Or that you're nearly frozen to death?"

"B-b-oth."

"Ok… but why are you here?"

Sam arrives at this exact moment with a hot chocolate, placing it on the side table, and a hot water bottle, which he slides across to Dylan, tucking it under the blanket to warm his chest. "That'll be my fault."

I glare at my best friend. "What did you do?"

"I was meant to remember that Dylan was driving up here. But then it started snowing and I forgot, so…"

"What? Wait. Why?"

He shrugs. "We wanted to surprise you!"

I sigh. "Well, congrats, I'm surprised!"

Sam smiles as if he did good then turns away to the kitchen, leaving me with Dylan.

"I still don't understand. Why are you here?"

He takes a sip of hot chocolate before answering, his voice still wavering as he says, "I didn't want to be alone with our family on New Year's Eve. I messaged Sam because I thought you'd say no."

"How do you have Sam's number?"

Dylan rolls his eyes. "That doesn't matter. I'm here because we're black sheep now and we have to stick together. You can't just swan off and abandon me with our family. I'm tired of being the loser."

"You're not a loser," I say, but right now, with him shivering on the sofa, it's a hard sell so I shrug. "Ok. You are a bit of a loser."

"Thank you," he says, as if that was in fact a compliment.

"I borrowed Dad's car to drive here but as I got closer, it started to snow. But, like, *proper* snow. Like I could barely see, kind of snow."

"Yeah, I get it."

"Well, the car got stuck on a bank somewhere. The wheels just spinning out. I tried calling Sam but I had no signal."

"Neither do I, to be fair," Sam adds from behind me. I don't look around. He shall be cold-shouldered for the time being.

"...I just started walking. But I didn't have a coat."

"Where's your bag?"

Dylan looks over at the door with a frown. "Oh shit."

"What?"

"I might've left my bag in the car."

"Might've?"

He cringes. "I did. I left it in the car. I was panicking. I thought I was going to freeze to death in the middle of nowhere, covered in snow, as the dark crept in."

"And your coat?"

He shrugs. "Didn't think I'd need one. I left it at home. I was meant to be driving up to the door."

I shake my head at him. "I'm calling Mum. Let her know you're insane but alive."

"Oh! And then I got chased by something, dropped my phone and couldn't find it."

"So, you lost your phone too?"

He nods.

"What did you get chased by?" I ask, eyes wide.

"A pig, I think. It was dark."

"*Oh my God.*"

"I slipped over. Don't remember the next part."

I hear Freddie mutter, "Wild bacon."

"You probably have concussion then," I say.

"I'm fine."

I roll my shoulders to ease the tension as I walk to my room to call Mum and let her know my idiot cousin has arrived at the lodge. The signal is patchy, but I manage to explain how he's waded through what now looks like at least a foot of snow. She tuts and huffs before promising to call my auntie. I mean, it's not as if Dylan isn't an adult with his own autonomy, but on the off-chance someone is worried about him, it felt right to make a call.

Sara is ushering Dylan to the bathroom as I re-enter the upstairs hallway. Sam is following behind with a towel. "You," I say, pointing at him. "This is *your* fault. You can stay with him and make sure he doesn't drown. You need to slowly warm the water up until he can feel his toes again. I don't want to drag paramedics out here in the snow."

Sam presses his lips together and nods.

As I descend the stairs again, Priya is in the kitchen. All I see is a plume of smoke as she opens the oven door, her arms batting around like crazy.

The fire alarm goes off. The screeching sound it emits runs straight from my ears to my toes, making my whole body tense. I try to work out which button to reach for but even though I'm tall, I can't get to it with these high ceilings.

Freddie runs up behind me, placing his hands on my shoulders before reaching up to turn it off. My instincts tell me to lean into his touch, but my brain reminds me it's off limits, so I squirm to escape him.

Priya opens the windows. "Sorry guys, I forgot the pizzas."

"There's no hot water left now," Sara huffs, storming back into the room. "Hattie, can you remember how to work the boiler…?"

"Oh my God!" I say a little too loudly. "I'm going to get some space. This isn't the chaos I was after for this trip!"

I jog across the living space to the door that leads to the basement games room. We haven't really used it yet as it's cold and dark down there with only one ground-level window, totally blocked up with snow. I switch the garish lights on and perch on the pool table.

I take a few deep breaths when the fire alarm goes off again, clenching my eyes closed to calm myself. I can hear feet shuffling above me before it's turned off. Voices are muffled. I bet they're wondering what the hell my problem is, running off sulking like that. But isn't it ok for things to just become too much sometimes?

Isn't it ok to need a break? Some space without chaos?

Steps finally sound on the stairs. I look across to find Freddie frowning at me by the doorway, his hands on his hips. He's wearing a plain, long-sleeved, maroon t-shirt with rolled-up sleeves. The firm lines of his forearms are clear to see. I bet he does forearm workouts. Are those a thing? He steps closer slowly, like he's worried he'll spook me, his blue jeans rustling. His thick, grey, hiking socks must feel nice on the smooth, concrete floor.

I look down at myself, dressed in black leggings and a grey, longline sweatshirt. He's right; I am plain. He looks disappointed, and it triggers something in me. There's a short burst of unwanted adrenaline spreading across my sternum. I feel like I'm going to have to pay for that moment in some way.

"Are you here to tell me off?" I ask, my protective walls closing me in.

His frown deepens. "No. Why would you think that?"

"Because Adam would've told me off for making a scene."

Adam would've been disappointed in me. Adam would've pointed out that his mates' girlfriends weren't as emotional and difficult as me. Adam would've made me feel like the brattiest person ever.

"You didn't make a scene," Freddie confirms. "It was already a scene. I don't blame you for needing to get away. That's why I left it a minute before checking on you. What Dylan and Sam did earlier... Ambushing you. It was out of order."

"Oh," I say, surprised. Something light and airy settles in my core. I'm ok. This isn't going to end in tears. I'm not being blamed.

"I'm checking you're ok," he says, his voice taking a gentler tone.

I fiddle with the end of my sleeves. "I'm ok. It's just... a lot. I feel really bad. I should've told Priya to go home earlier on before the snow got so heavy. You or Sam could've driven her. Who knows how long we'll be stranded now. I should've known why Sara was feeling off and I shouldn't have left Dylan to deal with my family on his own. He's right; I should've seen that. I could've invited him in the first place."

Freddie's frown stays right there. I want him to nod or confirm my selfishness but he just laughs instead, a kind of breathy, disbelieving sound. "Hattie, none of those things are your fault. You're not responsible for anyone in this lodge. They're all adults."

I roll my eyes. "I know. But this was my idea…"

"They all agreed to come. You didn't bundle them into the car and force them to come here. They agreed. They *wanted* to be here."

"I know. But Priya…"

"Could've left herself if she wanted to. She chose to stay."

"I know you're right, but it doesn't just make the feeling go away. I still feel like I've let them down."

He shrugs. "I just wish I could release you from that feeling. Why did you think I came down here to have a go at you?"

I look away. "I don't know."

He steps closer, and even though I can't bring myself to turn to him, I know his eyes never stray from my face. It's like my skin feels brushed wherever his gaze lands. If I was a braver woman, I'd take him on and stare straight back, challenge him and play with our chemistry, but I'm not anymore.

When I feel his warm thumb on my chin, I swear something bursts in my core, heat pooling everywhere. I've craved his touch for years.

He adds a light pressure to turn my face towards him, using his other hand to sweep my hair back behind my shoulder. His fingers linger. "Your hair is so soft," he murmurs; his steady, deep voice sends shockwaves rolling down my spine.

I finally look up. He's so close, I can see the gold flecks flitting out from his iris; it's like staring into a forest during the hot, glowing days of summer.

"I took this off the cards, remember," I say gently.

He nods. "I know. Want me to give you space?"

I don't respond. Instead, I take the opportunity to trace his beautiful, rugged face with my thumb. The fact he closes his eyes and sighs as I do it only fuels my confidence. I wonder what the light stubble around his mouth would feel like under my tongue. What would he taste like?

I laugh at myself, twisting and stepping away from the pool table to give us space. My thumb that touched him feels scorched. Freddie doesn't turn fully, and I secretly hope it's because he's hiding the swell in his jeans.

"I'm sorry," I squeak. "That was stupid."

Freddie sighs again and shakes his head. "I'm not sorry and wish you wouldn't be either."

"You're…" I'm about to say *terrible*, or *outrageously hot*, but I don't because there's a clanking sound throughout the lodge before all the lights go out. We're plunged into darkness. Not a speck of light.

I blink, disorientated.

There are a few screams and a yell upstairs.

I swear a sound comes out of my mouth but it's so feral, I can't work out if it was a scream or some kind of demented yelp.

Before I know what's happening, two large hands are on my waist.

"I've got you," he says.

I fall into him, placing my hands on his solid shoulders to ground me. It's not that I'm frightened of the dark. In contrary, the only way I get myself to sleep these days is by blacking out my room to match the deepest, darkest caves.

But this was unexpected.

There are voices upstairs and I imagine they all have their phone torches on, trying to work out where the hell the switchboard is. I bet Freddie knows. Hopefully, it's only that and not something to do with the snowstorm raging on outside. At least they have the glow of the fireplace up there. We have nothing down here.

Freddie's breathing is calm and sure, his chest moving slowly against my cheek as he rests his chin on my head. He moves to step away, but I can't help myself. I draw him in again, tangling my arms around his neck and running my fingers through his short, tawny hair.

But then, with a sharp, disbelieving laugh, I snatch my hands away, plastering myself to the cold wall behind me. "No, we can't. This needs to stop."

Freddie laughs deeply. "Want me to help you back upstairs?"

"You can't see either, can you? Do you have built-in night vision or something?"

"Yeah, all vampires have it."

I snort. "You could've gone with superhero."

"Nah. They don't suck the life out of people."

I blow out a long breath. "Freddie, that was *dark*." When he doesn't immediately reply, I say, "Have you left me down here? Because that would be really mean."

"Did you bring your phone down?" he asks instead.

"Erm, no?"

"Me neither. I'm sure we can crawl over to the door somehow."

"Sick of being stuck with me already?"

"We both know that's impossible."

I chew on my cheek. "Then why are you trying to escape?"

"I'm not. I'm strategizing. And distracting myself from the fact that I'm down here with you, alone, and you've just made it very clear we can't do this. Whatever *this* is. So, I'm thinking up next steps."

"We could talk?"

Freddie makes a strained sound. "Don't say scary things to me in the dark. It's cruel."

This only eggs me on. I think about asking him something about his dad but instead I go for, "What is it you actually do for work?"

"I'm a director of data."

"That sounds *thrilling*."

He sniffs. "It's a daily horror show. And it follows me everywhere."

"But pays well."

"Not always worth it," he says.

"Then quit."

"And do what?"

"What do you want to do?"

He groans. "You'll laugh at me."

"Oh, this should be good. Let me guess. A clown?"

"As if."

"You're right, too simple. Hmm, an actor?"

"I only know how to frown, remember. I'd be restricted."

I snort. "You're right. Plus, Hollywood already has enough grumpy arseholes."

"Hattie…"

"Can you sing?"

"No. Hattie, listen…"

"It's not something pretentious, is it? Like you're going to try and retrain for six years to be a marine biologist specialising in sea lions. They already have plenty of those."

"My God, shh," he says, one hand sliding onto my hip, the weight of it is exquisite, whilst his other hand finds my face skilfully, two fingers pressing against my lips. The pressure in my core slides down and settles lower. "If I didn't feel trapped in my current job, I'd quit and start my own business. But I don't have the start-up funds I need so... I carry on working away."

I swallow as his fingers slide away from my lips. "Well, that's not funny."

"What?"

"You said I'd laugh."

"It's not... You know what, don't worry."

TWENTY-ONE

The one where he leant me his sexy coat again

On our twenty-sixth birthdays, Adam agreed to host our new year's party in his first-floor flat in London. By this point, many of our friends from school and university were off doing other things but we'd picked up a few strays along the way from our jobs, clubs and general living.

I wasn't sure about city life.

It was full of people but it didn't feel like there was any sort of community. It often struck me how you could share a lift with someone from the same building once or twice a week but never ask them their name. I found myself falling into those same unsociable habits, trying to fit in and not draw attention to myself. I got an admin job at an art gallery in the city but was uninspired by the strange, abstract work that they sold there, and the insane money people were willing to spend on it.

When Adam suggested we have the party at his, I almost couldn't believe it. He was protective of his modern, shiny flat to say the least. Of course, there did turn out to be an agenda and a very clear reason why I was only meant to bring about six of my own friends. And that was because he'd invited *his* work mates. At least ten of them because he wanted to schmooze someone who could help get him a promotion.

I couldn't shake the feeling that he'd made my birthday about him in some way.

I guess because that's exactly what he'd done.

But it didn't matter because I was seeing Sam for the first time since I'd moved to London weeks ago. We were going to get shitfaced together and party like we were teenagers again.

An hour or so into the party, we were huddled around the TV playing the moustache drinking game on the music channel. Essentially, you put a stick-on moustache on the TV and every time a person looks like they're wearing it, you drink. A few of us were standing to work in crucial dance moves, some were perched on the edge of the sofa, and Sara knelt on the hardwood floor to be closest to the bottle of tequila for refills.

"My knees have dealt with worse!" she yelled, cackling.

Only *our* friendship group found that funny. Not Adam's friends. Or Adam, for that matter. They were all too busy judging our rowdy behaviour from the kitchen island.

I didn't care. I was turning twenty-six in less than two hours. So, fuck it!

Rihanna bobbed into the moustache on the screen whilst holding her umbrella.

"DRINK!" Sara yelled.

Priya managed to snort whilst sipping and some of it came out of her nose, which had us all cracking up, including her new girlfriend, Izzy. She got our vibe. She was a keeper.

Sam was noticeably drunk. He'd had a tough few years, flitting in and out of careers. Falling in and out of love with people. Then there was his tough relationship with his dad and brother. So, I didn't make too much of it, taking a mental note that he would need some care in the morning. We had makeshift beds to spread out on the living room floor for those who needed to stay the night.

Half an hour until midnight, I felt a hand on my elbow and turned to find Adam. I smiled, leaning into him, but his posture was rigid. I looked up to find his jaw was set. Brushing myself off, I maintained my smile and said, "What's wrong?"

"You know what's wrong," he said, his voice level but low. If anyone looked over, they would have seen a normal conversation between a loving couple. Sometimes, I thought that was the most dangerous thing about Adam – his ability to be angry but look fine.

I shuffled, peeking over at Sara, who'd caught my eye and wouldn't turn away. She was protective like that, but I prayed she'd stay out of it. I could handle Adam. He would just be disappointed for a few days. Maybe twenty-four hours of silence. It wasn't a big deal. It just made me feel numb and vulnerable for a bit.

"I think you and your friends have had plenty to drink. It's time to cut them off," he said, staring at me like he was hoping for a reaction.

I shrugged. "Ok. It's nearly midnight anyway. And we're just having fun."

"Yeah. Fun at my expense."

"Has somebody done something to upset you?"

"You're just embarrassing, Hattie. Acting like a child."

I ground my teeth. I wanted to tell him he was being no fun, to lighten up. But this was his flat and it wasn't fair to ruin his evening. That promotion meant a lot to him in a way I could never understand but tried to respect.

So, I forced out, "I'm sorry. I'll get them to rein it in."

But it wasn't a task I could achieve, and I think Adam knew that. Priya and Izzy were making out on the sofa. My friend from work had already been tactically sick so they could clean off the last bottle of prosecco and Sam...

Well, Sam was dancing around the living space, pumping his hands above his head and at some point, in the last few minutes, had taken his top off.

I was about to rush over and see if I could get some water down him, but he tripped next to the large, open window. Adam's friend was close enough to reach out and stop him, but he didn't. He laughed instead.

As if in slow motion, I watched Sam disappear into the dark street below.

My mind went to the darkest parts of my imagination as I sprinted over, my heart throbbing in my chest.

Sara was beside me in a split second, holding onto my arm like I might fall too. Sam was lying face up. He blinked then touched his head.

"I can't fly, Hatter!" he called up.

I laugh-cried as I shot towards the door to the stairs. I'm sure Adam sputtered something about it being my fault, but I didn't care. With Sara, Priya and Izzy hot on my heels, we rounded the place where Sam had fallen.

He was still lying there, and some kind passersby had waited with him to prevent him being run over. My heart was hammering as I knelt down beside him, the icy tarmac biting into my knees thanks to my stupidly skimpy, black minidress.

Sam was half-laughing, half-delirious.

"Where's the pain?" I asked, checking him over. There wasn't any obvious blood, but he also hadn't moved.

Sara gave me a worried glance before standing to call for an ambulance.

"This is going to be the worst hangover I've ever had," he said, nodding to himself.

"Sam. The pain? Where's the pain?"

He scrunched up his face. "Everywhere, pretty much," he croaked.

When the ambulance arrived, they let me travel with him to the hospital. It was chaos inside. A&E was heaving with partygoers. After seeing about ten doctors and being whizzed off for at least three different types of scans, they declared Sam a lucky, drunken idiot who had managed to only break bones for what could've been a fatal accident.

I finally managed to get hold of his mum once he'd fallen asleep, adrift on alcohol and painkillers.

He was allocated a quiet ward so I curled up as best as I could into the uncomfortable hospital chair and hoped they didn't kick me out.

At some point during the early hours of New Year's Day, I stirred, the yellow fluorescents glaring at me from the ceiling. I checked on Sam, who was still sleeping, his chest rising and falling softly. I'd never seen my friend attached to all the machines before. I felt uneasy and useless.

It was another moment before I realised someone had draped a thick, wool trench coat over me. I was still curled up on the chair. There were pins and needles in my feet and lower legs, so I hopped up to try and shake them out.

I held the weighty coat up as the sensation returned. My brain was slow with sleep, but recognition gradually returned to me. It wasn't until its owner popped his head back through the curtains that my heart started racing.

"Oh," I said. "You're here."

Freddie frowned, passing me a cup of something. "I am."

"I didn't think you would come. Sam said you two aren't talking at the moment."

He grimaced. "Mum was too drunk to drive but I was just having a quiet one, so she called me." He sighed, rubbing the back of his neck. He was in a loose, grey, gym sweater, but I could see the outline of his toned arms when he stretched like that. I tried to keep my face passive but gnawed on my bottom lip anyway. "Which was a big surprise since she hasn't been speaking to me for a while either. It's actually nice to finally see Sam," he said.

"Took falling out of a window," I muttered, then immediately felt like the biggest bitch on the planet.

Freddie dropped his arms to his side. His expression melted into sadness, and he blinked away. "It probably looks that way."

He dragged a chair into the cubicle and sat, not taking his eyes off his baby brother. He looked haunted. Dark skin under his eyes and pale lips. I took a seat too and sipped the hot chocolate he'd brought me. I wondered how or if he knew I didn't drink coffee.

"Could this have been avoided?" he asked, his voice its usual gruffness. It didn't sound like he was blaming me but more himself. He wasn't even there.

I stared at Sam for a second. I didn't know what he'd want me to share with Freddie. He hadn't explained enough about their fall out. Would he be cross with me for talking to him? Or being honest about how he'd been recently?

I offered Freddie his coat back, which was on the back of the chair, but he shook his head. "You need it more," he said. "You looked cold."

So, he'd noticed my minidress then. I thanked him and wrapped it over myself again. Something about the action made him swallow and drop eye contact. I checked my phone to make myself seem unbothered. No calls from Adam. No messages. Nothing.

Sara, on the other hand, needed consoling. I sent her a quick response.

"Sam's been struggling," I said finally. "But I don't know what I should be telling you. I don't know what he'd want you to know."

Freddie's face didn't change but he nodded. "You're a good friend to him."

I shrugged. "I definitely don't feel like one right now. I shouldn't've…"

"You didn't force him to drink," Freddie said with surety.

I swallowed, barely able to maintain his gaze. "I could've stopped it."

"It's not your fault."

"Well…" I frowned, thinking about how Adam might not agree with that statement. I stifled a yawn, stretching my face instead.

Freddie got up from his chair. "Come on. Let's get you home."

"Oh, I'll be ok. I'll get a taxi or something."

"At four in the morning on New Year's Day?"

I shrugged. "Good point. I'll walk."

He nodded. "Come on then."

Someone in a nearby cubicle coughed pointedly. I gave Freddie a silent, "Oops," then leant over to kiss Sam on the forehead. Poor, silly moron. At least he would be ok. That's all that mattered. I couldn't take my eyes off his pale, sleeping face, golden, sweaty hair swept back as I left.

In the hallway, the lights were down low and there was the distant sound of someone typing. I finally turned to hand Freddie his coat back before I made my way home. He stared at it but didn't take it.

"Who do you take me for, Hattie?" he said, not harshly but there was a hint of exhaustion in his tone.

"Er…"

"Put the coat on. It's -2 degrees outside. The roads are covered in ice."

I looked down at my heeled boots and bare legs. He was right. This walk was going to be torture. It would be nice to have a coat on at least. "How will I get it back to you?"

"You can hand it to me once we get to your door."

"Eh?"

He sighed, a disbelieving laugh escaping his lips. "You thought I was going to let you walk home alone? In the dark? In the tightest minidress I think I've ever seen?"

I snorted. "It's not even *my* tightest. There's no way it's the tightest *you've* ever seen." I blushed at my comment, wondering if there was accidental innuendo there. "I remember the girls you had at the parties."

He didn't even attempt to defend himself. "Please let me walk you home."

"What about Sam? I don't know if we should leave him."

"He's in the best place for him and he's not waking up any time soon. I'll come right back here after. He'll be absolutely thrilled to see me when he wakes up."

He said the last sentence without mirth, but I sniffed, knowing Sam wouldn't be happy to find Freddie there at all. Even if that was exactly what he needed. They'd not seen eye to eye in such a long time.

Come to think of it, had I ever seen them getting along?

"Put the coat on," he said again. "Please."

"You're going to freeze, though," I pointed out.

He just tilted his head as if to say I was being difficult.

"Fine. And fine, you can walk me to Adam's."

"You live with him?"

I didn't answer until we'd left the hospital and were breathing in the icy, misty air on London's streets. The cold hit my bare skin like a knife edge. I instantly regretted letting Freddie talk me into leaving, despite being exhausted and craving my bed. He had his hands tucked under his arms, so I knew he was feeling it too. Mine were tucked into his toasty coat pockets. I could feel a half-eaten pack of chewing gum in one and what felt like receipts in the other.

"I moved in with Adam a few months ago. It felt right," I finally answered.

Freddie nodded. "I don't live far from here. I'll pop by mine and grab Sam some stuff to wear. Take him some snacks too."

"That's a good idea."

"He still wearing shorts in the snow?"

I laughed. "Oh yeah."

"Good to know."

"He misses you, I think," I said. "But he's disappointed in something. He doesn't tell me what. I just know whenever he brings you up, he sounds sad, not angry."

"Sounds about right. Everyone is usually disappointed in me."

"I doubt that's true."

"No, it is. I don't ever seem to make anyone happy."

I chewed on my bottom lip. I'd need a million hot water bottles on my legs to warm up once I got in. "God, you're so brooding sometimes," I said in jest. "You're worse than Jon Snow."

"The news guy?"

"No! The *Game of Thrones* character. You know… 'You know nothing, Jon Snow.' That guy."

"I have no idea what you're talking about."

"Pfft. You should watch it."

He smirked. "Oh yeah? Will it teach me how to make good decisions?"

"Ha! Fuck no. Well, unless you're planning to overthrow a royal family or something."

"I'd better watch it then," he said, with that familiar sparkle in his eye.

My tummy flipped so I focused once again on the icy pavements.

We finally came to Adam's block of flats. Sara had run in to grab my phone and keys before the ambulance left so at least I wasn't locked out. She said everyone had decided to go home after the incident as it didn't feel right to stay anymore. I wondered how moody Adam had been with my friends.

"So, this is your flat then?" Freddie said.

I looked up at the modern complex and felt suddenly embarrassed by it. It wasn't very me at all. "Well, it's Adam's."

"But you live with him, so it's yours too, right?"

"No, it's definitely his. I'm not even sure if London is for me. Hopefully, we'll move back to the coast one day before we get married."

Freddie nearly choked. "You're engaged?"

My eyes went wide. "Oh. No. No, it's just a plan. Adam always talks about it. It's something he wants. You know, marriage, kids. He's serious about us."

If Freddie had an opinion on this, he kept it to himself. "All I know," he said, leaning in towards me, "is that if my girlfriend was living with me permanently, I'd want her to say *our* flat, not just mine."

I grimaced. "Yeah. It just doesn't feel like mine. All my art is still at my parents as there's no space for it here." That wasn't true. Adam just didn't like the clutter. And the way I did art was messy and generally chaotic. Which was funny, since my final pieces were always so serene.

"I still have that red boat painting you did," he suddenly remarked. "It's in my hallway, actually. So I see it every time I leave or enter the house. It reminds me of home."

I blinked. "I didn't know you had that. I gave it to your mum."

He nodded, a spark in his eye. "I might've stolen it and blamed it on Dad." He tapped his nose. "Perks of being a child of divorce."

"Are you still a child of divorce if it happened when you were, what, twenty?"

"Absolutely."

"Right. Makes sense." I had to look down at the road for a moment to hide my blush. Freddie had one of my pieces in his own flat. It felt weirdly intimidate. "That one wasn't perfect. I didn't get the sunlight quite right."

"I've never even noticed. I just stare at the boat in the middle of all that grey and think…" he paused, looking at my hair. It was probably frizzy from the damp, icy air but there was never any denying it had a tint of red in it. He swallowed. "You still paint, right?"

I gaped at him, unsure where he'd been going with the previous sentence. What does the red boat remind him of?

"Not really," I said, fiddling with the sleeves of his coat that were too long for me. "I'm working as a receptionist right now in some snotty, abstract art gallery. They seem to be really stretching the whole thirty-seven hours a week thing they promised. Besides, Adam pointed out it wasn't like I could make any money from it anyway."

Freddie didn't quite roll his eyes, it was more of an eye shake; either way, that statement pissed him off. "Hattie. I would pay good money for your paintings. And I know others would too. You're talented."

Was he trying to kill me with compliments? I was heating right up. I could've combusted right there on the spot. I couldn't look at him, kicking a stone on the road between my boots. "You're just being kind."

"Please start painting again," he practically whispered.

"I know you sketch," I said. Anything to divert the conversation away from me.

Freddie blinked. "Sorry?"

"That time in Brighton. In your hotel room," I was quick to explain myself. "You had a sketchbook."

The remaining colour drained from his face as he stared back at me in shock. "Did you look through it?"

"Oh, er…"

"I don't draw for other people. They're just for me. A way to clear my head of things." He laughed nervously, running a hand through his hair. "Did you look?"

"I…" I didn't think he was ready to know I'd seen the sketch of me, so I shook my head. "Only one. The bit of paper was poking out. It was a lamp or something."

He scrutinised my face, the colour finally returning to his cheeks. There was a question on the tip of his tongue, and I wouldn't have lied if he had asked me.

But right then, he visibly shivered.

"Oh shit," I said, hauling the coat off and practically launching it at him. In the process, I slipped on some ice, my boot flying up from underneath me.

I must've been inches from my arse hitting the floor when I was caught, one strong arm around my waist. His face was so close, I could feel the brush of his chocolatey breath on my nose. His gaze traced the line of my lips, my nose and finished at my eyes.

I swallowed, my tummy dipping like a rollercoaster on a descent.

This felt wrong. Adam was upstairs. It felt wrong that it felt right.

He must've read my thoughts because he helped me to my feet again. I fished my keys from my boot and waved awkwardly as he released me, heading towards the doors.

"Hey, let me see your keys," he said, before I could fully escape him.

He slid his arms into his coat. Damn. He looked good in that coat. It was akin to Mark Darcy in *Bridget Jones*. I wanted him to wrap me in it and rub my frozen nose against his.

Weird, Hattie. Very weird.

I knew what he wanted to see and smiled. I held up the storm-cloud charm. It had lost some of its shine from overuse. I dangled it in front of him.

He nodded, a big, bashful smile taking over his face. "Look after yourself, storm cloud."

"And you," I said.

"I want to see you get in. I'll get Sam to message you once he's awake."

"Thank you, Freddie." I finally stepped through the main doors, using my key fob to access the building. Once I was in the lift, I couldn't stop myself from grinning like an idiot.

TWENTY-TWO

I fidget in the darkness of the basement. I remember the sketches I'd seen before, and wonder if I should tell him about the one I found of me. Instead, I decide to goad him about sketching in the first place. I have no idea why he's so embarrassed about it. Not only is he gifted; it's something I know and love. There's no need to hide that from me. "I was hoping you'd say drawing."

I wish I could see his face. "I'm not an artist," he grumbles.

"You're good, though."

He laughs, frustrated. "Hattie, I don't draw properly. I'm not an artist like you. I just doodle."

"You doodle masterpieces. Got it."

"I've never even finished a sketch."

"Because you don't want to."

He scoffs. "Precisely." He moves away from me, his hand dropping from my hip. I hate it. I pounce clumsily, in search of him. In doing so, it turns out he hadn't moved far at all. Our heads collide and my hand practically stabs him in the chest.

He grunts as I duck down, crouching on the floor.

"What on earth…" he mutters, as his fingers land on my head like they were searching the air for me. "What you doing down there?"

"Hurting," I croak. "You have a really hard head."

Freddie seems to find this funny, which… *What the hell?* "You're so unpredictable," he says. "Honestly. I can never get a grasp on what you're going to do or say next."

"What? You weren't expecting me to give you concussion?"

"I'm fine. Are you?"

"Mmm," I mumble as he helps me back to my feet.

"Why you so interested in me all of a sudden anyway?" he asks. "You've never liked me before."

"Ha!"

"Oh, now I'm funny?"

"Don't act like you didn't know I've fancied you forever."

It's killing me that I can't see his face.

"*Whaaat?*" he says but I can tell by his tone and the slight pitch to his voice that he definitely knew.

"Oh, shut up," I laugh. "Just because you've always thought I was the biggest dork."

"You still are," he says, and I swear his voice is closer. I wonder how far I'd need to lean forward to find his lips.

Best not. I might actually knock him unconscious.

"Now who's the bully?" I say.

"You know the moment I saw you in a different light," he says. It's not a question. It's a statement. He really believes I know. But I don't.

"Do I?"

"You don't?"

"No. I didn't know you did now."

"*Please...*"

"You rejected me twenty-two hours, fifteen minutes and eighteen seconds ago," I remind him.

He chuckles heartily. "Is that exact?"

"Close enough."

"Maybe I didn't like your proposition."

"Ha. Was I supposed to ask you to fuck me in a different way?"

This earns me his other hand which lands on my waist, squeezing. I can feel his warm breath on my cheek. My head is entirely untrustworthy right now.

Bend me over the pool table.

Spin me and hold me against the wall.

Collapse to the floor with me.

"Maybe that's just it, though... What if I don't *just* want to fuck you?"

"Mmm, you have kinks. I didn't think about that."

I feel his smirk through the dark. It's like I have a sixth sense. And he doesn't even deny his quirks. I'm half-tempted to push him on it. Find out whether it's feet or armpits or something more extreme.

But he distracts me by dropping his head and pressing the stubble on his chin against the soft part of my cheek. I swear I gasp from the sensation of it.

How dumb. I shouldn't be like this.

Clearly, I'm still coming down from a minor adrenaline rush.

These actions are almost primal. Or, at least, that's my excuse.

Freddie's hands grasp handfuls of my sweatshirt as if to

keep himself grounded. His breathing quickens as I run my hands forward, over his cheeks and chin, letting my thumb trace his bottom lip daringly. He groans and I feel the vibrations through his chest.

I whisper, "Does it count if we can't see it happening?"

"God, I hope not," he says, his voice thick with yearning. Before I can say anything more, he presses his lips against mine, almost roughly. I haven't even removed my thumb. It's clumsy but hot. I feel like an idiot for not expecting it but he's unfazed.

He lifts his hands, swiping my thumb away before cradling my face, his fingers roaming from the tips of my ears to the slope of my chin. I can't help tipping my head back before realising this is exactly what Freddie wants as he takes my lips again.

He kisses slow and deep, taking his time, adjusting me carefully to get the best angle. His lips taste like coffee and mint. A delicious flavour on him.

He tilts my head just enough to run his tongue along my bottom lip; something about the action feels sort of filthy. I gasp against his mouth. Again, it's exactly what he was after. I swear I feel his lips curve into a smile as he seizes the chance to slide his tongue against mine.

I'm entirely at his mercy.

If my hands weren't already full of his t-shirt, I would drop to the ground in a horny puddle.

Freddie backs me up without even coming up for air and I become flush with the wall, the cold surface seeping through my jumper. It doesn't matter though because he's so hot on my front, I'm at risk of working up a sweat. He uses one arm to balance himself on the wall above my head, whilst his other hand stays firmly on my face, holding me, turning me, squeezing me in a way that feels close to desperation.

I've never enjoyed the darkness more than right now.

And something about realising I've never been kissed like this makes me want to weep. I feel vulnerable and powerful and fucking hot. I have no tools to manage these emotions.

"You've got… no idea… how long… I've wanted this," he says against my lips, his body enclosing around me. I free one of my hands from his t-shirt to explore his arm above me, feel the softness of the hairs there.

I hold onto him like he's my own personal scaffolding.

"Tell me," I demand, desperate to know when I finally caught Freddie Harrison's attention.

"The night you stole my wine."

"Borrowed."

"Thief," he whispers, leaning in again. His hand drops from my cheek, his knuckles dragging gently down my neck and over my sternum. There must be something about being touched in the dark that heightens the sensitivity of it because I feel like my body is about to burst into flames. And then his lips brush over the bare skin above my sweatshirt, along my collarbone. When he licks me there, I feel it reverberate in the places it shouldn't.

This is just a kiss. In the dark. It doesn't count.

It. Doesn't. Count.

I promise myself this to avoid the guilt. But I'd be lying if I said the thought of kissing Freddie, when I really shouldn't, doesn't stoke the flame.

A laugh bubbles up in my throat when I think about how long I've fancied him. Before he even knew I existed.

I rest my head against the wall behind me and bite my lip to prevent the thought whilst simultaneously giving him more space to explore.

His spare hand skirts below my sweatshirt, sneaking up and splaying over my warm skin. But his hands are huge, and his finger is practically grazing the underside of my comfy bra. Which reminds me.

Fuck.

I am not dressed for this to go further. The bra I'm wearing is elasticated and practical. Yes, it makes me significantly happier in my day-to-day life, but it does not look sexy. Or in this case *feel* sexy.

He figures it out fast, pausing. I can't see him and yet I know he's looking up at me with those dangerously sharp eyes. "What is it?" he says.

I huff, feeling completely unserious. "I have a shit bra on. I didn't know this was going to happen."

Freddie finds this enticing, his finger reaching up even further. He tests the feel of the stretchy material. "You actually think I'd care what you were wearing?"

"I don't know," I whisper, my heart beating slower and yet louder. I can hear it as if it's in my throat. "You forget, I don't know what I'm doing."

Freddie makes a throaty, disapproving sound. "You know what you're doing, Hattie. I don't know how to prove that to you without being crass."

I bark out a laugh as a thrill runs right through me. I search for his head in the dark and once I find his hair, smooth and thick, I tangle my fingers in it and pull him back to me.

Our tongues collide as he presses me against the wall again, his hand flat on my skin between us. I get the urge to push his hand lower; I just know he'd know exactly what to do to unravel me. I suck his tongue into my mouth, tasting his bitten-off groan, and the feral part of me wants to take it further.

I can imagine it. Imagine him hard and hot between my fingers.

But then the lights come back on and I'm bereft.

He pulls away.

I bite my lip and turn, using my hands to reorganise my unruly hair. It takes a good few seconds for my eyes to adjust again and for the stars to fade. There are footsteps on the stairs. When I look for him, Freddie is behind the pool table picking up a stick, acting like nothing's happened.

The door opens and I turn to Sam, who's surprised to find us there. "Oh. You're both here." He gives Freddie a strange look, who now apparently can't make eye contact with either of us. "I found the switchboard. All good. Thought it was the storm for a minute." He gives me a guilty look. "You ok? You look flushed."

This probably makes it worse. "Oh, yeah. Just a bit startled." I run a hand through my hair, hoping it isn't obviously messy.

"Well, I saved the day," he jokes.

I force a smile. "You have no idea."

"Hey, look. I'm sorry about the Dylan thing."

I wave him off. "It's ok. I'm glad he's here."

I follow him back upstairs where the smoke is still clearing from the kitchen and Priya is now making pasta, having binned the blackened pizzas.

Freddie doesn't come back up for five minutes and when he does, he heads straight for the shower. Not longer after, I copy.

I make mine as cold as the snow outside.

TWENTY-THREE

I swear there's fire coursing through my veins.

I'm lying awake, staring at the ceiling, and there's an ache between my legs that needs soothing or I'm going to start crying. Priya is snoring, one arm flung over her face, her silky, dark hair askew.

The cold shower has not worked.

Maybe I should go outside and frolic naked in the snow. *Fuck!*

That kiss. I can't think. I can't move. I can barely breathe right. How do you do it again? Air out, air in? Or air in, air out? Ugh, I'm trying too hard. I bite my tongue to focus.

I can still feel the pressure of his lips everywhere he touched. The trail of his fingers over my stomach. Oh God, I'm going to die from it. I can feel it. He's everywhere.

It has never been like this before. The way Freddie handled me, like I wasn't breakable. The confidence. The fact he couldn't even look at me and had to hide behind the table after.

I did that to him.

Me. I did that. It's unfathomable. I've never felt so wanted.

Damn those useless lights coming back on. I have the urge to go and mess with the switchboard just so I can stand there and hope he finds me in the darkness.

But it was a stupid, stupid thing to do.

The pure selfishness of it makes me want to weep. Freddie has been off limits to me for as long as I've known him. Sam would never speak to me again. And then to make it even worse, they're finally patching up their brotherly relationship which is the most amazing thing to see. I know Freddie thinks he needs Sam, but he has no idea how much Sam needs him too. They've been hauled apart by their parents' differences for too long.

I cannot be the one to spoil that.

I roll over to smother my face into my pillow, muffling a quiet scream. There's no way I'm getting to sleep like this. I mean, I can hardly get myself off with Priya in the room. She's flat out but I'm not quite brave enough to be caught in the act. Not that I imagine she'd mind; it just, you know, might be quite awkward in the morning.

And forever after that.

There's nothing else for it. I'm going to have to tuck into one of Sara's chamomile teas.

I hop out of bed, pulling on the oversized sweatshirt that hangs down to my thighs. I only sleep in a thin vest and knickers, so this leaves my legs and feet bare. Luckily, most of the lodge has underfloor heating.

I use my phone light in the kitchen so as not to wake anyone else up. I fill the kettle then flick it on to boil. It's louder than I remember.

Why is it so damn loud?

I glare at it, willing it to shut up whilst also leaving it on because this tea might be my last hope at soothing me. I grab a mug from the cupboard above and sneak one of Sara's teabags then wait for it to finish, playing with my hair in the meantime, which is still slightly damp.

"What're you doing?"

I fucking die.

My heart explodes. I grab my mouth to stifle a scream, spinning round to find Freddie staring at me from the other side of the kitchen island.

"Fuck!" I whisper-hiss. "What are *you* doing? Sneaking up like some kind of fucking sexy ghost!"

He runs a hand through his bed hair, which… I'm done for. How can someone look so hot straight out of bed? At least he's had the decency to put on a pair of jogger shorts and a white t-shirt. I'm practically half-naked.

And his eyes have dropped to my feet which means he's noticed my bare legs. I will the fire to ebb away before I'm forced to say something outrageous to my best friend's older brother.

"I needed a tea," I say. That's all I've got. I can't tell him the truth. I can't say, *Oh yeah, your kiss got me so riled up, I can't sleep, so I'm out here praying a chamomile tea will settle it when really the only thing that could probably achieve the required results are your tongue.*

Flipping heck.

I hold onto the kitchen side. I'm out of line.

He swallows but steps round the island to join me in the glow of my phone light. I can see the sharp line of his jaw.

216

The stubble there. I close my eyes when the memory of the sensation of it against my cheek rattles me.

I hear the scrape of the tall chair and open my eyes to find him sat, still gazing at me.

"We could make some rules," he says, his voice gentle but sure.

"For what?" Ok, it's official. My brain has turned to mush.

He smirks. Oh, the smirk he smirks. *He knows*. He is so onto me. It's totally unfair. How is he so relaxed? I'll just have to deny it until I die. Doesn't matter that I wear it all on my sleeve, he'll never get me to admit it. Probably.

"Sam doesn't have to find out," he whispers. "If you want me to help you, I'm all in."

"Bet you are," I joke, but I can't hide the nervousness in my tone.

The cretin takes my hand in his. It's too much. And then, to make matters worse, he starts massaging my fingers. I'm so out of my depth here but luckily, I don't think he's aware.

"I am. I want to kiss you again."

I look up to the ceiling. My conscience is catching up with me.

"You keep saying you don't want to be the villain anymore, Fred. But I'm worried this will make you the bad guy. I don't know why, but I do. And I really, really cannot be the girl responsible for that."

He's running a finger up the inside of my forearm, and I might collapse to the floor with need. How does such a small, insignificant movement make my ears hot and my fingers twitch?

"I always end up disappointing everyone anyway."

"Will I be disappointed then?" I say, dropping my head to look at him directly.

This makes him smirk even harder, his gaze burning. "Oh no. No, I won't be disappointing you."

My tummy falls from the sky. That familiar feeling. It's only ever been Freddie who could make me feel suddenly weightless in my core from just a look or a quippy sentence alone. I don't drop the eye contact, though. I let myself feel it. This energy between us… Have we always had it?

One of his hands grips my wrist gently, squeezing as he pulls me into him, spreading his knees so my body fits closer to his. I'm tall so we come nose to nose. I can smell the minty toothpaste on his breath. He leans in and doesn't even touch my neck with his lips, but I can sense him, leaving a forbidden trail of heat all the way to my chin.

I come to. "No, wait. You can't. Not here," I hiss, putting my hands on his shoulders to maintain distance. "Sam is asleep through that door over there."

"Ok," he says. He releases me, spinning on the stool and stepping away. My heart is thumping in my chest. This has not helped the "fire in my veins" situation at all. If anything, I'm 100 per cent worse than before.

I suck in a deep breath in the hope it might give me strength.

He walks away, albeit slowly. He knows. He's so bloody practised.

"Fine," I relent.

He pauses, looking over his shoulder. "Fine what?"

"Fine. Just fine," I say. "Help me."

Freddie watches me, a curious quirk in his forehead. "You don't really need my help. You know that, right?"

The ache has its own pulse now. "I promise you – I do."

"No one finds out," he says.

I nod, sure and firm. "No one."

"And it's only while we're here."

I don't know why that one makes me squirm but he's right. That's a very important rule, especially since I've vowed to go without relationships for a whole year. And besides, Freddie is well known for not being boyfriend material anyway.

So, I say, "Absolutely."

"We'll plan logistics tomorrow," he says. "Enjoy your tea, storm cloud."

"Wait," I sputter. I can tell by his side profile that he's smiling as he strolls casually back to his room. "Where are you going?"

"To bed," he says.

"But…"

"Get some sleep. You've got a late one tomorrow."

"Well, fuck," I mutter as his door closes. He's right. It's New Year's Eve tomorrow and we're going to have a proper party, fireworks and sparklers, booze and music. We're going all out. Sod the bloody snow.

I finish making my tea and decide it's better to drink it in the safety of my bed. There's a danger my feet could lead me in the wrong direction. And he'd be far too smug if they did. I'm not sure if he just started a game but the way he left just now felt awfully like a challenge.

Well, game on.

TWENTY-FOUR

Sara makes me a tea the next morning and suggests we hop in the hot tub before the others wake up. Freddie's bedroom door is ajar so I assume he must be out running. But in the snow? More has settled overnight. The news is saying it's the most snow the area has seen in nearly twenty years. Maybe he's just walking.

We get dressed into our swimsuits and return, me with my milky, sweet tea, Sara with her black coffee. I climb in and perch my mug on the side, letting the bubbles wrap around me. Last night, Sam used a broom to brush the foot of snow off the lid and Freddie shovelled out a path from the back doors so we could use it safely during our party later.

Sara has a sheepish look on her face.

"What's up then?" I say.

"Why do you think something is up?"

"Because you made me a tea."

She narrows her eyes. "I always make you tea!"

This makes me laugh. "Literally when?"

"I've definitely made you a tea before."

I press again. "Seriously, what's up?"

Sara scrunches her nose. "I feel bad. I didn't articulate things very well yesterday because it was the first time I'd said them out loud. It was the first time I'd really admitted any of my worries even to myself."

"But why do you feel bad?"

"Because I don't blame you, obviously. It's not *your* fault. Of course it isn't. But it was your break-up that's catapulted me into this weird, panic-induced brain fog." She sighs, taking a sip of her coffee. "Something feels off and I can't put my finger on it."

"Between you and Mike?" I ask, hoping it isn't our friendship group. Not that her having problems with her fiancé is any better.

She nods, her spare hand skirting the top of the bubbles like she's trying to round them up. "Like I said, I can't put my finger on it. It might be all in my head. You know what it's like up there." She taps on her head for effect.

For as long as I've known Sara, she has been a powerhouse of confidence and attitude. Outwardly, she comes across as formidable. This beautiful, tall, strong, independent woman who refuses to be knocked down. I once surmised that she dated men she knew would hurt her eventually because it meant she was right to not let her guard down, which is her comfort zone. When she met Mike initially, she thought he was too sweet, too gentle. She swore to me that he couldn't handle her but that isn't the case at all... She can't handle *him*. And now she's let her walls down and her world feels out of control. Having lived with her for nearly three years,

I have seen first-hand how she spirals into self-sabotaging ways and anxiety-driven decision making.

I'm not quite sure how to comfort her. I don't want to tell her not to listen to her own instincts. "Are you happy with him?" I ask instead.

She nods. "*Yes*. So happy. I've never felt so safe and relaxed with someone in my whole life. Not even during my childhood." She takes another sip then puts her mug down before looking up at the blue sky peeking through the branches above us. "I'm absolutely terrified. My brain is telling me my heart is stupid and not to trust it."

Something about the way she says it makes me chuckle. "Your brain is quite mean, though."

She snorts. "*Cynical*, Hattie. My brain is cynical."

"And your heart isn't stupid. It's bigger and more beautiful than you let on."

"Ugh. That was gross." She pauses, chewing on her lip. "There's something I was meaning to ask you, by the way. Something that keeps me awake at night and I don't know…"

"What is it?"

She tips her head back down to look me in the eye. "Did I miss something? With you and Adam? It's just none of it adds up to me. You know he was always kind of a secondary friend to me. Sometimes, near the end, I felt like things were off with him and I couldn't put my finger on it. He was trying too hard at something."

I take a second to consider her words. "I'm not sure what you're getting at really."

"Was he good to you? You know, when it was just the two of you."

"He wasn't bad to me."

"But he wasn't always good?"

"It was ok," I say.

Sara's eyes go round. "What did he do?" she whispers.

"Well, that's the thing. He didn't really do anything. He'd just shut down for days and I'd spend the whole time trying to make amends for things I wasn't even convinced were that bad."

"He gaslit you?" she asks, her voice raising a pitch.

"I don't know if that's what it was."

"I'm so sorry I didn't know you weren't happy."

I laugh at this. It feels absurd to hear it out loud. "*I'm* sorry I didn't know I wasn't happy. I'm sorry because if he hadn't have left me, I'd probably still be trying really bloody hard to make *him* happy so that *I* could eventually be happy too."

"Shit, Hattie. I had no idea. I just thought he could be an arse sometimes."

"I thought he was the love of my life, so I guess we're both idiots."

We descend into a comfortable silence after this. We need a moment to let life sink in, to really feel it as we listen to the gentle birdsong and the squirrels shooting along branches, occasionally knocking one so much it rattles, and snow falls into the tub, melting amongst the hot water. At one point, there's even a muntjac that strolls right up to the lodge, nibbling on the overgrowth. It's not even aware of us until someone pulls the sliding doors open, then it shoots away and is gone in a flash.

I turn to see my curly headed cousin squinting at me. "It's bright out here," he says.

Last night, Sam took care of Dylan, even letting him take his bed. Sam set up on the floor using blankets. Which good – he *should* feel bad for forgetting him. If that means suffering for one night, then so be it. Dylan could've died out there in the snow. Not that Dylan made good choices either.

"And how is my idiot cousin today?" I sing, as he comes to join us. "Where did you get those trunks from?"

"Oh, Freddie ran down to my car and back. Carried it back for me. Isn't that kind?"

"Isn't it abandoned about three miles away?" Sara asks, glancing at me disbelievingly.

"Yep. One way. In the snow too," he adds. "Lucky it was my backpack, so he didn't have to drag a suitcase."

"Wait up," I say, putting my hand up. "You're telling me Freddie got up this morning and ran three miles to your car in the snow and then back again just to get your bag?"

Dylan shrugs. "I told Sam I was worried as my meds were in there. And I can't go more than a few days without them," he explains. I vaguely remember him saying he was on anti-anxiety medication. There's a twinge in my stomach, and I think it might be guilt that I didn't think of that last night. "Sam must've told Freddie because I woke up half an hour ago with my bag by the door."

"Oh," is all I can say.

Freddie can't do things like that and then complain he feels like the villain all the time. Honestly. Villains don't do things like that. They're not selfless.

Dylan joins us in the hot tub and catches up with Sara. It must've been years since they crossed paths last – probably when he crashed our flat party in Brighton.

When Sam finally joins us too, we all cheer, "Happy birthday!"

Priya rushes outside, already in her apron to get to work on the festive food she has planned, to join in and Freddie leans in the doorway, arms folded across his chest, hands tucked under his armpits to keep warm. His hair is damp from his post-run shower.

I think about how smooth it was as I ran my fingers through it last night. I wonder if I'll get a chance to thank him properly for his heroic efforts this morning.

As if he heard my train of thought, his eyes flit to mine.

My tummy skydives but I don't look away.

No, not anymore. I take him on, staring back unashamedly until he smirks and turns to head back into the house.

A few hours later and I'm helping Priya in the kitchen. She's got a whole array of party food to make. I offered to buy the frozen stuff from Iceland, but Priya found that offer highly offensive. She's got me chopping massive tomatoes and adding slices of mozzarella with a pinch of sea salt. Meanwhile, she's caramelising onions for something else to do with cheese.

I can home cook but I'm nothing compared to Priya. So, I listen to instructions and do as I'm told.

Sam is decorating in a questionable style. We didn't bring much other than banners and random crap we already had stored away. I'm pretty sure we're too old for paper plates and cups now but Priya said they can be recycled, and it saves us having to stack the dishwasher later on.

She seems to be in better spirits now and has noticeably

been drinking less. I know she had an hour video call with Izzy and Ollie yesterday. I walked in during and quietly snuck back out so as not to disturb them.

Once she's finished most of the food prep, Priya pounces on Sam and me, sharing all the photos Izzy has sent her these past few days. They're basically all the same, except he seems to go through more outfit changes than a drag queen in a pantomime.

There are three more bags of Boobleys in the fridge at least.

I do wonder what she plans to do with it all. But like she said before, I shouldn't ask questions I don't want the answers to.

At some point in the afternoon, Sara is showing Dylan how to stack the wood right to light the fire. She's weirdly good at things like this. She tells me it's all because she did Girlguiding, but so did I and they never taught me how to light a fire. I hear a scraping sound outside and peek out the windows surrounding the front door to see Freddie out there with just a t-shirt and jeans on, shovelling snow from around the car. He's made two big mounds either side.

The way his arms tense and flex, I'm not sure how long I just stand there and stare. But I shake myself out of it as Sam calls, "Hatter, can you help me get the fireworks out the car?"

I snort, assuming he's joking. "What?"

"What?"

"*What?*"

He laughs, stopping in front of me. "What's so funny?"

"You haven't actually just left fireworks in the car these past few nights, right?"

He shrugs. "What's wrong with that?"

"I don't actually know. I feel like there's a hazard there somewhere."

"Maybe if it was hot outside."

I pull my boots on by the door and decide to forgo a coat as I'm only nipping to the car with him. I follow him out. Sam is saying something to Freddie already as I emerge at the top of the steps. They're laughing which, again, is a weird sighting for me. I can't help but smile at the two of them getting along.

Freddie notices me, raising his brows as I put my first foot on the top step. He says, "Careful..." and some other words too but I don't hear them.

As if in slow motion, my foot loses all traction below me. And then I'm looking at the sky. There's pain. But it takes me a second to work out where exactly.

Before I know what's happening, both Freddie and Sam are crouched beside me. They're asking me questions, but my ears are still ringing so I clench my eyes closed and will it away.

A rough, warm hand grazes my cheek and without even looking, I know it's Freddie because Sam's hands are much softer.

Slowly, his voice comes back to me. "Hattie, when you're ready, I need you to tell me where the pain is." He sounds calm and sure and yet worried all in one breath.

I peek one eye open. The sun behind his head is actually blinding. As if he works this out, he moves to block it out entirely. But now it looks like he has a ring of light around his head, which makes me chuckle, because he's no fucking angel.

Freddie isn't laughing though, and my reaction has him scowling even more.

"Where's the pain?" he asks again, softly, persistent.

I groan. "Butt and head."

"Right."

"Who's a butthead?" Sam asks, coming back to join us. He drapes a blanket over me and frowns at Freddie as they seem to share thoughts telepathically.

"Right. Can you feel your fingers and toes?" Freddie asks.

I wiggle both. "Yep."

"How does your head feel?"

"Bashed."

"And your vision? How many fingers?" He holds his hand up.

I roll my eyes because in hindsight, this is all very silly and I'm fine. "Three."

He nods, appeased. "I'm going to pick you up and carry you back inside."

I can't hide a nervous laugh which bubbles up and out of my throat before I can stop it. Sam gives me a strange glance, but I assume it's because he thinks I'm delirious. Honestly, I need more control.

"I'll get her legs, you grab her shoulders," Sam suggests, manoeuvring to my bottom end which... WHAT?!

Freddie just shakes his head at his brother. "I can manage."

"Really? She's quite tall."

"Trust me. I'll be fine." He swoops one hand under my shoulders, the other just below my butt, then hoists me up without even making a sound. I've never been carried like this in my life. This is for petite girls and girls who weigh barely anything.

I've always assumed tall girls carry themselves.

"Arms around my neck," he orders, as he works very hard not to make this a thing. I can see the glint in his eyes though, the slight quirk of his lips. He wants to do something silly, but he can't. Not here. Not now.

Same goes for me. I want to run a thumb up the back of his neck, make him shudder.

He smells salty from shovelling snow, a shimmer of sweat on his brow.

He strides up the stairs, into the lodge and places me carefully on the sofa.

It's all a bit over the top. I'm fine. I'm absolutely capable of getting up and walking this off. And to prove as much, I leap up the second he puts me down and shimmy. Except, I don't shimmy at all. I actually end up collapsing on the sofa again like a total fool.

"Do me a favour, storm cloud," he says, using a low tone so the others can't hear. "Don't make this difficult. I'm going to make you a drink and you're going to sit there until you feel ok again."

"Thank you," I call at his long, lean back as he heads to the kitchen and puts the kettle on.

Sara is watching me curiously but if she has something to say, she keeps it to herself.

Meanwhile, Sam is piling fireworks up in the lodge right by the radiator. I feel like he needs to be supervised. Freddie must be on the same wavelength as me as he calls to his brother, "Maybe store them *outside*, Sam."

To which Sam huffs and begins moving them back to the porch.

Freddie glances my way, catching me staring at his gorgeously rugged face. He smirks and shakes his head as if he heard my train of thought.

TWENTY-FIVE

I refuse to sit all afternoon whilst everyone else prepares for the party. Dylan has been assigned to cleaning duty since I've been told to relax but he's honestly useless. I catch him using a dirty dish cloth to clean the dining table and so begin to project manage, banishing him to hoover duty.

There's only the occasional moment when I feel the dizziness take over. I sit for a moment then I'm fine again. But it's the pain in my coccyx that keeps me from doing too much. When I sit down, I do so tentatively. There will be a nice bruise and a vivid reminder to go careful on steps when they're icy tomorrow.

The whole lodge smells divine when I join Priya in the kitchen to help set up the buffet. There's an array of cheeses (so much cheese) laid out along with everything from a bowl of homemade potato wedges to neat little vegetable spring rolls. We thought about doing a proper sit-down meal but then decided that having a buffet to pick from all evening was a far better arrangement.

Once everything is set up, we disperse to get ready. It feels a bit silly since we're not going anywhere but then again, it is New Year's Eve. I bought a short, black, sparkly dress with long sleeves and a high neck. Sam always loves to joke that I have the same colour dress in 500 styles and he's not far wrong. I pair it with a dainty pair of heels, blow-dry my hair and add a light touch of make-up with shimmer eyeliner which feels very noughties.

Priya wolf whistles as she comes back from her shower. She has a red playsuit for tonight that is currently hanging on the door. It's very her. I've seen her wear it a few times before.

"Who you dolling up for then?" she asks.

"*No one!* Why do you say that? I just want to look good for the party. I don't know why you have to make it weird."

She makes a face. "Ok…"

I laugh it off. Clearly it was only a throwaway comment. *I'm* making it something, which is in itself more telling. "Sorry," I shake my head. "I think the bash to my head has got to me a bit."

She smiles. "Go easy on the booze, yeah?"

I nod. "Yes. Sensible," I say as I neck my third glass of fizz.

At around eight in the evening, Sara calls us all into the main living space. She makes sure we've all got full glasses of champagne (well, apparently, it's British sparkling wine but who's going to complain?) and prepares us for a toast.

"Are we all here?" she says.

Sam perches on the sofa behind me, resting his arm on my shoulder. I lean into him. "Just waiting on Priya," I say. Dylan and Freddie are both seated too. I'm not sure why Dylan is double parked with a glass of fizz and a beer. Freddie just has a bottle of bear and looks suitably relaxed in his white Levi's t-shirt and black, vintage-look jeans.

We can hear Priya jostling down the hall before she appears with a smile. She's done something to her hair that makes it shimmer under the light. "Sorry, sorry. What a day!" She laughs, reminding us subtly that she's late because she has been slaving away over our food all day. She is *absolutely* off the hook.

"Where's my glass?" she asks.

Sara points to the kitchen island.

"Ok, sit down," she says, waving at Priya. "I want to tell you all a story about how I met Hattie and Sam and then we'll toast to the birthday people."

"Oh shit," I say, which gets Freddie's attention. He's bloody smiling again. His eyes gloss over me down to my legs which are about 80 per cent naked. I cross them and bite my lip.

Sara does a faux evil laugh before continuing. "So, Hattie lived in the same halls as me, two rooms down from mine. And there were about ten of us in total who all shared a big kitchen at the end of the hall. Thank God we had en suites. Anyway, I digress. One evening, during Freshers... Here's the thing about me – I can be quite unfriendly when you first meet me."

Priya mock gasps, which has me crumpling over with laughter.

"I had managed to avoid all the dreaded socials up until day three when I arrived home with the strangest boy I could find to spend the night with."

"Oh! Was that the guy who dressed as a pirate?" I ask.

Sara shrugs. "I can't remember. Don't interrupt, please. And we get back to the halls and there is this shrill laughter coming from the kitchen and the smell of smoke. I don't really want to investigate as it was probably two or three in the morning and I wanted to see if this weird man, who could tie knots with his tongue, was worth my time.

"But the laughter was sort of infectious and it was clearly more than one person. So, I poke my head in to find you two weirdos eating hash brownies, entirely off your fucking tits. And I remember knowing you would be a good friend when you looked me directly in the eye and said, 'Please don't call the police.'"

"I didn't say that," I said. "Did I?"

She nods. "Yes! You were so upset with yourself. And this one here," she says, prodding Sam with her finger, "was so spaced out, he could barely form words. My gentleman friend ended up finishing them for you. But I didn't want any as they were burnt. You'd clearly managed to source some weed on a night out and got home and thought you would bake. You were so alarmingly honest."

For a moment, I think maybe I'm in over my head with the whole Freddie thing. She's right, I don't really do things I shouldn't and if I do, they haunt me for weeks. I remember being anxious someone would find out about those brownies even months after. Sam was so hanging the next day, he's never eaten a brownie since.

We all cheers to this weird and sometimes dysfunctional found family then sing 'Happy Birthday' to Sam, who pretends to hate it as Priya walks in slowly with a Colin the Caterpillar cake, candles and all.

"Fuck, it's like being at a kid's party," Sara mutters.

"Time for shots!" she exclaims, marching over to the bottle of tequila that's been staring at us for the last few days.

We all take a shot except Freddie, who says, "Someone has to be at least half-sober," before eyeing me again like I'm about to pass out.

"Boo!" Sara chants as she starts refilling.

After this, someone puts 'Thunderstruck' on the speakers and turns it up to full volume. We all start dancing (ok, jumping) round the room. But when I look for Freddie, I find him leaning against the kitchen island, a humoured expression on his face. I stick my tongue out at him as he runs a hand down his face.

A strong hour of dancing and drinking later, we turn the music down and play a round of *Cards Against Humanity*. Even Freddie joins in for this one but doesn't laugh hard enough at some of the most outrageous rounds which means he is drinking much slower than us and probably none of this is even that funny.

Does this game even work if you're sober?

"Ooh, let's play hide and seek!" Priya suggests.

"Again, what's with the child's party shit?" Sara snipes.

"Hide and seek is the best! Ok, rules. You can't leave the house. No hiding in the snow! I refuse to go outside searching when it's -50 degrees outside."

"That's a stretch…" Sam mutters.

"Otherwise, everything goes. Loser has to do a shot of Boobleys. Wait no! Everyone does a shot except the last person I find."

"WHAT?!" a few of us exclaim.

And then she starts counting, covering her eyes with her hands, "Thirty… twenty-nine… twenty-eight…"

A spark of adrenaline pulses through me. There's no way on earth I'm doing a shot of Boobleys. This evening just got very real. I stumble through the house, Dylan hot on my heels, as I head for my room. I stop in there for a moment and realise this was the super obvious choice. Clearly, Priya will know. Dylan gets down on his tummy and shuffles under one of the single beds.

"Cover me up," he says, pointing to the unmade bed.

"It's every man and women for themselves, Dylan. Sorry, but I can't risk you beating me."

"Hattie!!" he mock yells as I duck back out of the room, down the stairs and into the living space where Priya is sat still covering her face.

"Nineteen… eighteen… seventeen…"

I fly towards the basement, thankful for the railing on the way down as I feel shaky on my descent. The light is on, which is weird. I pause, wondering where to go next. I could hide under the pool table or disguise myself behind the outdoors equipment. I'm distracted when I see a sledge and think it would be fun to use tomorrow.

"Ready or not, here I come!" Priya shouts from upstairs.

"Fuck," I hiss. Panicking, I dart to the cupboard which looks like some kind of boiler room. I shut myself into the darkness, only a hint of light coming through the vents at the top. It stinks like bleach in here.

I lean against the wall and let out a breathy laugh.

Who knew hide and seek could be so much fun.

"Nice of you to join me."

Again. Dead.

TWENTY-SIX

I instantly know the voice, but I must scream because he places a hand gently over my mouth and pulls me towards him. "Shh," he says, laughter in his tone. "She'll hear you and I will throw you out first in order to avoid the punishment."

I chuckle, my voice muffled under his palm as I say, "Scared of a bit of breast milk?"

"Honestly? Terrified."

I roll my head back as he keeps one arm around my waist holding me close.

"How you feeling?" he asks.

"I feel fine," I say, batting him off. "It was just a little fall."

"You couldn't hear me for a whole thirty seconds. That's not just a little fall," he says, and although it's dark in here, my eyes are adjusting enough to see him scanning my face for signs of something.

It's too tempting, having him all worried about me. It's

been sickening trying to behave around him all day. I reach up and let my hands roam over the rugged skin on his chin and cheek, really feel the bristle scrape over the soft parts of my palm. "Mmmm," I say. "You have no idea how good your face feels."

Freddie laughs quietly. "That's the weirdest compliment anyone has ever paid me."

"Shh," I say, before leaning in to press my lips against his.

This must be what he was waiting for because the next thing I know, he has me pressed up against the cool, concrete wall behind us. I can feel the chill of it through the thin material of my dress. I gasp against his mouth as he runs a stray finger along the top of my thigh, sneaking up and under my dress, teasing the fabric of my lacy thong.

I don't tend to wear thongs. In fact, it was one of Adam's many complaints about me. But tonight, I felt daring and sexy and ready to take on the world.

And that meant wearing a thong.

His finger stays there, tugging on the material as he deepens the kiss.

Now I feel dizzy.

But I only encourage him further by biting his bottom lip and sucking it into my mouth. And I'm aware, vaguely, that someone could walk in here at any moment. Once Priya has found someone, she'll get them to help too, and it could be Sam and then this is all ruined.

Maybe it's the alcohol but this doesn't stop me like it should.

It especially doesn't stop me as Freddie releases my lips and begins trailing kisses down my jaw, nibbling over my collarbone, scraping his teeth along the neckline of my dress.

Whatever it is he's doing, it feels like there's a warm swell expanding inside of me.

He hoists my dress up enough to kiss the bare flesh on my stomach and pauses there, groaning, as he uses his tongue to draw circles around my belly button before dipping it in, in a way that has me hopping from the wall and clenching my thighs.

But Freddie isn't fazed.

"Hold this," he orders, handing me my dress. I grab the material in one hand, using my other to brush through his hair, tugging lightly on the short strands there. "You want this?" he asks, peeking up at me from where he's knelt down at my feet. His green eyes are piercing under those long, dark lashes.

He doesn't need to clarify what he means.

All I can muster is a quiet, desperate, "Mmmhmm."

I'm not sure what I've done wrong, but he freezes, smiles then shakes his head. "No. Not here," he says. But he doesn't get up.

I drop my dress, feeling silly. Am I being rejected again?

"Sit down, Hattie," Freddie says. I twist to find him sat with his back to the wall, hugging his knees.

"I don't understand what's happening."

"I'm not getting you off in the boiler closet that stinks of bleach. You're too good for that."

I scoff. "No, really, I'm not." *Desperate much?!*

He just smirks, the faint light sneaking through the vents at the top of the door playing with the sharp angles of his face. "Sit down with me, storm cloud." He pats the floor beside him.

"Ok…" I say, positioning myself so our knees are

touching. Mine are bare, whilst he has smart jeans on. Hardly seems fair. And have you ever tried to sit on the floor with heels on? It doesn't work. My legs feel too long. I kick them off to the side and bring my feet closer into my body. "What now?"

"Tell me about your painting."

"Well, this will be a short discussion."

"You're not painting?"

I shrug. "I started one before… I wasn't in the mood for a bit. It has a base coat."

"I wish you'd never stopped. I need more of your art for my horrible apartment."

"I have a vision for one."

His knee nudges mine. "Yeah?"

"Why are we talking about my art?"

"Shall we sit here in silence instead?"

I glance at him. "Well, we *were* doing other things."

"What's the vision?"

"Freddie!"

"Hattie…"

"Are you trying to torture me?"

"Tell me the vision," he says. His large, warm hand finds my knee and squeezes. It's something, I suppose. I wish my instant reaction wasn't to press my thighs together. It's hardly encouraging him to be his usual self and behave badly.

"Well, it's about how I see the sea. I'm always running along the seafront. I've gotten used to seeing it as this kind of blur. And I want to capture that."

Freddie's fingers trace the small gap between my thighs as I take a deep breath trying to relax. "What's in the painting?"

"The sea…" I say like it's obvious.

"But what's it about?"

I snort. "The fucking sea, Freddie."

"Nah. I don't buy it. That boat painting is about more than the sea."

"Is it?"

"Isn't it?"

I press my lips together. "Alright, it's about staying afloat amongst it all. It's about that one thing that stands out against the background. The one thing that keeps you looking, living, breathing…"

"There it is," he says, a smile in his voice. "What's your new project about?"

"I don't know, actually. Maybe that's why it's not coming to me." And then, like magic, motivations for the painting start filing themselves in that little creative part of my brain. I close my eyes and let myself feel his fingers on my leg, the warmth and weight of them there, the way I always feel anchored and safe when I'm around him. So much so, I find the courage to be brave and misbehave.

And then I think about what it was that initially drew me to the blur of the sea, and I think it's life. Just life rushing by. I can't stop it. I've lost my entire twenties to someone because I didn't stop and pause and really consider what it was doing to me. I needed to breathe.

"I think it has to be about what life feels like as I pass by the sea every day. It's not just about the sea. It's about my life and how it feels blurred. The longer I live, the quicker everything feels."

"I like that," Freddie says, his hand squeezing.

"Shut up. That didn't even make sense."

241

He grins lazily. "It does to me. I've been so busy setting up my career, I've forgotten to make time for the people who I really care about. I got lost too. It's ok, I think, to get lost. Or even to just always be lost. Maybe it's good. Maybe being found is overrated."

At this, I burst out laughing then smack a hand over my mouth. I'm meant to be quiet, for fuck's sake. We're bloody hiding. Freddie's eyes go wide as we stare at each other but clearly Priya didn't hear as there's no sign of footsteps heading our way.

"What you going to do to stop the blur then?" I whisper.

I feel him shrug beside me. "I've been ignoring work today. Does that count?"

"Ah, that's why you've been so busy doing all the random jobs nobody asked you to do."

"You noticed?"

"The snow didn't need shovelling. And the six-mile run?"

"That was necessary."

"Thank you, by the way," I say, leaning my head on his shoulder. I don't really think anything of it, this natural feeling of wanting to be beside him, to rest on him, but once I'm there, I don't know if it's too familiar. And yet I don't move. "I forgot about Dylan's meds."

"I like to be useful. I've never felt needed or helpful and I've been trying to change that."

"Oh, I don't know. You helped me a few times. I never forgot."

We both turn to look at each other at the same time and I feel it in my core like a hot rock floating downwards. Freddie swallows, his gaze dropping to my lips. "Hattie, I feel like I haven't been honest with you."

I blink. "What do you mean?"

His hand is still on my knee, and I swear there's a slight nervous energy seeping off him now. Our faces are so close, barely inches apart. "I..."

"They must be down here!" Sam's voice calls out, echoing on the stairs to the basement.

I feel his voice like a kick to the gut. Freddie looks away, his eyes wide like he was just saved from himself or... actually, I have no idea. I want to press him on it. What was he about to say? Why isn't he being honest?

Sam is in the games room now. I can hear his feet padding about. I haven't had a chance to collect myself yet, but I sit taller and move an inch away from Freddie. "What do we say? Why are we in here together?"

Freddie tucks my hair behind my ear before climbing to his feet and offering me his hand. I let him help me up but can't stop staring at his face, my head spiralling about what has been left unsaid.

"I was here first. You thought it was empty. Nothing more to it," he whispers.

I nod, then the door opens and I'm clenching my eyes closed as the fluorescent lights in the basement blare into the boiler room.

"Found them!" Sam yells behind him.

I open my eyes again to find Sam looking at me for a long moment, a knot between his brows. Freddie doesn't say anything and for some reason, I feel like we've been caught. But caught doing what? Talking? Getting along?

How very scandalous.

I'm almost mad at Sam. I sort of want to push him back

out and close the door. I want to be with Freddie, alone. I want to know what's going on in that pretty head of his.

I nearly open my mouth. I nearly say something. I cannot tell you how close I am…

"Did we win?" Freddie asks, twisting to frown at his brother.

Sam shakes his head. "No, we still haven't found Dylan."

"Bugger."

"Yeah, Priya actually has Baileys, though. She was just fucking with us."

I snort, shoving past Sam. "I'll take a shot of Baileys."

I bloody need it.

TWENTY-SEVEN

Back upstairs, Priya has finally found Dylan, who jogs back into the main room and stops in front of me. "What's wrong with your face?"

"Rude."

"You look moody. Cheer up, it's your birthday in…" he checks his watch, "whoosh, only fifty minutes."

"Guys!" Sam calls. "It's snowing again!"

"What?!" Priya asks, jogging into the room. "But we're going home tomorrow, right?"

I walk over to the windows that look out over the hot-tub decking. The snow is falling thick and fast. Big, fat clumps of white fluff adding an additional layer to the already frozen-solid snow below that.

Even though I'm not dressed for it at all, it entices me outside. I step into the cold, dark night and watch the snow settle softly on my palm before melting. With the door shut behind me, there's only muffled noise from within. Outside, there's a gentle serenity.

The door opens again, and I look over my shoulder to find Sam coming out to join me. "Love the snow," he says, grinning, that familiar glint in his eye. He hands me my coat, which makes me smile. "Didn't want you to turn into Elsa."

"Trust you to pick a Disney character."

"It's called being cultured."

"I'm not sure visiting Disneyland Paris twice makes you cultured."

Sam sniffs. "I've been to Florida too."

"Ah well, then yeah, you must be cultured."

He nudges me with his elbow. "Why were you hiding in the cupboard with my brother?"

I swallow, heat pooling in my cheeks. "I wasn't... It wasn't..."

"It's fine," he says. "I know you're not stupid enough to fall for his swoony, moody man shit. I'm just checking he's being kind and all that."

"Oh sure. Yes. He's being kind." And then I think about what he just told me. How he isn't being totally honest. Totally honest about what? Has he got someone else in the picture? It's hardly like much is going on between us but Sam's mention of me falling for Freddie has me questioning everything.

I don't trust my own instincts anymore.

It makes everything terrifying because how do I know? How do I guess? Who is telling me the truth and who isn't?

I stuff my hands harder into my pockets, pondering.

"Sam?"

"Hatter?"

"You know I love you, yeah?"

"Has someone given you tequila? You only ever say that when you've had tequila."

I shake my head. "No. Well, yeah. I just... I need you to know. Because I worry I don't tell you enough. Obviously, we're not *in* love, but still. I do love you. Does that make sense? And... I just..."

"Hattie..." Sam says, linking an arm around my neck. He's not all that much taller than me so I end up crouching down a bit to make it work. So awkward. "We're good. I know where we stand. I feel the same about you. You're just soppy because it's nearly your birthday and you'll be as ancient as me."

"You're the same age."

"I'm older. It's important that you respect your elders," he says, squeezing me closer. "You're shivering. Let's go back inside. Priya has a punch on the go. And there's still some sausage rolls left."

"You know the more I think about it, the more I agree with Sara. Is this just a kid's party with booze?"

"I hope so."

We make our way back inside and Sam offers me control of the music. Although I turn it off and put *Jools' Annual Hootenanny* on to count in the New Year. Despite us being here together, we're so remote and stranded, I feel like I want to bring in a bit of the wider world into this space.

I can't see Freddie anywhere and I fight the urge to go looking for him. He's clearly slowing us down for a reason and that's fine. It's fine. I'm totally fine about it. *Did I say I was fine?*

It's just I'm starting to feel even more rejected, and my head is messy. Does he want me or not?

At five to midnight, Sam decides to go out onto the front

drive where there's at least a bit of a clearing without tree coverage to set the fireworks up. I go out to supervise but avoid the stairs. Although if I slipped again, would Freddie sweep me up in his arms like this morning and carry me off to his bed?

Hell, I need to get a grip.

I'm a grown arse woman. I don't need to be sheepish around him anymore. If I want something, I should just tell him straight. I need to stop being all girlish with it. No wonder he's being careful with me. He still sees the inexperienced girl from before, the one that's off limits, the one who would challenge him then dart away.

Well, that's not me anymore!

I'm bloody twenty-nine in… I check my phone. *Shit.* 30 seconds.

"Hey, Hattie, get in here!" Sara shouts. "We've got to count you in!"

Sam hears too and we make our way back inside where we huddle round the TV, the fire crackling under freshly added firewood.

Freddie catches my eye from across the room and swallows. The screen jumps to the London Eye where the countdown is on the wheel in great, big lights. I don't look away from him as I take a sip of my fizz.

"That's for after," Sara admonishes.

"Ten… nine… eight…"

What isn't he telling me? And why does it bother me so much? Am I missing something crucial?

"Five… four… three…"

What do I really want from him?

"Two… one…"

"HAPPY BIRTHDAY!" Sam yells from behind me, before throwing his arms round my neck and kissing my head approximately fifty times.

We all shuffle outside for an underwhelming five minutes of fireworks. I do sparklers with Sam for the hell of it. We try to spell our names in the dark with Priya filming, while Sara and Dylan stand on the sidelines judging our joy. Secretly, they wish they were us, I just know it.

Then we humour Sam by singing 'Auld Lang Syne' which is hilarious because none of us know the words at all. So, it's mostly hummed or made up.

Thankfully, after that, we go back into the warmth of the lodge where they sing my birthday song which feels silly. And, *damn*, we never really grow up, do we? Because why is it making me roll my eyes and smile like an idiot? Priya is bringing over the second cake in twenty-four hours and I'm blowing out candles and more drink is being poured and I'm feeling totally overstimulated when my phone vibrates in my pocket.

I think it must be Fliss or my parents wishing me a happy birthday or happy New Year and I open the message with a smile.

But no. It's neither of them.

I pause from celebrating for barely a microsecond, not wanting anyone to read the shock on my face.

Adam has messaged:

Happy birthday, Hattie. I miss you.

What the hell am I supposed to do with that?!

TWENTY-EIGHT

Why would Adam text me now? He's acted like I don't exist for over six months. He'll know I've seen it too. My tummy turns. I feel nauseous. I close my phone and bung it on the side face down like it burnt my hand. I step away and top up my glass.

Dylan says something to me and laughs but I didn't hear so I just laugh along too but it's very obviously the wrong reaction or a shitty, fake laugh because he grimaces at me.

"Sorry, what did you say?" I ask, shaking myself out of my state of horror.

"Ew, did you just fake laugh at me?" he says.

"Sorry, Dyl, I'm a bit distracted."

He nods. "Is it because your old now?"

"Hilarious."

"Do you need to go lie down?"

"Funny."

"Do you need help taking your teeth out?"

250

"Again, so funny."

But then my phone is vibrating on the side; it isn't even that loud, but I grind my teeth. It might not be him, I realise. I flip it over just to check but nope.

Adam is calling.

Adam is fucking calling.

Is he deranged? There's no way I'm letting him ruin my birthday and yet here I am, seething about the fact he's even had the gall to call me, and I'm faking a smile, trying to dance and have fun with my friends.

I hate him.

I hate him so much. It feels so deliberate and underhanded. I never did anything to him except try to be a good, supportive girlfriend and he was the worst. He was an ungrateful, shamelessly unemotional boyfriend who didn't deserve me.

Do I answer and tell him as much?

No. That feels wrong.

I march over to where the others are and plonk myself down beside Sara, who gives me a funny look.

"You're stewing," Sara mutters. Damn her eldest sister mood-detector abilities.

Freddie hears and looks up with a frown.

"Nope," I say, huffing and striding back to the kitchen. I hate how I can never hide my emotions from her. She sees through me like I'm bloody transparent. My stupid, pale, freckly skin gives me away in seconds. My phone starts to vibrate again. That hmmmm sound goes right through me so I unlock it, decline his call and turn my phone off.

WHO THE HELL DOES HE THINK HE IS?

I take myself away for a quick breather, perching on my bed in the darkness with only the sound of music playing downstairs. Sara and Priya have put on 'Saturday Night' and usually that would be right up my street, but I can't stop my heart from racing. I want to cry. I want to scream into my pillow.

I'm over Adam. But that doesn't stop the past from being dredged up and making me feel like shit. It's sickening that he has this kind of power over me at all.

There's a quiet knock at the door.

I startle, wiping at my eyes. "Yeah?"

Freddie pokes his head through the door. "You ok?" he asks. And why is his voice so gentle and sweet like he gives a damn?

"Mmm," is all I can manage for fear of letting myself go.

"Can I come in?"

I nod but he can't see me properly, so he doesn't move. "I'm nodding."

He closes the door behind him and sits beside me on the bed, our thighs brushing together. "Why you hiding in the dark?"

"If I tell you, you have to promise not to tell anyone else. It will kill the mood."

Freddie doesn't say anything for a moment then says, "I'm nodding."

"Adam texted me just now. And tried to call."

I feel him tense beside me. "What did he say?"

"The text said Happy birthday and that he misses me." Saying it out loud makes me realise it doesn't sound so bad. But it is. He has no right to be messaging me on my birthday and right at midnight too. He knows what this means to me. It's manipulative. But now I feel like a fucking idiot for telling Freddie when it just sounds innocent. "God, it doesn't even sound bad, does it?"

"He knows what he's doing. Want me to call him? Tell him to back off? Pose as your jealous boyfriend?" I can tell by his tone he's only half messing around. Part of me thinks he'd do it.

"You really don't like him, do you?"

"Nah. Didn't like him the first time I met him and definitely don't like him now."

"Would you actually call him?"

Freddie laughs but he sounds serious when he says, "Hattie, if you wanted me to do, I'd challenge him to a duel."

"On horseback?"

"I'd have to do some riding lessons first, but yes. I've always felt protective of you. At first, I put it down to you being my little brother's friend, but I don't think I can use that excuse anymore."

"I don't know if I need protecting," I say. I can't even fight the smile anymore. "But you know what, I'd like to see you duel him." Partly because I know who would end up on the floor crying for help and it sure as hell wouldn't be Freddie.

"Look, I didn't get to finish what I said before. I thought that's why you were stewing earlier."

I get to the point before he does. "It's ok. If you don't want this, it's fine. Just be honest with me. I can't take being played with anymore. It's killing me," I say and then the first lot of tears come, and I just want to suck them all back in.

I hate me!

"Hey," Freddie coos, tucking more stray hairs back behind my ear; his fingers linger at the soft part at the top of my neck. "That's not it at all. Before we were interrupted, I was going to tell you what I should've said from the start. That night in the hot tub, when you asked me to help you out… I've never felt so conflicted in my entire life. First and foremost, I'm a man. And a beautiful, sharp and funny woman is asking me to do unspeakable things to her, as a favour no less, and I have to be the idiot that says no."

"You didn't *have* to say no."

He nudges me. "You know my reasons. Well, you know one of the reasons."

My annoyingly loveable best friend is reason one but, no, I don't know reason two. "What are the other reasons?"

Freddie sighs. "You have no idea how jealous I was of Sam having you. I know it wasn't in the same way. That he doesn't think of you like I do, but it's so unfair. And I've wondered…"

"Wondered what?"

"You kept the charm."

I breathe deeply. "I never understood why you got me a gift."

"I wanted you to have something from me."

"But why?"

"Because I thought you were incredible, and I liked the idea of you having something on you that I gave you. I thought you were brave and clever and funny. And I couldn't go anywhere near you for fear of breaking what little I had left with my family. Still now. I'm thirty-two, you're twenty-nine, and apparently, this is still a thing we're not allowed. How does that work? What if I want to date you? Why should that hurt anyone's feelings? Honestly?"

"You want to *date* me?" My voice sounds small.

He nods once. "That's the other reason it couldn't be me."

"I don't understand."

"Come on, Hattie. I want more of you than that," he says, and I can just make out the whites of his eyes.

I reach across to him, craving the feel of his stubble under my fingers. As my hands graze him there, he leans into it, pressing a soft kiss to my palm.

"Freddie, I promised myself…"

"You need this year. I know."

"I…"

"You don't have to say anything now. You don't have to say anything *here*. It can be another time. When you're ready. I'm not going to change how I feel."

"Freddie…"

I'm not even sure what I was going to say. My head is a great, big jumble of things, like a washing machine full of boots and tennis balls. There's just clunking and noise in there right now.

But thankfully, Priya barges through the door, giddy from drink and dancing.

She stops short when she flicks the light on and finds us sitting this close, my hand still on Freddie's chin. "Oh!" she says. "Erm… Well, this is unexpected."

I drop my hand as Freddie gets up to leave. He doesn't say anything but gives me a small smile as he goes. I chew on the end of my thumb once the door closes behind him and Priya watches me curiously.

"So, well, that's a new development."

I grimace at her. "Please don't mention this to Sam."

She nods quickly. "Yes! No! No, I won't. But what is even happening?"

I groan into my hands and stamp my feet with frustration. "I don't know, Priya. I have no idea what just happened."

Priya sits beside me, wrapping an arm round my shoulders and smushing her face against my hair. "What's wrong, Hattie? Tell your weirdly adorable friend."

I laugh despite myself. "Adam texted me and then he was calling, and I panicked and then Freddie came up here and told me loads of confusing things. I'm meant to be going a whole year without dating. I'm meant to be doing things for me and being selfish. I promised myself."

"Do it then!" she says like that's the answer. "What's wrong with you? You can do anything you want! You're Hattie Tycer! You're invisible."

"I'm what?"

"Invincible."

"You said invisible."

"Well, I've drunk way too much Baileys tonight," she says with a burp.

"Angelic," I say, leaning away from her.

"Hey, get your arse downstairs. We're going to dance the macarena. You're not going to let any of these annoying men take away your birthday happiness. This," she says while waving her arms around me, "is already too much. They're not allowed any of you right now."

"Ok," I laugh.

"Let's go!" she says, pulling me up. "Oh wait! I came in here to use the en suite. Be right back."

When she returns, we stumble back into the living space, Freddie is nowhere to be seen, the door to his room shut. But Sara immediately gets us all dancing and laughing again. Sam and Dylan join us too, bouncing around the living room to the cheesiest music on planet Earth as the alcohol in our systems starts to wane and the sleepiness wades into our blood system.

"I'm calling it!" Priya says. "If we end up driving back tomorrow, I'm going to be knackered."

"I doubt we will with this much snow," Sara says. "But, yeah, time for sleep."

Sam gives me a big, droopy cuddle before skulking off to his room. Dylan is already passed out on the sofa. I grab a blanket and wrap it over him before heading to my bed.

Priya is already fast asleep, snoring her little head off. I stare at the ceiling, and it's like there's adrenaline pulsing through me. I can't drift off, no matter what I try. In the end, I find myself on my feet, heading back down the stairs, past Dylan on the sofa and pausing outside Freddie's room.

I'm not sure how long I must stand there, wondering what would happen if I knocked. I even raise my hand but then drop it again.

No, this is silly.

What do I even expect from him?

I guess I want to know why he didn't come back out to dance. Maybe he's sick. Or maybe he's embarrassed.

Ugh, no. I'm about to turn around when the door swings open and Freddie's tall frame appears, his eyes awash with hope. "Are you going to come in or just hover out here?" he whispers.

I swallow, my tummy swooping from the sight of his bedraggled bed hair. "I want to come in."

He nods, pushing the door wider so that I have to step under his arm to access his space. It smells so intensely of him, like bonfires and the seaside, that I end up standing there and closing my eyes, breathing him in.

"You couldn't sleep?" he asks.

"No."

"You can sleep in here."

I can't see him, but I hear him step up close behind me.

"What if I don't want to sleep?" I ask.

I feel his fingers in my hair first, followed by the gentle scrape of his stubbled chin on my bare shoulder. My lacy, satin vest is tucked into my not-so-sexy pyjama bottoms, tied at the waist. He tugs lightly on my soft curls, and I feel it everywhere, spreading from the roots to the tips of my toes.

"Do you still want more of me than just sex?" I ask, my voice as low as I can make it, knowing his brother is right next door.

Freddie's lips graze the base of my neck, his hands sneaking round my middle, pulling me into him from behind. His large frame curves over mine, almost protectively. I feel ripe with need. This is what I wanted. This is why I couldn't sleep. This beautiful and intense magnetic pull that belongs between us. I crave it.

"I want everything of you."

And that's all I need to hear. I spin round and throw my arms around his neck, pressing my lips to his.

TWENTY-NINE

Freddie runs both hands down my spine, and over my butt, encouraging me further. I grip onto him, feeling the way his shoulder muscles tense as he picks me up, my legs wrapping around his waist.

Finally.

I've wanted this for so long. I've got pulses beating where I didn't even know I could get them. My ankle, my ears, my... Well, you get the picture. I'm aching for his touch, for his undivided attention. I want him everywhere. I want him over, on top, underneath. I don't even care.

But... Hang on. He places me down on the bed, gently, rolling me back until my head hits the pillow. This is fine. We can work with this, except then he pulls away and brings the duvet over me.

Is he... *tucking me in?*

I scoff so hard, I almost choke. "Freddie…"

"Shh," he says, walking round the bed to climb in his side. He pauses first to remove his t-shirt in that sexy way hot boys do it. One hand yanking it over his head. A marvel. "You'll wake the others."

"Why… What is happening? Are you rejecting me again?" I whisper-hiss.

There's a muffled laugh as Freddie rolls onto his front, his face momentarily smothered by his pillow. He brings one gorgeously toned bare arm over my middle, pressing me into the sheets. "You fell and hit your head less than eight hours ago. You've drunk more than enough not to be making sensible decisions, and I am *not* going to take advantage of that."

I pout into the moonlit darkness, the outline of his face just visible. "But I want you to…"

He smirks. "Goodnight, storm cloud."

"You've got to be kidding me," I whisper.

"Nope. No joking here. You'll thank me tomorrow."

"I'd like to thank you *now*."

"Hattie…" he warns, his low, quiet voice sending vibrations through me. I'd be lying if I said I didn't enjoy it.

"Freddie!"

He shuffles upwards to get comfier before he uses the arm around me to pull me across the bed, tucking my body into him, his warm breath on my shoulder. I realise I'm enjoying the scent of him. That heady mix of forest and mint. "I said I want all of you. And I mean it. But it's important you understand that I'm going to want you more than once."

I'm too drunk to register the full meaning of his words.

"You could easily have me twice before the sun comes up."

Freddie scoffs. "Please.. At *least* three."

"Hey. Now that pushes my moral boundaries."

"You have moral boundaries?"

I stick my tongue out.

"Go to sleep, trouble," he whispers again, his lips pressing gently into the soft groove between my shoulder and neck. It feels so good, I roll my head back to allow him more access. I push against the bed so that my back is fully wedged up against him, shuffling in just the right places to be rewarded with one of his bitten-off groans.

His large, warm hand finds the bare skin at my waist, and he leaves it there, his fingers splaying. "Lower," I mumble.

I feel his deep laugh against my back. "Behave."

"Never…" I say, but I find myself drifting, the warmth and comfort from being held by him releasing me from my consciousness.

I'm nudged awake too soon. It can barely have been a moment's sleep. The crook of Freddie's shoulder is damp, and I quickly realise it's because I've been dribbling.

Hot.

I glance up at his face, squinting against the light from outside. He's frowning at the window. "What's up?"

"I think it snowed more."

"It's fucking freezing in here."

"And yet you're boiling," he points out. Which yes, I am, because I am pretty much skin to skin with my own personal radiator. I can't help myself from running my lips over his chest, feeling the brush of hair there.

He sighs contentedly. "You need to stop that because people are going to start waking up and I don't know what you want to do. But if you tease me, I will tease you back."

I groan. That's an absolutely terrible threat. It hasn't made me want to move at all. In fact, I might just stay forever.

But… "You're right. I'll talk to Sam."

I shuffle some more and feel the press of him against my waist. If I didn't have a heavy head, I would tease him even more but, alas, I am hideously hungover as he predicted.

Freddie breathes deeply, pressing me closer. "Please don't mention my brother right now. But no. I think it's better coming from me. He needs to know I'm not playing with you."

"When are you going to tell him?"

"I don't know if this is the right place."

I nod. "Agreed. So, we keep this lowkey until…" I pause, not wanting to be the one to assume anything about the plans for us.

"Until you let me take you on a proper date."

"Mmm. And that will be?"

"As soon as we get home."

"Literally?"

"If I get my way."

Then he uses his finger to run along my waistline, leaning in to kiss my throat. "You should go…" he mumbles, his lips roaming lower. Morning Freddie is my new favourite Freddie.

"Oh no," I mock whisper. "*Save me.*"

"I'm serious."

I can't help laughing. "So am I."

"They'll find out," he mutters as he runs his tongue along

my neck and nips my chin. "And I don't think you're ready for that."

"Ugh," I sigh. "Fine." I roll from under the covers. I still have my pyjamas on but it's so cold, I search the floor for more layers. A stray hoodie of Freddie's has been left on the floor. It's big on him, so would swamp me. If it wouldn't be horribly noticeable, I could live in that for weeks.

He sees me eyeing it. "Put it in your bag. It's yours."

"Oh, well now this is boring. I was going to steal it."

"Fine. You can't have it," he says, leaning half out the bed to grab it before I can, but I swoop over, snatching it from the floor and smushing it against my face, breathing him in. Fuck, why does it smell so good?

"Happy, thief?" he murmurs, lying back again.

"I can't take it now, though. You'll have to care for my stolen goods until I'm home."

He just smirks at me, taking it from me but pulling me down towards him in the process. I melt into him. "Hattie... I hate to kick you out but..."

"Right. Yes. Must leave. Or get caught." I get up from the bed, the chill of his room firing up goosebumps all over my arms. I give him one last glance before I go. My heart swells at the sight of him lying back on his bed, hand behind his head like a fucking underwear model.

He winks, which is diabolical, and then I pop my head out of the door, surveying the area. I swear Dylan stirs but other than that, the living space is abandoned as I creep through on my tiptoes and up the stairs.

When I sneak into mine and Priya's room, I find her lying with her back to the door so hopefully she's none the wiser.

I climb under the covers and pretend to sleep, smiling to myself at the outrageously good night's sleep I just had.

Happy birthday to me.

But I must actually fall back to sleep because the next thing I know, I'm being woken by a booming voice downstairs. I half-panic, wondering if Sam and Freddie are fighting again. I roll out of bed, pulling on a sweatshirt, and jump down the stairs.

"What's going on?" I ask, finding Sam and Dylan pulling their coats and boots on.

"We're taking this bad boy out in the snow," Sam says, holding up the sleigh from downstairs.

I cringe. "Is it safe?"

"Of course it isn't. You coming?"

I laugh. "Let me get some caffeine down me first."

Freddie takes this moment to walk out of his room, his gaze swiping over my body without an ounce of shame. "Morning," he says. "You joining us?"

"You're going too?"

"Someone needs to supervise," he points out, which, fair. He's probably the most sensible of the three of them when it comes to the snow.

"Are we leaving today?" Priya asks, stepping into the room. "It's just Izzy is back to work tomorrow, and I need to have Ollie… and if I don't hold my baby today, I'm probably going to spontaneously combust."

She's talking to me, but I've not had my cup of tea yet so I'm still half-insensible. I put the kettle on and turn to Freddie with a questioning stare. This feels like his responsibility.

Why's that? I'm unsure.

Maybe because it's his car we're travelling in?

"We'll go scout the drive down to the main road and see how passable it is," he tells Priya. "I need to get back too, so I'll do my best."

He glances at me again on the way to the door and I just know my face is betraying me, so I distract myself by adding bread to the toaster. Priya and Sara decide to make use of the hot tub one last time, while I head to the front porch to watch out for the boys, in case they get injured.

After about an hour, I hear their voices, laughing and joking as they tow the sleigh back towards the house. I seize this opportunity to throw my coat and boots on and sneak to the side of the lodge, careful not to slip again.

I ball up a pile of snow, wincing at the ice burn. I always forget how bloody cold it is. My woolly gloves are already damp through.

Then I wait, poised like the yeti monster, ready to attack.

When their voices are near enough, I don't think, I just pummel them with snowballs. One after the other. I miss a few, granted. I'm the running-in-straight-lines sporty type – I'm not much for aiming.

"What the…" I hear Sam exclaim as one smacks him right in the cheek.

I snigger as the next one gets Freddie on the forehead, just as he looks me in the eye. He pauses for a dangerous second, calculating. Sam bends down to ball some snow but misses as I duck behind the lodge. It thwacks off the wood.

I throw another one at Freddie, because he's closest to me now, having stepped in my direction. It slams into the groove above his neck, and I swear he sucks in a breath. A lovely bit of icy snow trickling down his t-shirt.

"Oh, you're dead," he fires back. I scream, flying round the back of the lodge below the balcony where Sara and Priya are spectating from the hot tub. I'm quick. I can totally escape him, except the fucking snow round the back is like two foot thick and partly frozen over uneven, untrodden ground. It's honestly lethal.

I try to use big steps to escape, but at some point, I stumble and slide down a slope. Luckily, I stay upright, shooting further into the snowy forest. I spook a creature – a squirrel, maybe – which goes sprinting up into the trees.

All the time, I can hear the crunch of his massive boots in the snow behind me, his hastened breathing, half-panting, half-laughing as he stumbles along in pursuit. My heart is firing like my life depends on it, which is insane, especially since I absolutely want to get caught.

I know he's getting closer, so I use a tree as barrier. I grip hold of it, peeking around at Freddie, who's charging at me, his face lit up with the biggest grin I've ever seen on him. Everything in my body softens, the adrenaline washing out through my fingers as he throws an arm around my waist and tackles me to the floor.

"Oh, my fucking God! It's so cold," I screech as the snow infiltrates the top of my coat and around my hips where it's ridden up.

Freddie's laughing, his breathing ragged as he lies on top, his weight pressing down on me, exquisite. He places one frozen hand on my cheek, which has me gasping.

"Argh! You're so mean."

"Says the girl who just pummelled me with snowballs."

I grin, teasing. "What you going to do about it?"

He can't seem to knock the smile off his face. "I'll think

of something appropriately evil," he says, before pressing his lips to mine. I greet him easily, enjoying the taste of him.

He has one leg between mine and I can't help fidgeting against it, hoping to rile him up even more.

"Brat," he mutters, pressing into me further. I snicker against his lips.

But our fun is short-lived when Sam shouts, "Where the fuck did you go?"

We're buried in the snow, thanks to the weight of Freddie as he took me down. He climbs off me, getting to his feet and helping me to mine. With his spare hand, he runs his thumb over my bottom lip, his palm squeezing my chin before retreating.

Not yet. He hasn't spoken to Sam yet.

And that's ok. This isn't the right time or place.

I head back towards the lodge too, noticing that Freddie is checking behind him to make sure I'm at least following. That is until I spot another figure a few metres to my right.

I slap a hand to my chest. Dylan blinks at me, his lips twisted into an impressed smirk. He gives me two thumbs up. Which... *gross*. No!

My eyes go wide, and I shake my head at him.

"Nice work," he says, nodding as I stride towards him.

"Shh. No, no, no."

But he's turning and heading towards the lodge too. I bolt after him instead, grabbing his arm.

"Sam doesn't know. Don't..."

"Hey, I won't reveal your dirty secrets."

I sigh. "It's not dirty."

"How disappointing."

"Dyl..."

"I'm only messing with you. And hey, you took my advice."

I shake my head. "What?"

"I said something super wise about doing something, or *someone*. And I mean, fair play, fucking bullseye. I knew you were cooler than you let on."

"Ok, but I think it's more than just…"

"Oh no," he says stopping beside me. "How long has it been going on?"

"Like two days."

"And you think it's more than what? Just a shag?"

"Well, yeah." I cringe. "And we haven't… I hate that word."

He gasps. "Why didn't you shag him?"

"I'm not discussing this with *you*."

"Fair. But it's probably not *more*. You need to chill out. Want me to push you back into the snow? Your aura is horny."

I scoff. "I don't think that's a thing."

"Trust me, it is."

"Whatever, Dyl. Just promise to keep your mouth shut."

He nods, serious. "Oh yeah. This would *blow up* between those two. Christ. You're actually quite messy. I'm sort of impressed. It must run in the family."

"It won't blow up," I argue.

Dylan leans back to give me a telling look. "Hattie… I'm going to need you to be serious for a minute. You understand what you're doing, right? You and Sam's hot brother just…" He pauses as he catches my expression.

I'm not even sure what my face is doing. But it probably knows more than me because my body feels deflated, my heart beating a little too hard.

He's right, isn't he? I said I wouldn't do this. I said I wouldn't dive head first into something new and it's like I can't even help myself.

I gasp. "Oh no."

"Oh, babe," he says. "You know casual is casual. And you're very *not* casual."

"Yes. I do know that."

"Ok. Ok, don't panic. I've done this loads of times. You just need to prepare for impact."

"How do I do that?"

"Well, I just stock up on Ben and Jerry's, to be honest."

I laugh, exasperated. This isn't going to end well. I stride away from Dylan, who walks behind me, cooing about how it'll be fine and… "Don't get your knickers in a twist."

"They're already in a twist. I let him twist them."

And I take a deep breath before walking back into the lodge.

THIRTY

A few hours later, after a round of hot drinks to warm me up, I've calmed down, reminding myself that Dylan is not one to be accepting advise and warnings from and find Freddie shovelling snow again. The bend and scrape does wonderful things for his arms. And to be outside in what is apparently -4 in only a t-shirt and jeans has me thinking inappropriate thoughts.

Dylan ruins my moment though by coughing loudly from the kitchen. I glare at him before striding back to my room to pack the final bits of my bag. But he's right, isn't he? I can't be trusted to make sensible decisions right now. I've made a pact with myself and that shitty paper napkin from the pub.

No relationships. Not for a whole year.

I take the opportunity to check my phone whilst nobody is around. It riles up the horrible kind of adrenaline in me. I can't ignore the creeping feeling that if I don't call Adam back, I'm going to be dealing with a cold shoulder for days.

It's there whether I like it or not. I spoke to a therapist about it for a few weeks in the autumn. And she explained it could take time to unlearn this reaction. It could be years and still I will experience that tummy-wrenching moment whenever I perceive danger.

He's sent another text message, but I decide not to read it this time. I delete it before I change my mind.

He doesn't get to occupy any space in my head if I can help it.

I spend the next fifteen minutes working on calm breathing to rid myself of the anxiety, cramming my clothes into my suitcase only to realise I should've put my shoes in first. Thankfully, I just need to bung it all in the boot of Freddie's car, so I grab a plastic bag and toss them in there.

Why is it always harder to pack everything on the way home?

"Are you ready?" Freddie appears at my bedroom door with his hand out, offering to take my bag for me.

"I've got it," I say but he stays where he is. He squeezes the back of his neck, his gaze running over me like he's trying to memorise what I look like. It's the kind of intense thing he does that turns my core muscles to jelly.

I laugh, suddenly nervous again. But the good kind of nervous: the warm, fizzing kind. "What?"

"I just... I'm worried when we go, you'll see this differently."

"Differently?"

"Yeah. Like I'm just playing you." He grimaces. "I heard Dylan."

"Oh, God, I'm sorry. He can be quite loud."

Freddie nods. "What does all this mean for us? I don't want to be the guy who ruins your plans."

I wilt. "You're not that guy."

"Then tell me how this works without breaking your own rules."

I shrug helplessly. "I don't know right now. I still have a lot of figuring out to do. I feel like I was honest about that…" I think about how Adam's text made me feel and it hits home just how badly I need this time. Even if it means losing out on this, with Freddie.

"You were honest. I don't want you to run into something new with me if you still have things to figure out. So…" He sighs heavily, leaning on the door like it's a kind of life support.

I pout. Am I experiencing the fourth rejection of the week from this man? Or is this me rejecting him? "So…"

"I guess I'll wait."

"You'll wait?"

He nods. "I've waited a long time for you. Although I never actually thought it would happen. So, yeah. I'll wait for you. Just let me know if you need a travel partner, yeah?"

I can't even fight the grin. "You'd travel with me?"

"Of course I would. I'll go anywhere with you," he says as he reaches out to tuck the loose strands of hair behind my ears. He holds me in place, tracing the line of my chin until he pinches the end softly and brings me closer; his other hand fists in my sweatshirt and pulls me into him. I gasp as his lips press against mine.

I reach up, tangling my arms around his neck, feeling the warmth of him. It's a gentle, familiar kiss that's more intimate than before, as if we're relaxed enough to take our time and revel in each other.

But we're distracted by a sharp laugh.

I pull apart. Sam is in the upstairs hallway. His eyes are wide, flitting between Freddie and myself. My heart races in my chest. I grab Freddie and try to push him behind me, but he doesn't budge, staring back at his brother.

"Sam..." Freddie starts, but Sam holds his hand up.

"No."

"It's not what you're thinking."

"NO."

"Sam, I swear we were going to tell you when..." I start.

He scoffs, his eyes falling back to me. "I'm not mad at *you*, Hattie." Then he turns and strides away.

"Come on, Sam, wait up," Freddie calls, striding behind him. I jog down the stairs and across the living space to keep up with them.

Sam just keeps walking, shaking his head and muttering expletives. He storms straight out of the lodge, past the car and down the snowy drive until he's disappeared amongst the trees.

Freddie doesn't follow him far as he hasn't got his boots on.

I pause at the door, hugging myself against the chill and chewing on my bottom lip.

Shit.

"Did Sam finally figure it out?" Sara asks.

I turn to see all three of them waiting by the kitchen, their bags already loaded into the car. I give Priya an admonishing glance. "Did you all know?"

Priya snorts. "Hattie, you snuck out the room and back in and thought I wouldn't notice?"

"You were snoring."

"I still noticed you weren't in your bed. And besides, you were sharing a very cosy discussion in the dark last night. I'm not stupid."

Dylan nods. "I caught them frolicking in the snow."

"Dyl!"

"I noticed them eyeing each other on the drive here," Sara says. "They thought I was listening to music, so they didn't know I could hear them flirting. Seriously, it was so obvious. I feel a bit sorry for Sam, actually. He's oblivious, isn't he?"

Freddie comes back in flustered, stripping his thick socks off which are now damp from melting snow. "I need to go after him."

"He won't get far," Sara says, waving a hand dismissively. "Let's pack up and go. We'll catch him up."

I run upstairs to grab the last of my things, throwing my coat and shoes on. Freddie hovers by the stairs outside, ready to catch me, I assume, which is pointless because I've damn well learnt my lesson now.

We all clamber into the car then realise it's full even without Sam. "Oh bugger. I didn't think about that," Freddie remarks. "Someone will have to sit on someone's lap until we find Dylan's car."

"I volunteer Hattie on your lap," Priya says.

"Hilarious," I say.

Sara snorts. "Sam would seethe."

"Can we stop with this line of joking, please?"

The car has been running for twenty minutes already to warm up and defrost so at least it's cosy. Freddie puts it into first gear. I instinctively grab the door handle, but it drives onto the track Freddie spent all morning digging out smoothly.

We relax.

"Gosh, it is pretty, isn't it?" Priya remarks. "Like a winter wonderland." Which is funny since she had zero interest in actually exploring said wonderland while she was here. "Thanks for inviting me, guys. I've felt a bit left out since having Ollie."

"But we always invite you," Sara says, a bit stoney for someone who's barely even seen *me* in the last six months thanks to her insane work schedule.

"I know. But it's different now, isn't it. I don't expect you guys to be super interested in Ollie, but I can't just go out in the evenings like I used to. And neither of you want to go to a soft play."

"Ew, no," Sara agrees. "But we still love you."

"I'd go to a soft play. Sounds fun," I add.

"But neither of you are even free during the day. I've had to make loads of new mum friends. Which is lovely. It is. But the only thing we have in common is we all own small humans who don't sleep, poop a lot and sometimes publicly ruin all your clothes with sick when you don't have spares. I've never been around a group of women who can all pull out a pack of wet wipes at a second's notice like they can. It's both fascinating and jarring."

Sara's face in the rear-view mirror is a picture.

"Doesn't sound like your cup of tea?" I ask her.

She doesn't even try to hide it. "Absolutely not."

"Well, I've hated being so far away from Ollie," Priya adds. "But it's nice to feel like I have my friends back."

I twist in my seat to squeeze her hand. "You'll always have me. I guess we're all just experiencing life at different paces. And I'm sure one day, I'll be coming to you will all the baby questions."

Which, oof. I can't help but check what Freddie's reaction is to that statement. Sara's eyes go wide, and I inwardly kick myself.

But Freddie is unfazed. He's too busy concentrating on the drive to pay me any attention. I swallow, pleased to have survived that awkward moment when he says, "I'll add that to the list."

"Right. Good." *Mortifying.*

Napkin rules, Hattie. Napkin rules.

The car drifts a little on one of the bends. I spin back into my seat, pressing my feet against the floor like I have invisible brakes. But Freddie handles it expertly.

We drive for about fifteen minutes at barely five miles an hour when I spot Sam stomping off up ahead. Freddie exhales audibly at the sight of his brother. I fight the urge to reach across and squeeze his leg. I've never seen him so worried before. He's almost protective and I wonder if he was ever secretly like that growing up. A part of him I didn't get to see.

But I keep my hands to myself as we have an enamoured audience across the back seats so it's not the time.

The lane is less snowy the further we drive down the hill. But the surface is still frozen over, the ice compacted by tracks, wide enough to be tractor tyres. It makes for a smooth drive, despite the wheels making a crunching sound.

That is until we close in on Sam, the lane getting steeper and steeper… He's barely twenty metres ahead, his red coat very easy to spot, when Freddie tries to slow down, but all the car does is make an awful, grinding sound as if it's fighting for friction.

"*Shit*," Freddie hisses. The car begins to swerve. He hits the brakes but all it does is speed us up.

At the bottom of the slope, there's very clearly a vertical drop between the trees. And if Freddie can't stop us, we're going over.

Should I open the door and roll?

I tense all over, squealing.

"Oh hell, we're going to die!" Sara screeches from the middle seat.

I grab hold of the handle as Freddie clambers with the steering wheel, yanking on the handbrake. He tries his best to right the car. He turns it into the snowy drifts either side of the lane to gain purchase.

The wheels crunch and groan.

But Sam doesn't look back. He's right in the way.

Freddie hits the horn to warn him.

Sam spins around, his eyes wide. He slips a bit when he sees how close we are and dives to the side, disappearing into the snow. Freddie finally manages to ram the car into a bank to stop it.

We both fly out to look for Sam, trying and failing to walk up the ice-covered surface where he bailed.

"Sam?" Freddie calls out when he doesn't automatically spot him. There's a steep bank where he fell.

"Down here!" Sam grunts.

We bend over the muddied drift. Freddie holds onto a tree trunk at the top of the bank to help grab his brother and haul him back onto the path. Sam brushes himself down of mud and snow and grit then stands tall, staring Freddie down.

Freddie nods. "Go on then. Give it to me."

THIRTY-ONE

Sam scoffs. "It's not even worth it with you. You were meant to be here to patch things up with *me*. You coming on this trip was supposed to be about *us*. I would've never invited you if I thought you were going to… I don't even want to know what you did to her."

"*Her?* I'm right here." I mumble. "I think I'm going to sit in the car," I say, turning away.

"Uh, no," Sam says. "You can stay. The more I think about it, the more annoyed I am with you too."

"*What?* You said you weren't mad at me."

"I *knew* you fancied him. You always lied about it. But I knew."

"I valued your friendship more and besides, Freddie was never going to be interested in me," I point out. It makes sense in my head but they're both looking at me now like I'm an idiot, which I guess is true. I roll my eyes. "Well, not back then anyway."

"She isn't one of your conquests!" Sam shouts at Freddie,

who just takes it. Not even trying to defend himself. "You *don't* get to play with Hattie. This isn't some game. Do you understand that?"

Freddie nods. "I'm not playing with her," he says, his tone calm and factual.

"Bullshit."

"I'm not, Sam."

"Ugh. I just… I don't trust you. I don't trust your motives. I never have. You're so hard to read."

Freddie swallows, his jaw ticking. "Go on then. Say what you want to say. You've never just said it how it is."

Sam puts his hands on his hips and looks down at his boots. "I don't know how you chose Dad."

"I didn't want to. I never wanted to be forced into picking a side."

"Well, you had to!" Sam yells. "You had to pick a side, and you picked *wrong*."

"He needed me."

"You needed a career, more like. You sold out."

I try to step back towards the car; this feels like it's taken a new direction. Maybe none of this is even about me at all.

But Freddie notices and points at me. "Stay. *Please*. We need a referee."

"I don't know…"

"Please stay," Sam adds without even looking at me.

"Right. But no hitting anything like last time. I don't want any bloodied knuckles."

This makes Sam laugh but not in a good way. He's agitated and I've likely just nudged him towards a dark memory.

"Dad deserved to be lonely after the way he treated Mum. And *us*, for crying out loud! He was an arse for years. He treated me like shit, and you just picked him like it wasn't even a hard decision."

"It was a fucking *agonising* decision, Sam! You don't get it at all." Freddie raises his voice for the first time.

"No. I don't get it."

"You and Mum had each other. You were ok. You didn't need me."

"YES, WE DID!" Sam practically screams.

"Ok… I think we should take it down a notch," I say. "There's a lot of snow. We don't want to cause an avalanche or something."

"Hattie…" Sam begins but then shakes his head. "A fucking avalanche? *Whatever*. Fred, you're my older brother, and you were barely there. Mum was heartbroken that she lost you to him. I just don't think you understand…"

"Why did you guys make me pick?" I swear Freddie's eyes are growing damp. He swallows thickly. "Why did it have to be a choice?"

"Because we hated him. You were at uni those last few months. You didn't see it."

Freddie rubs his chin. He's already told me how guilty he felt about not being around for Sam at that time. I just don't think he's ever told him. "No, I didn't see it."

"It was like you didn't believe us."

"He was sick."

"He was a prick!"

"He needed someone."

"It doesn't matter, Fred. He didn't *deserve* someone."

Freddie throws his hands up. "Well, I did it anyway."

"Why? Because you wanted his support and money?"

"No!" Freddie rears back, his face appalled. "I did it because when I went over to see him and tell him I was done picking up his slack, he was passed out on the floor, covered in sick."

Sam clenches his jaw, his breathing heavy. "What?"

"It doesn't matter what happened. But he needed someone to take care of him. He needed someone to check in on him. He's not just the grumpy arsehole we grew up with. He's our dad. And he needed someone."

"Ok, fine. So, you helped him. But then you made him a whole feature in your life. You let him run your bloody career. He set you up for life."

Something about this statement seems to rile Freddie. "I tried to bring you into it. You could've done that too. Dad was trying to help us both. I came round that time you punched the wall to offer it to you."

"I didn't want his help!"

"That's *your* decision. Don't judge me for mine. I never asked for them to fall out. I never asked for any of it. Why do you act like it was all my damn fault? I hated it as much as you did. I was heartbroken to lose you."

"Come off it. You hated me."

"I didn't *understand* you."

"You never tried! You hated everything I did. You hated that I wasn't sporty. You didn't get that I wasn't like you."

Freddie laughs. "You wouldn't let me. Ok, I wasn't always the best brother, I'll admit. But I had shit to deal with too. Dad wasn't just an arse to you, you know. I've been in therapy trying to get my head around some of the manipulative, fucked-up crap he put into my head. I'm trying really hard, Sam. I'm trying so hard to be the good guy. To make the right decisions.

"I've been told my whole life that I need to be the winner. I need to be better than everyone else around me. I need to earn more, be more, fight more. Just always more, more, more. And I'm tired of being his hobby. I'm tired of always being the fucking bad guy. I hate it. I fucking hate it."

"Oh yeah, good job," Sam remarks, the sarcasm dripping from his tone. "Must be why you chose to do this whole thing with Hattie and then hide it from me. Over my birthday, no less!"

"I'm sorry," Freddie sighs. "None of this was to hurt you."

"Again, great job. You're doing a brilliant job of persuading me you're not a massive fucking dick."

"What do you want from me?"

"I want you to be my brother!"

"I *am* your brother. I'm here, aren't I? I'm trying."

"You're… *doing things*… to my best friend. The one person who's never had anything to do with you! And I swear to God if you ruin that for me, if you mess with her in any way, I will never speak to you ever again!"

Freddie stares at his brother, his eyes narrowed and, if I'm totally honest, more intense than I've ever seen them before. "I would *never* hurt her or do anything to ruin… whatever it is that's going on between us."

Sam's gaze flits to mine. I know my face will be betraying me. I'm hot and sweaty from the stress, despite it being freezing outside. He presses his lips together. "Well? What the hell's going on?"

"It's my fault," I say. "I don't think you want the details, but you should know, it was me who initiated things. Nothing really happened. And I don't want you to blame him."

"Why him?" he asks; he sounds tired now.

"Er, do you really want the details?" I try to brush it off with a smile.

But he just shakes his head, groaning as he looks up at the sky. "This will take some getting my head around."

"Guys." Sara pokes her head out of the car window. "So great you're all finally having it out. But it's literally freezing right now, and you left the car doors open without the heating on."

Freddie and Sam both exhale audibly at the same time.

"Come on," Freddie says. "Let's hit the road. Hopefully, I can reverse out of this. You'll have to figure out how you're going to sit until we drop Dylan off as there aren't enough seats."

"Even better," Sam complains, striding past me to the car. I feel a pain my chest when he doesn't so much as glance my way.

Freddie gives me a sad smile as he walks back to the car.

THIRTY-TWO

"There it is," Dylan says, pointing from his squished spot in the back at a black car abandoned on the side of the narrow country lane. It's been left in a sunken layby, his only hope as the snow became too heavy to see and his wheels started to spin out.

Freddie parks beside it. The road is deserted so there's no concerns about holding anyone up as we all climb out of the car to assess the situation.

There's still a foot of snow on the roof, the doors frozen shut and the windows iced up. Dylan pulls on the driver's door roughly until he hears the familiar cracking sound. He climbs in, his breath visible as he fiddles with the keys. Thankfully, the engine starts first time, so he turns to me with a triumphant grin.

I'm freezing outside and regret getting out of Freddie's warm car but I'm feeling that familiar trickle of anxiety that I've done something I shouldn't have. That I, Hattie Tycer, am the reason somebody else isn't happy. And that breaks my heart.

To solidify my point, I turn my gaze to Sam, who is staring at his boots as he kicks the muddy snow on the side of the road. He's lost his shine and I'm to blame.

So, instead of sitting there doing nothing, I'm going to help get Dylan's car sorted. We all set to work using our coat sleeves or random branches we find lying about to help clear it off. Sara squeals as Sam brushes a ton of snow right off the corner and into her shoes. Freddie produces some antifreeze spray and a scraper from his car. Once it's in a semi-driveable state, Sara and Priya both get back into the car, snatching Freddie's keys so she can turn the engine on and get the heating firing up again.

I clench my damp-gloved hands into fists at my side. I swear my fingers are now blue.

"Hey, I'm sorry," Dylan says, walking round to give me an awkward half-hug.

I frown. "Why are *you* sorry?"

"I shouldn't have just turned up like that. I should have warned you. And made better choices."

"It's fine, Dylan," I say, finding the ghost of a smile to reassure him. "It's been nice having you here. You get on so well with everyone and I'm just glad you didn't have to suffer our family's party."

"And I would've suffered."

I nod. "Utter torture."

"You know I've always looked up to you, Hattie."

"Really?"

"Yes, really! You're the golden child in our family."

I snort. "Not anymore."

"Pfft. No, they *hate* you now. How dare you get broken up with?"

"Despicable."

"Wait, stop. Let's be serious."

"Are we not always serious?"

"You're going to be fine and you're going to make the right decisions because that's the woman you are," Dylan says, nodding to himself. "Whatever happens, you're going to be ok."

"Thanks?" I laugh, unsure how to respond. "You know, you have similar genes, right. So, if you say these things to me, they probably apply to you too."

"Oh no. I got all the bad genes. All of them."

"Stop it."

He shrugs. "I was actually going to ask you about career stuff at some point. Get your advice on how to be a grown-up. You know, things I should've figured out a few years ago."

"I really don't have much of a career," I point out, fidgeting on my feet to warm up.

"You're doing something you enjoy. It pays you enough to feed yourself and not live with your parents. So, you're definitely somebody to look up to. And I'm going to be channelling that this year."

I smile. "Tell you what, let's have dinner at mine once a week. That way, we can catch up on your antics and I can help you find your happy career."

"I'd love that," he says before climbing into the driver's seat and fiddling with the mirrors that are still glazed over.

"Oh, and Dylan," I say before he closes the door. He grins up at me. "You should know I've always sort of been jealous of you too."

"Ah yeah?"

"I wish I had even an ounce of your spontaneity. It's your special thing and even though it might be good to settle a bit, don't ever lose that."

Before he can respond, I shut the door and he shakes his head. We're not really the family for sentimental stuff. "Drive safely," I shout instead.

That's when the boot of his car opens and I see Sam chucking his bags in.

"What you doing?"

"Going home with Dylan."

"Sam…"

"I'm not ready to sit in the car with you for the next four hours. I need space. I just…" He stops at the passenger side. I can just make out Dylan trying to act like he isn't listening, fiddling with the heating vents in my peripheral vision. Sam sighs. He can barely look at me. There's that sharp ache again building in my chest. "I don't know how to handle this right now. I'm angry. And partly at you. But I'm not going to say things now that I might regret later."

And with that, he climbs into the car and slams the door. I fold my arms across my chest as I watch them speed off up the lane and out of sight.

"Hey," Freddie's deep voice calls to me from the car. I turn to find him leaning on the bonnet. "You ok?"

"I've hurt Sam."

He twists his lips. "You're not alone. He'll come around."

I chew on the end of my thumb. I want to have this conversation with Freddie, but it doesn't feel like the best time. Especially when I know Sara and Priya will be watching unashamedly from the back seats. "Let's go," I say.

As soon as we hit the main roads, where the ice and snow had been cleared, it's plain sailing. It's probably the longest time I've ever gone without talking when we reach the service station two hours later. Is it because there's so much to say, it's easier to say nothing at all? Or is it because I'm not even sure what I'm meant to say? And in addition to that, I keep going over what I'm going to tell Adam to get him to back off.

He doesn't just get to call me whenever he wants.

Priya and Freddie grab some drinks (non-alcoholic this time – I've had enough alcohol this New Year to last me months) for the last half of the drive. I follow Sara back to the car, having been entrusted with the keys.

"Hey, I've been thinking about what you said," I say as we climb into the car.

"What did I say?"

"All your worries about getting married."

"Ok..."

"You know, I didn't expect that from you. I think it's because I've always seen you as this super confident, independent woman who fights. You're always fighting. You fight your family. You fight for your career. You fought that old man just now because he tried cut the queue."

"And I would have won if that had become physical."

"Well, yeah, but only because he was about eighty."

"It's just disrespectful, you know? I don't care how

old you are. This is Great Britain. We queue in an orderly fashion, even when there isn't a clear need to queue. We like queues."

I snort. "I was being sentimental. If you could please take your own advice and wait your turn."

"You know I'd fight you too."

"You'd have to catch me first. And stop it. Sara, I want you to know that your wedding is going to be perfect, and I can't wait. But if it isn't or anything didn't work out for whatever reason, I still love you. We love you. And it doesn't make you a fool, it makes you human."

"Ugh, you're going to make me sick."

I grin and continue to torture her. "You need to tell that voice in your head, that makes you doubt whether you deserve love, to get lost. Because you do deserve to be loved. And you do deserve happiness. I'm going to need you to buck up and be less afraid of it."

Sara looks away, staring out into the distance. The distance being a seagull chasing a squirrel who just took quarter of a pasty that's fallen from a bin beside the pasty truck. Never let it be said that the UK doesn't have beautiful scenery. "You know, you don't get to throw really lovely words at me and not receive some in return, right?"

"What? You know how to be *nice*?"

"No, not really. But I'm going to say some things, so brace."

I hold onto the overhead handle. Ready.

"You're not going to believe this. And I think I know why, but I won't go into a full character analysis right now. Did you know…" she pauses for effect, leaning closer to the front seat, "you can break the rules."

I scoff. "Well, no, you can't break the rules. That's the point of rules."

"But sometimes, rules are there to be broken. If no one ever broke the rules, this world would be a hideously dull place."

"What rules are you even referring to?" I ask, but I think I know.

Sara just gives me a telling smirk as Freddie and Priya return, climbing into their respective seats and popping drinks into the cup holders. He checks my face briefly, barely even a glance, then we're on the road again.

Back to silence.

When I look in the rear-view mirror as the sun drops below the horizon, I notice both Sara and Priya are fast asleep. I allow myself a moment to stare at Freddie's side profile. I take in the hard lines of his face and his gentle, sloping nose. Is he a rule I can break?

I swallow, thinking about why we organised this party in the first place. The need to do something Adam would've hated. The need to do something fun for me again. And the catalyst to my year alone, independent and adventurous.

"What're you thinking? I can see you staring at me," Freddie says, his voice barely above a whisper.

"You'll be going back to London later, right?"

He flexes his fingers over the steering wheel. "Yeah, I have work tomorrow. And I haven't logged on for two whole days so for all we know, the company has crashed. That, and you know, I kind of live there."

"Right. Yeah."

"Hey," he says, reaching out to touch my knee but then wincing and taking his hand back, thinking better of it.

I hate it. I want to feel the weight of his hand on me. I already miss it. Which is absurd as it was less than twelve hours ago that I was dribbling on his chest. But I think my head is telling me he's something I still can't have.

He's always been this untouchable thing.

And maybe, outside of the lodge, that's who he has to be because Sam means the world to me. It was Sam who was at my door within minutes of Adam breaking it off. It was Sam who stayed at mine for a whole week just for support. And it was Sam who's been relentlessly my friend through all these years. From the nerdy girl who had no friends to the heartbroken woman who needed a hug.

It was always him.

God. What if I've ruined it?

It's all I can think about as we drop Priya off, waving at Izzy and baby Ollie, who are already there waiting for her by the front door. Then Sara, who we drop at the station so she can get the train back to Brighton where she lives with Mike.

Then it's just us and he's driving me back to my flat a few blocks away from the sea. It's dark outside, the sky a deep navy, seagulls cawing into the wind. There hasn't been so much as a drop of snow in Seaford, which doesn't surprise me at all. It never really snows down here on the coast.

I'm tongue-tied the whole way trying to decide how the hell I'm going to leave this with him because, honestly, I feel like I'm just going to end up wanting to kiss him again.

And that's not going to solve any of my problems.

Freddie finds a gap to parallel park, effortlessly reversing into the spot. It shouldn't be as hot as it is. I suspect the attraction to sexy, careful driving hits in around the same time as a fully developed frontal lobe.

"Is that Adam?" Freddie asks, peering out the passenger's side before he's even got the handbrake on. I flinch like someone's thrown freezing-cold water at me. My heart practically descends to my toes because...

"Oh my God..." It *is* Adam.

He's sat on the wooden bench outside the main doors to my apartment block, slumped over with his phone in his hand. There's that dark, long hair falling over his face that I've been so familiar with for so long. And yet I don't experience the ache that usually comes with seeing him. I don't feel like I'm missing anything anymore. He hasn't moved so I don't think he's noticed us.

But, of course, he wouldn't expect me to be in this car – let alone with Freddie.

"Huh. How did you handle the text incident last night?" Freddie asks, his eyes still trained on my ex.

I shrug. "I ignored him. I kind of hoped he'd just leave me alone."

"Well, I don't think he got the memo."

Clearly. I bite my lip, pondering my next move.

"Come on," Freddie says.

Part of me expects him to drive us away again. I could stay at his for the night and hopefully, by the time we're back, Adam will be gone. Except that's not what is happening. Nope. Freddie is climbing out the car.

Panic kicks me into motion.

"Wait! What are you doing?" I hiss, launching for his arm and hanging onto his firm bicep like I own it. "He'll see you."

Freddie pauses, halfway out the door, the chilly evening air seeping into our perfectly snug car. There's really no

293

need to leave. His gaze lands on mine, a warm confidence there. I don't release his arm. "Good. What's the worst that can happen?"

"I don't actually know." I frown but my mind is catastrophising. I'm seeing a brawl. I'm seeing Adam in my life again. What if I do something stupid and forgive him? I've done it before.

Freddie waits, his stare unwavering. "What do *you* want to do? If you really want, we can leave. Or I can go see him off myself?"

I can't fight a surprised laugh. "You'd do that?"

He tilts his head. "You know I would. In fact, it would be an honour. I would enjoy it. Honestly, you'd be doing me a favour. But you shouldn't enable my ego."

I laugh again. And... just how. This is a stressful moment. My ex is but metres away, but Freddie is putting me at ease and I'm laughing. I take a deep breath. "I know. I know. But no. *No.* I need to do this."

"Want me to stay here?"

I scoff. "I'm being brave. Not mental."

"Is that a yes?"

"Yeah."

He smiles. "I shouldn't be this excited."

"No, you shouldn't. This will be a boring exchange."

"We'll see. Give him hell, Hattie."

I release Freddie and ready myself to climb out my side. His door slams and then before I know it, he's opened my door like a gent, even offering me his hand to help me out. Oh, he's going to really enjoy this performance.

"You don't have to do that," I say as he slams my door just hard enough to gain attention. His devilish grin when I look at him tells me he knows exactly what he's doing. I pretend I have no idea Adam is there, but I swear I can feel his eyes on me. Freddie steps ahead, opening the boot and looping my bag over his shoulder, and I don't even bother resisting him.

Because maybe this whole show is exactly the performance Adam needs.

Freddie offers me his arm as we begin to walk, and I take it. Why not? Might as well give it my all. Adam is standing when my eyes finally land on him. He's in his nice jeans and smart boots. I don't recognise the coat he has on. It's weird. I would've usually helped him pick something like that.

"Adam?" I say, and I sound surprisingly candid.

His eyes trail from mine to where my arm is linked through Freddie's before he finally looks up and acknowledges him with a nod. "Hattie, erm ... aren't you Sam's brother?"

"That's right," Freddie says. "And you must be Alex?"

I fight a snigger. Instead, I press my lips together and look down, squeezing Freddie's arm tighter.

"Hattie, don't you hate this guy?" Adam asks, gaining my attention again.

I feel Freddie tense beside me.

I make a face at my ex. "Clearly…"

"Right. Well… I was hoping we could talk."

I can feel Freddie fighting the urge not to speak and ruin my moment to shine. I take a second to breathe and order my words. I have to do this right. "There's nothing to say."

Adam scowls. "I have something to say. And I'd appreciate a moment alone."

Freddie doesn't budge. But I feel a sudden need to do

this on my own. He's got me this far. It has to be me who confronts my literal demon. I release his arm, and we share a brief, silent exchange. *I've got this*, I hope I portray.

With a twist of his lips, he steps past Adam and walks towards the main doors to my building.

It's a statement, alright. If he'd returned to the car, it would've given Adam the impression Freddie was leaving. But, oh no, *he is staying*.

If only that were true.

Once he's out of earshot, I feel a blast of rage run from my chest to my tongue. "Why did you text me?"

Adam swallows thickly, his gaze landing on mine. I hold him there, waiting to see if he'll be honest. Maybe, after all this time away, I'll finally be able to read him. "I miss you. Things haven't been the same without you."

"But at midnight?" I ask. "You know I'm up and celebrating my birthday at that time. Why then?"

"I guess I just remembered…"

"Remembered what? All the times you weren't there whilst we were together?"

"Hattie. You're not being fair."

I pause for the briefest of seconds. Blame lodges itself in my throat. I almost swallow the pill and accept I'm the one in the wrong. It's amazing how fast that works. But I throw it up in the form of word vomit. "No!" I shout, way too loudly. People are going to start peering out of their windows. "I *am* being fair. I'm being very fair. And I don't owe you anything."

Adam is shaking his head. "You always do this. You try to twist things. I'm here trying to say sorry…"

"I don't want your sorry, Adam! And I don't want you!

I'm tired of feeling like I'm the one messing up all the time, or overreacting, or being difficult. Newsflash! I'm none of those things. You had no right to make me feel that way about myself."

Adam laughs, the bitter sound making my blood boil. "You *were* all those things. You still are! Look at yourself. What the hell are you doing with that guy? How did Sam take that, huh? Or does he not know?"

I blanch. I'm not ready to confront that just yet. "That's none of your business."

"So you're an item?"

"What do you care?"

"Oh my God, Hattie. I'm glad we did this. I am. Because now I know I was right the first time."

I scoff. "Yes. Me too. I'm glad you've shown me that you're exactly the person I thought you were. It's taken time to bleed the poison you fed me."

"You need to grow up," he mutters before shoving past me back towards the road.

"Never contact me again!" I yell at his retreating figure.

Once he's definitely gone, I feel instantly lighter, as if he's taken some of the weight I've been carrying away with him.

THIRTY-THREE

Freddie has an impressed grin on his lips when I round the corner, which makes me suspect he heard everything. He's leaning on the wall beside the building's intercom. I can't stop smiling. I feel like I've levelled up in a game. Defeated the enemy.

He walks me up to my flat, insisting on carrying my bag and coat. I play with my sleeves in the lift and then invite him in for a drink. It's only fair considering he just drove four hours and has another hour drive into the city all by himself. And besides, I'm not ready to say goodbye just yet. I'm sort of hoping he doesn't go.

But isn't that what I'm trying to avoid?

I can almost hear Fliss asking me if falling into something new so fast is right for me. I made the rules and I should stick to the rules. Why can't I get a grasp on any of this? It's still so new but I've known Freddie for what feels like forever and so surely, it's not the same.

I *do* know what I'm getting into with him.

"I take it you want something with caffeine in it?" I ask, flicking the kettle on to distract myself.

"Please." He nods, strolling around my cluttered flat. I let him look. I know he'll be most interested in the canvasses on my walls. He pauses at one of them and I instantly know why. "This is just like mine," he says, running his finger along the bottom.

I grin shyly from the kitchen. I painted that one back at university, sat on the beach during one of those rare winter days when the winds are low, the skies an epic blue, but the temperature subzero. There were a few of us all wrapped up in thick coats and hats, praying the seagulls didn't ruin our canvasses with their own paint. I mapped out the layout that day then spent the next few weeks painting and tweaking it until I felt at peace with what I'd achieved.

"I didn't know you had my other one back then. But I knew Mandy didn't have it on her wall anymore and I missed seeing it, so I added that red boat. It wasn't actually there. In fact, I seem to remember there was a hideous, great big tanker and I cut that out. This one is more refined than yours. I'd learnt a lot about the craft in the year before I painted that one."

"Mine's perfect," he says.

"It's not as good."

"It's better. Because it's mine."

I laugh. "Well, you stole it so…"

"Then we're both thieves."

"I'd like to steal one of *your* sketches and frame it for *my* walls. Seems only fair."

He peers around the room at the severe lack of wall space in here. "If, for argument's sake, I would ever agree to share my sketches, where would you put it? Your walls are full to the brim."

"I'd make space."

"Even if it was the one of you?"

His comment catches me off guard. I just stare back at him, unsure what to say.

He nods as if my reaction was expected. "I knew you'd seen it."

"It was…"

"Not finished," he says. "It was an indulgent thing I felt like doing. I rarely ever saw you and I just really love your freckles and your smile. And that night, when you sang that godawful rendition of 'Thunderstruck'…"

"In hindsight, it was way out of vocal reach."

"…it was horrendous, but perfect."

"What every girl aspires to. Horrendous but perfect."

"You weren't meant to see it."

The reminder of that sketch sends my pulse racing. It was the first time I allowed myself to even wonder at Freddie showing me an interest. And now I know. "Everyone needs a portrait of themselves really."

Freddie laughs at this before catching sight of my bedroom through the door. The light is off in there, but he can just about make out the blank canvas I have propped up by the windows.

"You going to finish that one?"

I shrug. "I don't know why I bought such a huge canvas. It's mocking me. I'm intimidated by it. And I just feel like I've lost that part of me somewhere along the line."

"I loved your idea for it. How life is moving so fast

sometimes, it feels like a blur." He turns his gaze on me and my tummy dips, a flicker of hope alighting in my core. He might stay. I want him to stay. If he stays, then I'll be able to keep this feeling I have around him. The one that makes me feel like I'm whole.

"Please paint it," he says. "Do it for you. You deserve it."

I press my lips together. "I'll finish it if you do the same."

"Do what?"

"Finish one of your sketches. Properly. Frame it. Own your skill. For you."

He runs a hand over his chin. "There's a reason I never finish them," he says. "I wasn't allowed to draw as I grew up. Dad wouldn't allow it. I had to focus on more important things, like exams and sports. He didn't see any value in it and I kind of believed him back then. I knew it wouldn't earn me money. It was just for fun to begin with. But then I found I quite enjoyed it. It came back to me that time I discovered him."

He swallows, pausing as if the memory takes him out of himself for a moment. "My head is so focused and quiet whilst I'm sketching. To begin with, I'd sketch whatever I could see. One time, after Dad was in hospital again, I just sat there and sketched the IV pole that was bringing him back to life. He was in and out of consciousness and I thought he wouldn't approve so I ended up shutting my sketchpad a few times. Even told him I was taking notes for an exam at work.

"Once I was home, I started sketching properly again. I'd sketch whatever caught my eye." I don't miss the way he looks at me before flitting away again. "But I never finish them because it feels wrong to. Like finishing them would make them real. I prefer them to just be sketches. I'm not an artist like you."

"Everyone's an artist."

I bring our drinks to the table, hoping he'll join but he doesn't sit. He lingers nearby, sipping. The silence stretches. The tightness in my chest suggests my body knows before I do.

"What a day," he says.

I laugh but it sounds sad. "You can say that again." I woke up dribbling on his chest and now my best friend won't talk to me and he's about to leave me. "You've got to go," I start for him when he doesn't say it himself.

He nods. "I've got to go. My work…"

"They need you."

"I hate it," he says, looking at me like it might just break him to leave.

I take a deep breath. I don't want to sound pathetic. But I do want to know if I'll see him again soon.

"Hattie… Sam and I… We've been through so much."

I look away. "We shouldn't have done this, I know."

"I don't know how this works without hurting people."

"It wasn't meant to. Ugh!" I groan. "This is silly, isn't it? We've known each other for years but this doesn't have to be serious right now. It doesn't have to be anything." Although saying that out loud makes it feel much worse. "I made a promise to myself that I wouldn't be in a relationship with anyone for a whole year."

"Now why did you do that?" he asks with humour in his tone. "Didn't you know I was right around the corner?"

I bite my lip to prevent myself from smiling. "It felt right at the time. And no, I didn't think *you* were ever on the cards. I had no idea you were coming on this trip and I think Sam might be regretting the invite now."

Freddie plays with his hands. "Maybe I should go. I don't think any sensible decisions are going to be made whilst we're so tired, hey?"

I get up to walk him to the door where he pauses.

"Take care, storm cloud. And happy birthday again."

I suck in a deep breath, an ounce of panic washing through me that he might not ever walk through those doors again. This could be it. But it's for the best. It's what I need. I need space and sleep and resetting to be able to see this properly.

"Drive safe, Fred."

I close the door like the sensible woman I am. Look how mature we are. Not even a kiss goodbye. I'm almost proud of myself. That is until I experience that little snap of adrenaline and run back to the door, swinging it open.

Freddie hasn't moved, hands braced on either side of the door. I swallow at his intense gaze, his heavy breathing. Then I launch at him, pressing both hands to his warm, bristled cheeks as his lips press down hungrily over mine. He makes this bitten-off groan that has me clenching everything below waist level. Desire thick in my bones.

THIRTY-FOUR

He lifts me, both big hands cupping my bum, as I wrap my legs around his middle. He walks me back into the flat, kicking the door closed with his foot. I drop a hand, fisting it in his t-shirt, his muscular back firm against my knuckles. I want to explore every inch of this gorgeous man. And thankfully, he seems to get the hint, heading towards my bedroom.

"I swear to God," I manage to say between kisses, "if you reject me now, I will die."

"I never rejected you," he argues. "I was just playing hard to get."

I crack up, arching myself against him as his tongue traces the crease between my lips. I open to him as I drop my other hand from his hair, feeling across his muscled shoulder, his strong back.

Freddie groans. "Is this ok?" he whispers.

"Mmm-hmm," I say, nodding, tugging at his t-shirt. "*Very*. I would sign a waiver. I want this. Yes."

Freddie's lips never leave mine as he props me on the chest of drawers beside my bed. He stands between my thighs, running his hands along them as I tug him closer. I moan, frustrated, when his mouth trails softly, warmly down my neck, to the curve of my shoulder, lingering in spots that make me hop. He runs a finger along my baggy sweatshirt, kissing the line of it.

He looks up, testing my reaction as he pushes it over my shoulder, his finger trailing lower until it will give no more. I smile, swiftly pulling it, with my vest and bra underneath, over my head, leaving me topless, and lob it across the room.

I press my lips together, but Freddie doesn't notice; he stands taller as I wrap my legs around him, enclosing his body into mine. He's focused as he plants both hands on my waist, his fingers splaying. The tips stroking along the underside of my breasts.

I lean towards his ear, whisper, "*Freddie, please.*"

He shushes me and I can feel the curve of his smile against my cheek like he's planning on playing with me. And he does just that, paying particular attention to my earlobes, which he pinches with his teeth, tugging exquisitely. The same buzz whips up and down my spine, teasing the spot where the ache is building, begging. I want to press him closer, feel the swell of him against me but he keeps a couple of inches between us.

Freddie's hands lower to the hem of my leggings, sneaking underneath, grazing the bare skin at the top of my thighs. The scratch of his rough fingers there is promising. I think about where else I want them to scrape over and my impatience grows. I fiddle with them myself, a sudden urge to rip them off.

Freddie smirks into my lips. "Steady. I'm not rushing this."

His eyes feast greedily over my bare nipples, now firm and budded. He runs his hands up the back of my spine, then around the front, under my arms, his fingers gentle, achingly so, as he finally slides his knuckles over them.

He bites his lip. "*Fuck*. You're so fucking gorgeous. I don't think I can handle it."

"Well, you're going to have to pull yourself together and try."

He takes a breath, laughs. "*Fuck*."

I grab his t-shirt again, fisting the material and pulling him closer till his lips are on mine. This time, he's quick to tip my chin. Our tongues slide together and I feel the answering swell in his jeans. His fingers splay at my waist, sneaking upwards until they're tracing the underside of my breasts again. He groans, stepping even closer, his hands lowering down my belly to the waistband of my leggings. He tugs a little, but I have to lift my weight off the side for him to peel them off me. Then he pauses again. Breathes deeply.

"Look at you," he whispers.

For the briefest second, I feel that familiar sludge of self-consciousness. He's looking at me like I'm more than I am. What if I can't live up to the hype?

As if he can tell, he fits his lips with mine again, distracting me from wherever my head has gone. Expertly, his hand traces along my waist, over the curve of my hip and then down my left thigh, grazing the skin with his knuckles. I hop in my seat as he trails the inner part of my thigh, higher, slower. It's so sensitive, so wanting, I can barely retain my groan just as the tip of his thumb finds the most intimate part of me.

I groan almost immediately again when he removes the pressure.

He laughs. I hate him.

"*Don't*," I say. "Don't be mean."

"Shh. I've finally found something I can tease you with," he says in return, his voice husky. I throw my head back as he leans in to kiss my throat, his tongue trailing up the side of my chin where he takes a tactful nip. "Promise me this won't be our only time."

I gasp. "I…" But words aren't forming as they should. I'm riled up and insensible. This isn't time for promises, surely. And yet, "Yes."

"Yes, you promise? I don't want to just be your rebound, storm cloud. I want more of you. All of you."

"Yes, yes."

"Hattie…" Freddie leans back and it's awful. It's so cruel. I sigh, my legs hanging off the drawers like some kind of bedraggled doll. "I need to know this isn't just a one-time thing. I'm not fucking this up with you."

I reach for him, grabbing his t-shirt. "I want more of you too. I want *you*. I want you. *Please*."

This seems to be enough for him. Encouraged by his sudden attention to my body, his lips returning to my belly, roaming all over, from my cheeks to my earlobes, down my neck again, my nipples, pulling, teasing, then lower still. Fire spreads through me, heat bubbling just below the surface of my skin.

I feel his warm breath graze my clit before he kisses gently above it. It's enough to make me gasp, as I claw onto the side, my fingers gripping. He smiles against my belly button. I want so desperately to kiss him. I almost pull him up to me, but I get the urge to tease him instead.

"Don't you know where it is?" I ask.

At this, he chuckles deeply. But the challenge works; he masterfully demonstrates, sucking me in, that mischievous spark in his eyes. A breath catches in my throat as the ache intensifies.

"Was I right?"

I shake my head. "Missed."

This time, he gently scrapes his teeth over it, his tongue pressing hard. I hop right into his mouth, one hand gripping his head.

"Brat," he mumbles in triumph, his hands sliding behind me to hold me to him.

I collapse against the wall as he drives me closer to the edge.

God, it's been too long to be teased like this.

A growling, hungry sound emanates from his chest. I feel the vibrations of it against my skin. The ache that's been building starts to overflow. I hang onto Freddie, with zero control over the wanton sounds falling from my lips.

As every part of me starts to unravel, I tip my head back again. Freddie pushes me harder. I can feel the strength of him under my hand. Stars in my vision. The whip of sensation sprints up my spine. The heat in my core spreads until I'm my own wildfire.

Freddie stands again, kissing me, the taste of myself rich on his tongue.

"I've been dying to do that for a very long time," he murmurs into my lips.

"Thanks," I say, my lips pressing to his shoulder. "You can go now, I guess."

Freddie scoffs good-humouredly, a low rumble from his chest. He picks me up, guiding my legs around his still fully clothed waist as he walks me to the bed. I let my head rest on his shoulder. He places me carefully on the sheets, yanking a blanket from the end and folding it over me.

I start to object; no way is he going to tuck me in again! But he kisses my forehead, using his lips to push me back.

"Are you sure you…"

"Yes!" I sputter. "I feel like I've made that very clear, Freddie."

"Ok, well then I'd love it if you didn't judge my next action." He tucks his hand into his back pocket and produces a condom wrapper.

"You brought that into my flat?!"

"I asked you not to judge me."

"When?"

"Are you annoyed?"

"No! I'm impressed. And very grateful."

I kick off the rest of my clothes, including my socks.

He chucks the wrapper on the bed as he strips down to his boxers, climbing in beside me; the heat of his skin next to mine is divine. I take that as a cue to abandon the blanket, sliding across his lap. His hands find my hips, squeezing. "Take your boxers off," I whisper.

I kiss him long and slow as he fiddles with his boxers, jumping from his seat beneath my thighs to free himself of them. Once he's naked, I sit back to take him in. He watches me, cautious. I bite my knuckles.

"Oh." Yeah, ok, now I'm nervous.

He's bigger than…

"Don't overthink it," he says.

"What if I've been underthinking it, though?"

He grins, and I can see by his expression, this isn't a surprise to him. Must be nice being so fuckable. He grabs the condom wrapper beside him and is about to roll it on, but I jump to it.

I take him in my hand, feel the width of him between my fingers. The gorgeous solidness of him. He closes his eyes, groaning, as he tips his head back. This fuels me further. I lean down to plant a kiss on the tip of him, to taste him there.

He grunts then before I know what's happening, he grabs me by the shoulders and flips me onto my back. He rolls the condom down as I sort my crazy mane out and then we both gasp audibly, forgetting ourselves, as he guides himself in. The hard, hot slide of him, his body snug between my thighs, as he encourages my legs around his waist again.

Everything else, except me and him, blurs. I want to paint this moment. The pause between us as the world slips by. All I know is the feel of him everywhere. His weight. His beaded sweat rolling down his back as I try to grip onto him. The perfect anchored sensation building, slowly, slowly.

As he increases momentum, he kisses me again. It's a hungry, leave-nothing-behind sort of kiss.

"Hold onto me," he says against my lips, his elbows braced either side of my face. Somehow, me squeezing my legs tighter around him catches the perfect spot. I gasp into his lips, tensing all over, clawing at his back.

"Fuck," he groans, as he finds his release.

He drops his head onto my shoulder, my fingers tangling

in his hair, holding him to me. He tries to move, to remove his weight, but I like how it feels. I like how it's keeping me breathless. Grounded. I squeeze him tighter.

"You're going to kill me if you do that again," he groans. He holds still, collapsing into me some more.

Before we get too sleepy, the perfect mix of post-sex haze washing over us, he rolls to the side, his arms never leaving my body. "You," he says.

"Me?" I ask, curling into him, finding the perfect spot to rest my face in the crook of his shoulder.

"Yeah, just you."

The night fades into morning, the sunlight pushing through my blinds, birds stirring in the trees nearby. We've barely had any sleep, our bodies restless with the need to be touching, kissing, feeling. I managed to find more condoms in my top drawer, which was a relief to us both. But now he has to go. He should've left last night and now here we are, with no time left.

"I'm going to be very late for work today," he says. "And underdressed."

"It doesn't matter if I'm late so I might go back to sleep," I say with a dramatic yawn and stretch. Freddie throws the duvet off me, his eyes taking in my naked, stretched-out body. He runs a finger from my belly button up to my breasts, softly grazing my nipples, entirely entranced.

"Can't believe you weren't going to kiss me goodbye last night," he mutters.

"Rookie error."

His finger trails lower again. I'm suddenly breathless.

311

"I think I corrected my mistake, however."

"Mmm," he hums. "I'm going to have freckle withdrawal symptoms."

"My withdrawal symptoms will be far more extreme. You should go before you don't go at all," I say, but I'm already experiencing his departure in my gut and I don't like it at all.

He kisses my belly then my lips once more, brushing my hair back behind my shoulder. I'm sure he almost says something else, but whatever it was, he keeps it to himself and hops out of the bed. I pull the duvet back right up to my chin while I watch a naked Freddie, in all his muscularly lean perfection, roam my room, bending to grab his clothes and pulling them on one item at a time. It's almost surreal. I wonder if fourteen-year-old Hattie, who was entirely obsessed with him, would believe me if I told her.

I'm almost bereft of the sight as he pulls his t-shirt back on.

"I'll call you."

"You *can't* say that. Haven't you watched any noughties film, ever? *I'll call you* means you don't want to see me again."

"That's not a thing," he says, smirking. "*Is it?*"

"Watch *He's Just Not That Into You* and revert back to me. It's homework."

"Ok, I'll watch it. And I won't call you?" he asks, now entirely confused about how to manage this.

"Well, obviously don't call me. A text will be fine. This isn't the nineties."

He chuckles softly and kisses me again, perching on the

edge of the bed. "I'll show myself out," he says. "You look too cosy to move."

"That is correct. I might even take a sickie."

"What've you come down with?"

"Orgasm-induced fatigue?"

Freddie nods, working hard to keep a straight face. "Hattie?"

"Yeah."

"I am going to call you."

"What did we just talk about?"

He squeezes my thigh over the duvet. "I have things to sort out with my brother and I don't know how *we* fit into that just yet."

I swallow and nod. "I know."

"And so I'm telling you this isn't the end. But…"

"Freddie… I get it."

He nods, his eyes scanning my face for a sign that isn't true, but he finally relents with a sigh before stepping out of my room. Moments later, I hear the front door click shut.

THIRTY-FIVE

In the end, I didn't call in sick. Who was I calling anyway? I run the place. The owners rarely answered their phone. I spent the day planning the events calendar for the year ahead, drafting Fliss an email with messy ideas that I hoped she would organise for me. When I get home that evening, I'm working hard not to stress about the lack of texts from Freddie and the fact Sam still hates me. I tell Alexa to play 'The Black Parade' and dance around my flat like I'm fifteen again, just without the thick eyeliner and Impulse spray all over me.

Alexa uses her magical powers to play more classics from the era and the volume is so loud, I almost don't hear the knock at my door.

"Alexa! Shut the hell up!" I shout.

There are only three people who can get up to the main door without calling first.

My mum, who has a key for emergencies, but she

wouldn't knock on my door; that would be too respectful. She simply walks in like she owns the place.

Sara has one too, but whenever she visits now, she calls up and I'm sure it's because she secretly lost the key. She would never admit it, though.

And then there's Sam. Sam just took a set one day because he doesn't like waiting outside. But the same as Mum, he wouldn't knock.

I stand stock-still, wondering if maybe it's Adam. But no. I don't think he cares enough to chase me down again. It would be too much effort. And besides, I hope I embarrassed him.

"Hattie, let me in. I'm worried you're dancing naked again."

Sam.

I bolt across the room and throw the door open. He's pouting, his eyes narrowed like he's here but he's still mad.

I hold my hand up, pointing at him. "It was one time, ten years ago. It was the middle of summer. And the lyrics were literally about liking your body better when you're naked."

"I still haven't recovered."

"Is that what you came to talk about?"

He frowns. "No."

"Do you want to come in?"

"Not really."

"Then why you here?"

Sam sighs, shaking his head. "Because sometimes, I like to be the bigger person."

"Oh yeah?" I work really hard to hide my smile. "Sam, I'm really sorry. Please can we talk?"

He sighs again, this time with comedic exaggeration. "He's not here, is he?" Sam mutters as he follows me in and shuts the door, before lounging on my sofa, which he's so used to doing.

"Listening to emo music?"

"Good point." He nods. "He's too cool for us."

"Have you spoken to him?"

He shakes his head. "I'm conflicted."

"Then why are you here?" I bring him a glass of squash because that's what we usually do whenever he comes over. It's like we never grew up sometimes. Maybe that's the problem.

"I thought about it some more. Turns out Dylan's a good sounding board. And I know you're going through things right now. I don't know if I approve of you using my brother as a rebound but if that's all it was…"

"Is that what Dylan told you?"

He glances at me. "He said he felt responsible. That he'd encouraged it."

I roll my eyes to the ceiling, throwing my head back. "I think everyone needs to stop treating me like I'm this vulnerable, susceptible person. Everything that happened with Freddie this weekend was *my* doing, Sam. It was completely on me. I made that decision. Nobody tricked me. Nobody seduced me. Nobody encouraged me to do anything."

"Right." Sam blows out a breath.

"If you're going to be mad at anyone, it's me. Be mad at me."

"Fine. I'm mad at you. *What the hell, Hattie?*"

"I know."

"You're the worst!" he says, but I can see from his expression that he's trying not to laugh. "You're such a hussy."

I snort. "A hussy?!"

"How could you? My *brother*!" But then he laughs, covering his face with his hands, which makes me crack up because this doesn't feel anywhere near as serious as it did this morning.

"I'm sorry. It's not as sudden and random as it seems."

"Ugh. Is this going to make me even more angry with you? How long has it been going on?"

"It hasn't! It's not like that. It's just… well, you know I always said I didn't like him. And that he was an idiot."

Sam nods, eyeing me suspiciously.

"That wasn't always true."

"No shit." He smirks. "I knew you fancied him. What happened? What did he do?"

I huff. "When are you going to accept that I'm part of the problem? He didn't *do* anything. It was all me. Remember that night I went out in Brighton alone because your girlfriend was mean?"

"Yeah?"

"Freddie found me. He took care of me. And I *needed* taking care of. Trust me. Then he brought me home. And when you fell out of the window…"

"You saw him in the hospital?"

"You were asleep, and he walked me home."

"What a dick!"

"Sam…"

"He was flirting! That's flirting."

"It's being nice."

"So naïve," he mutters.

I faux-punch his arm.

"Ok, ok. Whatever. Fine, so he's not always a total arsehole."

I sober up, sitting back into the sofa beside him. "How you feeling about the thing with your dad?"

He shrugs. "I didn't know any of that went down. He shouldn't have shielded me from it like he did. If I'd known, I would've... I don't really know. I was very angry at him back then."

"You should go see him. Your relationship means the world to Freddie. You know, we're not going to pursue this, Sam, if it's going to hurt you."

Sam blows out a breath, watching me with surprise. "What do I say to him?"

"He's your brother. You'll figure it out."

There's a beat of silence as Sam absorbs this and I can see he's considering it. I'm desperate for them to get along.

"Are we ok?"

Sam picks up my TV remote and turns it on. "Anything new on Netflix?"

"Erm? Probably."

"Get me some snacks and I'll think about forgiving you."

I nod, getting up and heading towards the kitchen. The snack cupboard in my flat is regularly replenished. "Hey, you have to admit that childish rule was a little redundant though, right? You can't be annoyed at me for breaking that. We're nearly thirty."

"Bring that up again and I'm leaving."

"The rule or nearly being thirty?"

"Nearly being thirty."

I press my lips together. And just like that, I have my friend back. He never was one to hold a grudge, really.

My phone chimes to tell me someone is at the door downstairs, and I get that familiar rush. Is it him? But when I answer, it's Sara. "Please let me in. It's bloody freezing out here."

"Er, ok…"

Once she reaches my floor, she strides in with two bottles of wine. I groan. "No. Take them away. I'm done. I'm not drinking for at least a month."

"Me neither. That's why I brought them. I don't even want to look at them." She eyes Sam. "So, you guys made up?"

"We're still mortal enemies," he says. "But we're talking again."

"Obviously." She turns back to me. "I'm here because Adam messaged Mike to say something happened. And that's all I know. Are you ok? Was he horrible?"

"You saw Adam?" Sam's ears prick.

"He kept calling me. And he texted me at midnight on my birthday."

Sara gasps. "Why didn't you say? Is that why you tried to jump Freddie?"

"Hey! Brother's present!" Sam yells.

"Ok, I'm done talking about this. I'm knackered. I'm somehow still horribly hungover and I just want to bum around with snacks and a film. You can join or you can go. No more inquisitions. For anyone. Agreed?"

Sara relents, joining Sam on the sofa. We snuggle up to watch a shitty film that Sam picked, I bring some blankets in to cover us and the next thing I know, my morning alarm is bleeping from the coffee table.

I sit up, alert. We've all fallen asleep right there.

"Get up. Work," is all I manage to mumble as I clamber off to the shower to get ready to open the gallery. The sun is shining bright through the big windows in my bedroom. I hear shuffling so assume Sam and Sara are off to work too. When I come back out to my deserted flat, I find a tea already made on the side.

I practically inhale it before heading to work.

THIRTY-SIX

Over the next few days, I'm distracted, throwing myself into my job. I chat with prospective clients, have a meeting with a new artist that's moved here from Copenhagen and would love to contribute to the gallery. It's quiet at this time of year but I sit behind my desk and enjoy the view of the waves lapping at the stoney coastline.

I get back to my morning runs, waking early and taking on the coastal paths, breathing in the salty fresh air. The weather is calm for the most part, if a little windy. All the time, I imagine I'm running the same route with Freddie. I wonder where he is and what he's doing. I type out messages to him about the weather. I snap a shot of the sun rising above the sealine one morning. But I don't send them.

I made a promise to myself. A rule. A whole year.

One day, Fliss comes by the gallery. She's wearing a bright-blue sweaterdress that clashes with the calming pastel colours inside the gallery. I make her a tea and she pretends to peruse the artwork as if she's shopping. Not that the owners are even around to see. I'm sure they forget they own a gallery sometimes. Luckily for them, I make it my business to run the place as if it were my own.

"I've booked an event in May," Fliss says as I pass her drink to her.

"Oh yeah?"

"Mmm. A wedding."

"Not Sara's?"

She nods. "Yes, actually. Did you recommend me?"

"Absolutely. I said you were very intense, but get shit done. Sara liked the sound of you."

"Well, at least you're honest," she says. "She booked me to take control of things. And thank God she did. She has so many guests and hardly any of them have booked accommodation yet. She doesn't have enough room for them all at the venue, so I made a deal with a hotel down the road. And then I asked her to email me her itinerary, plans and stuff like that and she just blinked at me."

"You're meant to have those things for a wedding?"

Fliss stares at me for a moment too long. "Hopeless. You're both hopeless."

I take a seat behind my desk, entirely unoffended. "I'm glad she reached out to you. She's been quite stressed about it all."

"Well, of course she is. She doesn't even have any lists.. Not even a proper bloody guestlist! But it's ok. I'll handle it."

"I have no doubt."

"She told me something," she adds, pressing her lips together.

I look up from sipping my tea. "Oh?"

"Just said something happened at your house party."

I bite my lip, willing the heat away from my cheeks, but there's no hiding it. "What did she say?" I ask guiltily.

"Nothing. Honestly. But I reckon I could give it a good guess. Did you actually get with Sam's hot brother?"

There's no point denying it. I feel like Fliss is trying to make it into something funny, something silly and exciting. And, in a way, that's what it is. But I can't fight the feeling that I've gone about it wrong and now he isn't messaging me.

Oh God. He isn't messaging me. What does that mean?

Fliss reads the horror on my face. She takes the seat at the other side of my desk and frowns. "Talk to me."

"It was only meant to be... I don't know."

"You can say a shag. If that's all it was meant to be. You can say that."

"I *hate* that word."

"Shag?"

"Yeah."

"Shag. Shag. Shag. Shag. Shag."

"Stop it!" I say, batting my hands at her. "Yes. Ok. That's how it started but we have this weird, flirty history that nobody knew about except for us, and I don't know... Getting physical sort of..."

"Brought the feelings to the surface?"

"I have no idea. But I feel bereft of him this week. It's pathetic, honestly. And it's very frustrating because I set myself rules for the next year. Which I'm sticking to because that's what I do. I'm a stringent rule follower. But it probably doesn't matter anyway because after he left, he hasn't messaged me once."

Fliss sighs heavily. "Do you still have the napkin?"

"The what?"

"The napkin with the rules on it?"

I lean across to my handbag and pull it out, laying it out in front of her. "It's very clear. You, yourself, pointed out this might happen. That I'd fall into relationship territory right away."

"I did, didn't I?" She eyes the napkin. "You know, you can barely make that rule out and you've already completed the last one."

"What are you saying?"

"That maybe these rules can be broken?"

I gasp at her. "Who are you and what have you done with Felicity Rainer?"

She shrugs. "I think sometimes, rules are bullshit. And if you made them, then you should be able to break them too."

"Are you encouraging this? You know Sam was livid, right?"

She nods, her eyes wide. "I can imagine."

"Doesn't matter anyway. Sam and Freddie aren't talking again because of me. And Freddie isn't messaging so I guess this all just fell apart. He probably got home and realised he wasn't that into me anyway."

It's a bitter pill to swallow saying that out loud. But maybe it's true. Maybe I need to accept the fact that Freddie just can't be for me.

"No. I don't buy it," Fliss says. "I bet you haven't messaged him either. He probably feels the same way. Especially if he's worried about your relationship with Sam too."

Just then a client comes in and has so many questions

about one of the larger canvasses of Brighton Pier that Fliss ends up waving goodbye before we can finish our discussion.

She sends me a message that evening just as Dylan arrives for dinner. I have him dicing onions as I put the oven on with one hand and hold my phone in the other.

I thought about it on the way home and I should have told you this at the gallery. James and I sort of fell into a whirlwind romance too even though we'd known each other for years. It all just suddenly fell into place like we found the lost puzzle piece, and everything finally made sense. But me and you are thinkers. We've been tried and challenged by love, and it makes us question and overthink things which I don't think want to be overthought. This is becoming waaaay too profound. What I'm trying to say is, maybe we're so used to using our heads that we forget to listen to our hearts. My heart was right about James. I want you to follow your heart too. Hopefully, it knows what to do. Speak soon. xx

"Why are you crying? Is it the onions?" Dylan asks, glancing at me with concern.

He's right; my eyes are watering. It isn't the onions. "Yes, this always happens. Hang on, I'll go splash some water on my face."

"Does that work?"

But I don't answer, stepping into my bedroom and closing the door. I perch on my bed and think about what to message Freddie. What do I even say at this point?

325

I dare myself to type.

Screw my rules

I hit send.

THIRTY-SEVEN

I don't start to panic and regret sending it until the next morning when I can see he's seen it but hasn't responded. Dylan is sleeping on my sofa because he had one too many wines and couldn't be bothered to walk home. I don't want to wake him before I have to, so I leave him a note on the coffee table to say I've gone out running, which route and when I should be back.

Sick with dread, I pull my running kit on and step outside onto the pavement in search of the sea. I run until all I can think about is how hard running is. I blast dance anthems to keep me focused on putting one foot in front of the other, hoping I don't publicly humiliate myself by crying.

How could he not reply? Surely, he understood the context. What if he's regretting everything that happened? Did Sam speak to him? My heart feels too big for my chest, and I keep having to swallow lumps that form in my throat.

I'm two miles away from home when I realise, I didn't check the weather before heading out. Fat raindrops slap my cheek, blown sideways by the gales chopping off the water. I pause on a quiet, wide stretch of the seafront, holding onto one of the black, metal railings separating the walkway from the pebble beach.

I check my phone. Still no message.

The winds pick up. Without my music on, it's just the constant roar of the winter waves crashing and retreating from the shore. As the clouds separate and the rain starts to tip down, proper January, British rain, I turn for home.

That's when I notice the tall, wide-shouldered figure heading my way, running in jeans and a drenched jumper. His hair is plastered to his head, his eyes intent on me.

I feel his gaze like a shockwave.

I can't move, except to run a hand over my face, wiping away the rain so I can see.

He stops a few steps in front of me, his face unsure.

"You're here," I shout over the weather and the waves, fighting to be heard.

He nods. "Dylan told me you were out running."

I swallow. "You didn't reply to my message."

"I didn't know how to convey what I wanted to say in a text. I tried. I just... Sam came by last night. We spoke for hours. I didn't see your message until right before bed. I left first thing this morning."

"Is Sam ok?"

He nods, raindrops dripping from his fringe. "We got a lot off our chests. It feels like there was so much we just held onto. And it's no surprise really. The things he thought I did to him. The betrayal. I get it."

"And does he?"

Another gust of wind nearly knocks me sideways.

Freddie steps closer, his hand holding my elbow to keep me upright. "He's going to try," he says with a frustrated laugh. "I don't think we're ever going to see eye to eye. Not fully."

"What about…"

Freddie smiles. "Us?"

I can barely nod. I'm too afraid of the answer.

He swipes a thumb over my cheek, sweeping up raindrops. "It's pretty simple really. Because I don't care. I love you, I'm sorry."

A feral, gurgled laugh bursts from my lips. It's the most unromantic sound. "I love you too."

My lips quiver. From the cold or because I'm on the verge of tears, I can't tell. But it doesn't matter because then his hands are hot on my neck, not a care in the world that I'm covered in sweat from running. And we're kissing and he's so warm, it feels incredible. He tastes salty, like the sea air has tainted his lips.

But he breaks off, now cradling my face in his large, warm palms, our noses practically grazing. "But I refuse to be the villain in your life. You're not breaking your own rules. We'll use them to prove this is it for us."

I frown. "How?"

"We'll date, exclusively. We won't call it a relationship. If that's what you want, that is?"

I smile and nod. "Date exclusively? Isn't that the same thing."

"Shh. Don't complicate this."

"Will you travel with me?"

"If you want me to. I'll do anything with you. I'll go anywhere with you. I want to run this route with you in the morning. I want to sit there and watch you paint. I want to buy you a house overlooking the sea. I want you."

I swear I'm crying but it's such an overwhelming statement, I can barely work out what's up from what's down. *He wants me. Freddie wants me.*

"What was your other rule?" he asks.

"Rule?" My brain short circuits but then I remember. "Oh. To live alone for a year."

Freddie scrunches his drenched face. "Then that's the rule. And I'll respect it."

"You've really thought about this, haven't you?"

"It's important. You wrote those rules because you needed them. I'm not going to be the one to trample all over your boundaries."

I shake my head in his hands. "What if *I* want to break them?"

"Don't. Don't break them for anyone. We'll just bend them slightly."

I throw myself at him, kissing the rain drops off his rugged face, tasting them on his lips. He presses me up against the railings behind us, picking me up and propping my butt on the cold metal so that he can stand between my thighs.

It's completely indecent in public but I don't care. All I can think about is him. He's every bit of me.

And he loves me, he's sorry.

THIRTY-EIGHT

New Year's Eve, a year later

My blurry seaside canvas is up on the gallery wall. The imposter syndrome is a heavy sludge in my veins. It isn't good enough. All I see are imperfections.

"Shh, it's perfect," Freddie says, reading my mind for the tenth time this evening. He leans in to brush his lips across the bare skin at my shoulder.

The owners have allowed me to host mine and Sam's thirtieths at the gallery. I'm both excited and nervous. I'd like to think we're old enough now to be sensible and not destroy any artwork but I'm eyeing up Dylan and Sam, who have been in the kitchen out back concocting a party punch since they arrived.

I chew on my lip and stare up at the massive canvas again. I didn't get the light exactly right and it's more obvious when it's dark outside. The blur of the pebbly British seafront turned out more beautiful than I thought it would. It's all greens and blues and greys combined, with the softest hint of sun pushing through the clouds.

I'm momentarily distracted as some of Sam's nerdy friends arrive. Freddie welcomes them with a glass of champagne and makes a point of telling them which piece of artwork is mine. Somehow, it's both sweet and entirely embarrassing in the same breath.

Freddie returns to my side. "Will you please relax. It's…"

"Perfect. Yeah, you said. I just wish I'd added those seagulls in the end. You know, just to give it some life."

"It's perfect, I promise."

I sigh. "Well, I'm only giving it a month up there. If it doesn't sell, I'm not wasting wall space."

"It's going to sell. I'd buy it, but you keep saying I'm not allowed."

Just then, Priya arrives with Izzy. She's flustered, her hair not as shiny as it usually is. Come to think of it, her face is rather pale. "Are you sick?" I ask as she comes over to give me a hug.

"Lovely to see you too. You look great."

"Ok… Point taken. How are you, dearest friend? You look wonderful and spritely."

"Liar," she snorts. "I'm pregnant, if you must know, and I'm currently fighting off constant nausea whilst battling with an eighteen-month-old."

I gasp. "Congratulations!" I give her a gentle hug, but she shrugs me off.

"No," she says, holding a hand over her mouth. "Your perfume is making me sick."

"Oh. Charming."

Izzy joins us. "It's been a long week. If we make it to midnight without falling asleep, it will be a heroic effort."

"I'm just grateful you're here."

Freddie leans across. "Have you seen Hattie's art?"

"You don't have to tell everyone."

"I do and I will," he says close to my ear. That deep voice still takes control of my heartrate, I swear.

We grab drinks and I'm glad I stocked up on Shloer. Priya takes a seat on one of the stylish loungers we have positioned around the gallery for clients to rest on. In all honesty, they don't really get used during normal opening hours. The occasional lonely pensioner comes in from time to time and pretends they're going to buy something. I'm onto them but I don't mind their company for a while.

"Have you heard from Sara? How is she?" Priya asks.

"I have actually. She called me earlier today. She is living her best life, chasing the sun right now. But we can't talk about Sara," I say, partly because there are people here who might not know who and where she is and it isn't my secret to reveal.

We move onto discussing my canvas on the wall. Sam and Dylan come out of the kitchen to join us, and I realise we're all finally celebrating in a very grown-up, sophisticated way. In the last year, I've watched my best friend in the whole world adapt to the fact that his brother is often in my flat at weekends.

And he's only had one or two jump scares.

Of course, it changed our dynamic. It would be unrealistic to say it hadn't. I've seen slightly less of Sam this year, but it hasn't weakened our friendship. If anything, it's allowed us both the space to build on ourselves separately.

And I've lived on my own for a year. (Even if I did have a regular overnight guest.)

Oh, and I've travelled to five different beaches. California, Santorini, Vancouver, Amalfi and finally, the secret place where Sara is. Freddie travelled with me to two, Dylan came to California, and I went on my own to Vancouver and to see Sara.

It's been quite a year.

"Right, listen up," Sam yells to the whole party. "We have less than ten minutes until countdown. Make sure you've got full glasses."

Freddie finds me talking to one of my old school friends and loops an arm around my waist. He sticks right there by my side until we begin the countdown.

We toast as the clock strikes midnight.

"And so, I guess I'm thirty," I say to Freddie, pretending to be horrified, but honestly, it's sort of freeing. I have a sneaky suspicion my thirties will be my best decade yet.

"Hey, come with me," Freddie whispers in my ear, his large body curving over mine from behind.

I twist, reaching up to stroke his face, feel his tidy yet bristly chin under my fingers. "Where we going?"

He doesn't say, just takes my hand, grabs our coats and gently tows me outside until we're crunching over the pebbles on the beach. The wind is biting cold, and Freddie looks like he regrets asking me out here, his lips pressed into a grimace.

"What's up?" I ask, fidgeting on my feet.

He takes both my hands, and I gasp. "You're not going to propose, are you?"

"Well, thank God I'm not or that might've hurt my ego."

"Oh shit. *Were* you going to propose?" He stares at me for a long moment and my panic stretches. "Freddie?!"

He shakes his head, but I can see the glint of humour there. "What if I did? What would you say?"

334

"Ok, but this better not be your actual proposal."

"It's not. You'll know when it's time."

"Well, then you'll have to wait for my answer."

He scoffs. "You're the one who brought it up. No, I wasn't proposing. But I do have another kind of question to ask you."

"Oh yeah?"

"The rule period is over now, right?"

I nod. "I should think so, yes."

"Good. Move in with me."

"Where was the question?"

"I'm serious."

"In London?" I ask, and immediately feel myself recoil.

"No. God, no. Here. Or somewhere on the south coast. Hell, anywhere you want. I'll commute. I can do that now I'm self-employed. That's part of the beauty in being your own boss. It doesn't matter where I am. I just want to wake up with you next to me every day and not just at the weekends. I would've done it sooner, but we promised each other the time."

"We're not even official yet," I point out. But I'm only teasing and I'm pretty sure he knows.

"Ah yes. We're dating exclusively."

"We're *exclusive*?" I joke.

"How much have you had to drink? You're being extra gobby."

I laugh but it's gurgled. "I haven't even drunk that much, I swear. I'm just giddy."

"Giddy?"

"Well, yeah. My date, who I'm apparently exclusive with, is asking me to live with him. Of course I'm giddy."

Freddie stares at me for a beat, his mouth slightly ajar as if there's something right on the tip of his tongue. Then he nods, running his tongue over his teeth, before getting down on one knee.

"Shut up!" I squeal.

He just laughs, that deep, perfect rumble. "Hattie, will you do the honour…"

"No, you can't now. I've been mean!"

"…of being my girlfriend."

I bend over to kiss him. "Well, thank God for that. Yes. Yes, I will be your girlfriend."

He climbs to his feet just as we hear squeals and clapping from inside the gallery. We both look at each other at the same time and crack up. He picks me up, his arms wrapped around my legs and spins me. I laugh, holding onto him.

"Well now they're definitely going to think we're engaged."

"Let them," he says, placing me back down. "I have a present for you, by the way. But you're not allowed to judge."

"I never judge."

Freddie swallows, fishing something out of his inside coat pocket. "This is just a copy. I've framed the original."

He passes it to me and I'm not gentle as I unfold the paper to find the sketch of me, aged nineteen, singing my little heart out. "Oh, Freddie. You finished it."

"The only sketch I've ever finished. And it's been easier since I've seen a lot more of my muse recently." He takes a deep breath. "Is it ok?"

I smile up at him. "It's perfect. You got the freckles just right. And my hair! Look at me."

"I always am."

I kiss him then, the paper flapping about in the wind as I throw my arms around his neck. He pulls me into him, tucking me into his long trench coat until we're just one four-legged blob out by the ocean, the wind lapping at our sides.

Every year, this party will come around.

Every year, we'll celebrate a friendship, two birthdays, and for me, well, I'll also celebrate a love story.

ACKNOWLEDGEMENTS

WRITING ACKNOWLEDGEMENTS always feels somewhat surreal – this time two years ago my dream of publishing a book still wasn't a reality. And yet, here I am again, thanking all the wonderful people involved in turning my random order of words into a physical book. I am deliriously lucky to do this, fuelled by delusion and kind encouragement (read: enabling) from those around me.

Firstly, thank you to everyone at Head of Zeus for supporting and championing my writing from the start. Aubrie – thanks for loving my characters as much as I do. It's a dream to work with you! Thanks to Shannon for all your marketing prowess and promoting my books so brilliantly. Thanks to Holly, Sophie, Yas, Zoe and Aliisha – I see you and all the work you do for me. I really, really appreciate it!

Endless thanks to Safae El-Ouahabi, my wonderful agent, who is always available and ready to support when needed. Thanks, in extension, to everyone at RCW for all they do.

Thanks to my writing and reading friends. Thanks to Kayleigh, Steph, Anna and Rhian for reading early drafts of *House Party* and providing fantastic feedback. As always, early feedback forms part of the bigger picture and helps me catch the things that need the most work. Anna Britton – thanks for being my good chum and an ear for writing rants. Thanks to Lauren, Maggie, Kat, Katie, Annie, Georgia, Carlie and so many others! Just knowing you're a message away for support is priceless.

Thanks to all the Booksta, BookTok & early reading community who come out in force to support debut and up-and-coming authors. You are worth your weight in gold! Thanks for doing what you do to promote my work. You have no idea how amazing it is for an author to see a reader aesthetic of their book. It's like some kind of magic!

Finally, so much love to my family. Mum – you always read my books early and I love your biased motherly praise each time. Thank you. To my husband, I hope you're enjoying your shows while I write in bed for evenings on end. One day, I'll be back to annoying you all evening, it's a promise. Thanks to my siblings, my dad and my extended family for showing up and supporting my books.

Thank you to you, the reader, for picking my book up. I hope it was everything you wanted!

ABOUT THE AUTHOR

CHLOE FORD grew up in rural Sussex but is now based in South Gloucestershire. She has an affinity with all things country, from riding horses to muddy walks. Her love for writing began at secondary school when her English teacher would set a writing task for the whole hour. An avid reader, she started sneaking Mills & Boon books out from under her mum's bed as a teenager and hasn't stopped devouring romance books ever since.

DISCOVER THE HILARIOUS ENEMIES-TO-LOVERS
ROM-COM FROM CHLOE FORD

'Bursting with sparkling wit and crackling tension'
Catherine Walsh, bestselling author of *Snowed In*

AN UNEXPECTED
OVERNIGHT

WORK
TRIP

WHAT COULD
GO WRONG?

CHLOE FORD

THEY SAY YOU SHOULD KEEP YOUR ENEMIES CLOSER...

For Fliss, the prospect of a team building work trip fills her with dread. Mostly because she cannot stand her pushy colleague James, who often attempts to derail her brilliant plans. But when the two arrive in the Scottish Highlands, they find themselves facing a unique challenge: their boss has abandoned them in the middle of nowhere with only one tent, two sleeping bags and a few protein bars.

Cut off from the outside world, the pair are forced to put aside their differences to weather the unpredictable elements of the Highlands and get home. As they set out on a journey across miles of rugged wilderness – pushing each other to survive and testing their physical and emotional limits – they remain fully aware of their boss's manipulative plan to orchestrate a hook up between them.

But even with only each other for company, Fliss and James stand firm in their resolve: they won't give in to any romantic notions. *Or will they?*

TURN TO READ THE FIRST CHAPTER

ONE

He's done it again.

I can hardly believe it. No, scrap that. I can absolutely believe it. He does it all the time, actually. The words in his email roll through me, soaking into my blood system until my limbs are rattling. I breathe in for three then slowly exhale away the stress for ten. Amongst the background noise of work chatter, gossiping and coffee machines hissing, I find peace in this modern glass building. I will not let him destroy that peace.

"How do you say, *'You're a total dipshit, I hope you and your idea fall into a pit of misery and despair,'* without it sounding unprofessional?" I ask my assistant, Gemma, who looks up from her desk, her hazel eyes blinking over her screen.

"I think it's 'I appreciate your interest in this matter. However, the situation is in hand'?" Then in a lower voice, she whispers, "What's he done now?"

I massage my eyebrows as I stare furiously at my laptop. Gemma is used to these altercations now. She's a seasoned employee here. "He's trying to say he can make more money using our cosy lounge area for our VIP customers by putting another hospitality marquee there instead."

I delete my last comment: *Are you actually kidding? Or are you maybe a bit stupid?*, and try for something less sassy whilst also retaining that tone of – *you're a sneaky weasel and I'm going to get you back.* Professionally, of course.

"Is it direct to Michael?" Gemma asks, a flit of concern in her expression.

I peek across the modern office and notice our CEO, who is the key decision-maker around here, talking to someone in the main kitchen.

Well, at least he isn't reading his emails yet.

I nod at Gemma, angry-typing as I respond. I write, *Thank you so much for your idea. I can see you put a lot of thought into this. However, as you already know, we are far too close to the event to incorporate these changes.*

"Yes, it's direct to Michael," I say. "And I've only seen it because Fiona copied me into a reply. He's a sneaky..." There are too many rude words to choose from so I trail off, undecided.

Fiona, our Head of Finance, tends to take my side on things, but I'm pretty sure she enjoys fuelling the drama. She's always the first to hit the karaoke at work events. And since she mostly organises them, there is nearly always a karaoke. Often Abba themed. Her red hair, once fairly natural looking, has been getting brighter by the month. She mentioned she was battling greys, now in her early fifties, and she's often trotting off to the hair salon down the road. I imagine her colluding with the stylist, picking a colour closer to atomic red each time she goes.

"Rajesh has already shown his support of the new idea," I add with a pained sigh. Rajesh being the Head of Operations. He's almost impossible to get to respond to an email, so I assume the enemy had to practically lean over his shoulder to get his written endorsement.

I take a deep breath, trying to push down the tight pang of panic building across my abdomen. I've done well to secure Head of Marketing by my thirtieth birthday. Even if I must say so myself. But it's taken sheer determination, long hours, magically forgetting I haven't used even half of my annual leave and networking with the Board of Directors on what some might describe as arse-licking levels. I have dignity, it's just not as much as other people. I'm driven and I know where I want to go.

I joined The Starr Agency six years ago and progressed my way up the ranks by showing dedication to the cause. We work with local parks in the city, throwing pop-up musical festivals. The company has been growing fast because we offer a range of options to suit those on a lower budget and corporate clients who want to spoil their customers with a suave dinner in a specially designed pop-up restaurant.

It's been growing in popularity, to the extent we are now being invited to major sporting events to run mini festivals within their larger events.

It's great for business. It's bad for my social and mental wellbeing.

But it's worth it. Michael Starr, our esteemed leader and creator of the company, has been hinting about making me a director. Only last week, in my monthly appraisal, he said, "You're now portraying all the behaviours we'd expect to see in someone even more senior than yourself." And the other day, his email to the heads of departments very clearly set out his plan to promote internally since his very strange (incredibly handsy) and elderly uncle stood down from the board. When I've finally shown my worth, I can start reeling in the money in a big way, and all the sweat and tears I've committed to this point will be worth it.

Only problem is, there's a hurdle.

A greasy-salesman-shaped hurdle.

James Boatman.

And he's a real pain in my arse.

I growl as another email comes through. Gemma sits taller, rolling her chair back to stand and make her way to the kitchen. She knows how I like my coffee and I'm guessing she's sensing an incoming implosion. The machine rumbles to life, hissing the liquid into my mug. Our little kitchen is mostly a cupboard with a sink beside our cubicle. I got it installed so I didn't have to waste time going to and from the main kitchen all day.

"Michael's just replied suggesting we discuss James' idea further in this morning's meeting. *But what is there to discuss? Seriously?* We're three weeks out from the event and we've sold seventy per cent of the VIP tickets. We'll easily sell the rest. What do we do for those who've purchased it already? Downgrade them? That'll go well." I suck in a big gulp of air for mental strength before pressing my fingers to my eyelids. "Why is everyone trying to make me cry? Why can't Gloatman just back off this one time!?"

James' surname is Boatman, but since he makes a point in the end-of-month company "show and tell" to make a huge song and dance about every single bloody sale he makes, it was my genius idea to call him Gloatman.

Ok, so it's not particularly clever.

It was annoying when he found out what I was calling

him, and instead of being incredibly offended, wrote it at the top of his sales board as if he was proud of it.

I don't know what he calls me, but I'm sure he does call me something.

Oh god, there's a prickling behind my eyes. I shake out my limbs. I will not allow myself to cry. Part of being a successful businesswoman is being able to offset the tears in a moment of weakness and let them flood out at a point when nobody can see.

Which, admittedly, is becoming increasingly frequent.

"Drink this," Gemma says, placing a milky coffee down in front of me. It'll have three sugars in it. The rich aroma wafts into my nostrils in a sensational way.

My battle drink. My sweet kick of fury. My caffeine booster.

I nod, murmuring a thanks to my loyal colleague as she returns to her desk. I roll my shoulders, slap my palms together a few times and sip in between aggressive typing. Then I hit print on our ticket sale statistics for last week.

Once I'm ready, I leave our corner of the skyrise office opposite Liverpool Street station and head towards the other side where Michael's conference suite resides. I try very hard not to bristle when I spot James already sitting in the chair closest to Michael's, leaning back casually as if he hasn't purposefully beaten me by arriving seven minutes early. He has his usual classic salesman appearance. Matt-black hair gelled immaculately. Gleaming shoes. A fine, expensive-looking three-piece suit with a teal tie that brings out the blue in his eyes. I'll give him something, he has a nice nose. It's long, with a little bump in the middle. James's appearance oozes with an irritating confidence that I've always thought gives off Matthew McConaughey vibes.

"Gloatman," I say.

He smiles, but it's not a friendly smile, more calculating. I imagine he's saying my nickname in his head. The fact that I don't know what that is only irritates me to the extent that I want to turn this building upside down in order to retrieve it.

But no… deep breaths. *Deep breaths.*

Finally, his smile fades as he turns his chair back towards the table where he has a notepad. He fiddles with it in his lap, using his long fingers to spin his pen. "Felicity."

"It's Fliss."

"I know," he replies without looking at me.

Then say, FLISS!

My christened name is Felicity and nobody except for my parents (and Gloatman) have called me it in about twenty years. Granted, it was an error on my part. James started at Starr a few months before me, and on my first day, as I was being shown around and introduced to everyone, my nerves got the better of me. I said my name was Felicity. And he's never forgotten it, even though I sign off my emails as Fliss.

I take my seat opposite his. This way I'm close to Michael if not exactly closest thanks to the oval shape of his office. I'm a stark contrast to James, in his dark tweed suit, with my flowery patterned dress that flares from the waist down to my knees. My dark brown hair, which I attempt to straighten every morning into a semi-acceptable state, is naturally thick, pulled neatly backwards by my fuchsia Alice band. My nails are currently painted a pastel blue, my kitten heels are from Irregular Choice and are exactly that, covered in sequins.

James always looks as if he's about to step onto an episode of *The Apprentice*. Whereas I look more like I'm going to a summer wedding.

"Did you see my email?" he asks, raising an eyebrow in a telling way.

I look up, fixing him with a narrowed stare. He knows I've seen it. "Did you get a chance to read my reply?"

He makes a face, a sort of arrogant smirk, which suggests he did. Damn it. I should've added a read receipt. "Unfortunately, I haven't had the pleasure. I'm sure it was incredibly insightful."

Bastard!

Before I can load a useful response on my tongue, the rest of the team starts filing in. There are five main departments at The Starr Agency: Events, Sales, Marketing, Operations, Finance and HR. HR is literally Mel in her own little office where people go to be fired or hired.

They take their seats, sipping on their drinks whilst I watch my nemesis across from me. We smile overly politely. The room is too hot, or at least I am, so I remove my cardigan and hang it on my chair. James has gone back to making notes on his pad. What's he writing? Does he have a plan for this meeting? He often comes prepared with his irritating ability to woo people.

Except me, that is.

I see right through his appealing front door, past the lavish exterior, the dark blue eyes and toned arms – tight against his sleeves, and see the arse that he really is. He knows the consequences for me and my team if we don't hit our targets for ticket sales. We don't earn as many bonuses as the sales team. In fact, we earn only one a year and our success is hinged on this event he is trying to ruin for us.

"Good morning, Dream Team," Michael sings in his jubilant way as he enters the room, walking round to take his seat at the head of the table.

Admittedly, Michael's a strange one. Some would call him quirky. I value his input and calm leadership here. But he does have this tendency to sway between marketing and sales like one of those old-school gameshows with the spinning wheels. He could land anywhere. It makes me both tense and agitated, whilst also maintaining a sense of hope that I have a fifty per cent chance of taking the enemy down.

He's pretty reliable in some ways. He always wears a white shirt, no tie – a few buttons undone at the top and a pair of standard grey work trousers. Even when this office is verging on chilly, he'll only wear the shirt. And yet, he's also the most unpredictable decision-maker I've ever met. It makes him hard to work for. Never really knowing what he's going to do next.

I try not to grind my teeth when he touches James' shoulder as he passes. "How were your weekends?"

We all look around waiting for someone to speak first. It's one of those frustrating moments because none of us actually care how each other's weekends were. However, it is an unwritten rule that we should at least pretend to.

"I went fishing with my cousin," Rajesh offers. I inwardly sigh. Rajesh is in his late forties but looks older. He's lovely, but frustrating to communicate with when his stress levels peak at ten, yet mine can launch well over a thousand in a matter of minutes. It's hard to get him to understand the sheer depth of importance of some tasks. For example, branded signage being positioned in the correct places for maximum visibility. Or sponsored merchandise being worn by our event staff. I suspect he thinks we're all a bit mad.

"Marvellous," Michael grins, his teeth glinting.

Michael, the man behind this whole enterprise, comes from money, I think… Actually, I only assume. We don't know very much about him at all. With his silvery-dark hair and spookily pale eyes, he's a mystery to me in many ways. He never seems to be tired. I regularly receive emails from him in the middle of the night and I'm still yet to see him eat.

Obviously, there are rumours. I don't involve myself in them. But I know people around the office joke that he's a vampire. Or a ghoul. Someone once suggested he was a cannibal.

I silence my mind in case he can read it. At that exact moment, he turns his head to smile at me in his eccentric way, full mouthed, stretched cheeks, as if he heard me thinking. I open my mouth to say something, but James beats me to it.

"How was *your* weekend, Michael?"

Slimy git.

"Exactly as you'd expect it to be, James. Kind of you to ask," he replies. Ever the mystery.

James gives Michael a polite nod before turning to me with a slightly less enthusiastic grin. "What about you, Felicity? Get lots done?"

I laugh in polite corporate. He knows I did. The reason he knows is because we were the only two sad fools to be logged in on Saturday afternoon, replying to Michael's many emails. "It was sublime, thank you, James. And how was yours? Did you manage to get away from your laptop for a few hours?" I round this off with a pity face.

"Hilarious," he mutters, his grin faltering. "Yes, thank you, Felicity."

There's a moment of strained silence. I physically feel it in my chest but force myself not to fill it with some unhelpful nonsense. No. We need to get to the heart of the matter. I, however, will not be the one to cause the friction in our first meeting on a Monday morning.

James purses his lips before finding his stellar grin again, leaning towards Michael in his typical flirtatious way. "What did you think of my idea then, boss?"

Let's bloody go...

I say, "If you had gotten to my email before this meeting, James, you would have seen that it is *far* too late to be incorporating changes..."

"As I said a moment ago, Felicity, unfortunately the sales team were very busy this morning, so I was unable to make time for your reply. However, if you had fully read the email thread, you would've noticed my idea has already been endorsed by the ops team."

He means Rajesh. He means he walked up to Rajesh and told him to write a response.

My smile is corporate cyanide as I lace my fingers together on the table. "That's really great. I'm so glad you took the initiative to get this project signed off by Rajesh. And I did see that part of the thread. Thank you for highlighting it to me again. The trouble is, you have forgotten that you need both Marketing and Finance to sign this off too."

Michael looks between us, as James blinks at me. I notice the quiver in his cheeks and along his rigid jawline. He knows he's got to play his best cards to win this because I'm not going to budge.

He talks quickly, clearly. "As Marketing will remember..." I'm *Marketing* now – hilarious. I'm not a person, I am an entire department. "... we've almost sold out of hospitality places for the final event of the summer. We could easily close out another marquee. The profit would absolutely annihilate anything VIP tickets can achieve. Although I admire and support all the work Marketing have done to bring this about, Marketing should be realistic about the way business works."

The way business works? What a patronising...

My smile is making my jaw ache, but I must win this battle now. Time for some swift blows. "Of course, Marketing is very aware of how business works. Thank you for your concern in this matter." I cringe as I say, "It would help, however, if Sales were more aware of the work that goes into the last efforts of organising the events, as it mostly comes down to the dedication of the other departments to achieve this. For example, where would you put the kitchens?" I ask, tilting my head in a patronising way to mirror James' tone. "What about the menus? Sales have less than three weeks to finalise it. And the sales team aren't always as reliable as we would like—"

James laughs with volume to interrupt me. "Don't go for my team," he says, his pitch raising slightly, his teeth gritted. Ooh, he's protective of his aggressive slime bags. I'm yet to meet a salesperson in his team who has any kind of office-kitchen etiquette. At work events they're always the loudest, rudest and most inappropriate. Annoyingly, Michael tends to turn a blind eye.

We, being my lovely marketing crew, are usually trying to have a pleasant evening of laughter and food whilst they're mashing it up with *shots, shots, shots* and glugging beer back like it's going out of style.

"Sales needs to consider the fact that there's absolutely no guarantee you can sell the tables in that timeframe," I reiterate. "And even if you can, what about the sixty people who've already paid for the VIP tickets? Marketing sold another twelve last week alone. We're at seventy per cent capacity. Marketing can easily get this to the one hundred per cent."

Gosh, even I'm talking about myself as if I'm an entire department now.

"The sales team deserve the chance to exceed their bonuses, and this would allow them that," James says directly to Michael, not even bothering to include me now. He gets straight to the heart of the matter. Money. That's all he cares about anyway.

"Erm… excuse me? When making business decisions, please consider all the departments it will affect," I say. In other words, stop being a selfish prick.

"Thank you for pointing this out, Felicity," James says. "Unfortunately, when you look at the bigger picture success of the company, you'll know the bonuses your department achieve are incredibly minimal compared to Sales so—"

I scoff. "Marketing *deserve* their bonuses too."

He makes a face. "Sorry, I wasn't aware the middle of my sentence was interrupting the start of yours."

Ugh. Shots fired. I have no response to this. I glare across at Gloatman. In fairness, I did interrupt, but he's done it to me too.

After a moment, he continues, "And besides, you're only marketing. You don't mind working on your salaries. My team require bonuses for motivation."

"Isn't selling their job? Like marketing is ours?" I ask through the last shreds of my cheek muscles.

James gives me one of those oh-you-poor-thing expressions, wrinkling his nose. "You don't understand how this works."

I laugh, frustration lacing the sound. "Although I appreciate your concern about my understanding, sales are in constant need of financial incentive. Their motivation levels are lacking, and it may be time for their leader to look inwardly at this challenge. They've already hit their bonuses. Why do they need to *exceed* them?"

James turns back to Michael again as if I haven't even made an iota of a point. I notice I'm clenching and unclenching my fist on the table. The line between professional behaviour and physical violence is sometimes scarily thin.

"The profit target has been met. Sales can exceed it. Let us do this. It will look so, *so* good to the board. You know it too. Rajesh has already endorsed my idea. The kitchens can be extended. The furniture can be hired. It's all ready to go."

"No, no, no…" I say, leaning in towards our leader too. "What about our clientele? We can't just let them down. I thought your vision, Michael, was to bring joy to local communities. If we continue to remove affordable options in lieu of expensive corporate stuff how does that impact our long-term goals?"

"Our long-term goals don't mean shit unless we're driving a steady profit," James retorts.

"Which we are…"

"No thanks to Marketing. You'll find the real profit is achieved through Sales."

"Which is consistently supported by Marketing," I grin, but my teeth are set together.

"Entirely against the point. That is the purpose of your department."

"As is Sales to… erm… What is their role again?" I make a show of tapping my chin. "Oh yes, that's it. *To. Sell.*"

Gloatman is giving me his full attention now, nervous energy seeping from his pores. Maybe it's the way he's gripping his pen. I have a feeling he's already committed to his idea. I have a feeling he's already sold some of the tables. I have a feeling he's not going to let this one slide.

Well, hard luck for him. Neither am I! We stare each other down as if the other might crack.

"I see this is quite the debate," Michael intercedes. "I support both your points of view here. You make very strong arguments. As you know, I like to be led by my team, and if Fiona is in support of Fliss, then it means we are split down the middle."

We all turn to Fiona for her wide-eyed nod of confirmation. She's an angel. Always has my back. I'm convinced I hear James curse in response.

Michael is no longer smiling but watching us with a worried expression. At some point during the discussion, he's rolled his shirt sleeves up, and I notice his arms are completely hairless.

Vampire…

"I think the whole team needs a break," he says calmly. "A nice corporate away day to boost morale and rejuvenate."

Oh, absolutely not. We're three weeks out from an event.

There's so much to do. He's done this before, dragging us to some random event in Paris for a "learning experience", and it was a nightmare. I ended up working through a whole night to get everything done.

"No. No, it's fine—" I say, as James says, "I would advise against—"

Michael holds up a hand. "I think we *all* need a break." He smiles again in his unnerving way. "You are my team. I can't have you disagreeing like this. I will make a decision about James' idea after our... away day." He nods to himself as if he's having his own internal discussion about this. "Yes. I think some team building will be good for all of us. An adventure. Somewhere different... Yes. Somewhere but nowhere."

"We really need a quick decision," James pipes up.

He's silenced with a calm but stern expression. "No decisions should be made in such a rushed way my fearless leaders. You require time to choose wisely."

James opens his mouth to object again, but Michael goes on. "Don't worry. I think we should go away imminently. Clear your calendars for the rest of the week. No exceptions. I'll let you know the details by end of play today. Team dismissed."

COMING IN 2026

GLAD YOU CAME

SHE WAS MEANT TO BE ON HER HONEYMOON. HE WAS SUPPOSED TO BE A POPSTAR.

When Sara is jilted at the altar, she does what any
self-respecting woman would do: boards that
honeymoon flight to Croatia anyway.

But she doesn't expect to find her ex-fiancé and his
smug new beau at the same beach resort.
Enter meltdown . . . and then enter Gus.

Fresh off the breakup of his world-famous boyband,
Gus has no career plans, no bandmates, and no idea
why the gorgeous, slightly unhinged woman next door is
knocking on his door with a proposal: a fake dating
plan to sabotage her ex's loved-up getaway.

It's all fun and games until fake dates start to feel
a little too real. What could go wrong?

AVAILABLE TO PRE-ORDER NOW!

Stories to fall in love with.

Aria

THANKS FOR READING!

Want to receive exclusive author content, news on the latest Aria books and updates on offers and giveaways?

Follow us on X @AriaFiction and on Facebook and Instagram @HeadofZeus, and join our mailing list.